# Ta Khut

## (...The Light...)
### Science & Myth Entwine on a Quest for Truth

## K.C. HOGAN

Ta Khut

Published by Kivas Publishing UK

First Published in Paperback January 2017

Cover Illustration By K. E. Hughes

By

# K.C. HOGAN

ISBN-13: 978-1542545341
ISBN-10: 154254534X

# DEDICATION

For Ken – with me in all that I do.

I love you always.

# ABOUT THE AUTHOR

K.C. Hogan is a successful writer of short fiction, published both in the UK and abroad. Though circumstances demanded she abandon school at the age of thirteen, she continued to harbour a dream to finish her education and become a writer. A determined effort in her thirties led her to achieve both – the First Class Honours degree in Applied Psychology and the paid publication of her first short story. Having worked in a variety of jobs – from dishwashing, to lecturing at university, writing remains her way to escape to other places. She shares her life with Ken, her husband, and their wayward, but loveable, rescue dog, Gypsy. This is her first novel.

# CONTENTS

# PROLOGUE

As the hum of the city retreated Thomas Begvious slowed his step. Tonight there was no plastic laughter invasion of his thoughts, just a cold crystalline clarity to the images of his past. A life caught cruelly in freeze frame.

He stared along the roadway, devoid now of traffic, across to the empty warehouses that ran alongside the embankment. It would be no great loss, he told himself. Unpleasant, yes, for those unfortunate enough to find him, but life was filled with grim discoveries.

He crushed the two-week-old obituary, his own grim discovery, in his fist. Chance, that bugbear of academics and statisticians, was a mysterious phenomenon, the fall of the dice, the cut of the cards – a change in the wind that could lift a single page from a newspaper and carry it in low level flight to rest at his feet.

"Why?" he asked of the sky. The night delivered no answer, only a muffled distant sound like thunder, evidence of an aircraft cutting through the blackness.

He walked on. Conscious of the possibility that the answers darkness gave were those that the mind projected outwards. Easier to believe you were inspired or cursed from some external force than to take responsibility for influencing and imposing the patterns of the Universe. Maybe in reality there was no such thing as chance or providence, all events being determined mathematically. Life no more than one huge equation – the answer fixed. Not malleable.

Had he placed his faith in madness? Delusion, he knew, was a strange fellow. The mysterious guest invited into the mind. The eternal conjurer who performed to cast shadows over truths the mind would rather deny, or light upon the evil it wished to perpetrate. It was always the hidden things that he, like most, was afraid of, yet sought – things which lay in wait behind closed doors, barricaded fortresses, never that illuminated by the lamp.

But now the locked doors of his past had been prised open. He could see himself as if from a distance. A man like the madmen remembered from his childhood, bundled up in overcoats, unshaven. No more than a beggar. The boy he'd once been gone.

Escaping the path his father had hewn for him, a path where the edges

I

were sharply defined, directions clearly signposted, the equation exact and correct, had led him here.

He stumbled, remembering the idealism of his youth – the belief that one could fulfil an external plan and had been chosen to do so. Chimerical thinking. Searching to find the essence of the meaning of life in dark places, spiralling into drug use then vagrancy, believing he was breaking away when in truth in league with the conjurer. Now the final trick had been played. His father was gone. Dead. The two-week old obituary confirmed it. The finality seared him. Now there could be no forgiveness or reconciliation. He'd likely own it all. Everything he'd wished to turn his back on.

Finding the broken fence at the side of the warehouses he squeezed the bulk of his body through, making his way across the muddy wasteland and down the soft damp slope toward the railway bridge. The trains, after the eleven o'clock cargo train, did, he knew, not run again till sometime around dawn. By then he would be asleep, unaware of the sudden roar that would serve to silence his thoughts and complete with one stroke the final summation.

Feeling the excitation of fear he wondered if he was brave enough to go through with the plan. Thought again of the impact his death may make on the person who discovered him. Of the train driver who would live with the discovery and the question of 'What If?' He ran a hand over his face, still cognisant of his responsibility to others. He stilled. Listened to the silence, barely registering the sound at first, merely conscious of, and giving vague acknowledgement to the background whine reminiscent of nurseries and fairy tales before the heightened awareness and recognition.

By the time he located the sound he was fully sober. The child hidden beneath the rags and boxes lifted and concealed within the warmth of his greatcoat in seconds. Within minutes he was clambering up the slope of the embankment toward the highway, the long forgotten taste of purpose sweet upon his tongue.

# 1 TICK TOCK

John paced. Checking the clock that hung within the entrance to the chapel building at each turn, almost eight; still no sign of Dr Franklyn – why did the guy do this? Hadn't he given the man enough to demonstrate that what was happening cosmologically needed rapid intervention? He rubbed at his jaw. Wished he could move on what he already knew. Instead he was waiting, controlled by the tick-tock of time – straitjacketed.

An entire life spent waiting – for people and processes to reach some sort of fruition or closure, while endlessly trying to fathom the mysteries of the Universe when he couldn't even untangle the mystery of himself or his beginnings. Instead he kept returning to the blank space where his past should be, constantly quelling the sense of urgency to move forward.

He glanced at the door to Franklyn's office. Hating the power game Franklyn enjoyed playing, tried to shake off the blanching feeling of anger evoked by failing to set personal rules to play by. He could sit all night and day and Franklyn wouldn't show up. It wouldn't be the first time.

Feeling the increasing agitation quickening and thickening his blood he curled his hand around the mobile phone in his pocket. Retrieving it, determined he'd just text Franklyn and then be gone.

The Chapel doors swung open. "John," Dr Franklyn acknowledged him without making eye contact. "With you when I'm ready," he spoke as he unlocked the door to his office, before disappearing inside and closing it behind him.

John slipped the mobile back in his pocket. Cursing for not leaving before Franklyn arrived. But he needed a response. He'd emailed Franklyn a brief draft of his findings. He laughed to himself. Brief draft – it had taken him over three weeks of sleepless nights and a hundred rewrites and edits to make the paper as concise as possible. Franklyn would likely rip it apart if he hadn't done so already.

It made no sense. It seemed so clear. Was it in the writing down of his thoughts that the essence of what he was trying to convey became fogged – distorted? Maybe he was chasing down too many different avenues. Yet no single discipline could explain what was happening. The mathematics of the Universe was not discrete.

Each time he thought he'd captured the time frame or the

measurements there was some other factor he couldn't define. But there was no denying the evidence. There was something going on – an increasing rotational pull, the Universe itself or the core of the Earth out of synch. If it wasn't then why was it that certain distant planets evaded discovery? The solar system was dependent on its component parts. New planets were discovered not always because some saw them, but because, like an algebraic equation, something had to be if something else was. Something wasn't adding up.

He'd expected answers. The Earth's rapidly diminishing magnetic field, the repulsive forces of the Universe, the rotational shift of the axis of the Earth. Instead he was finding more questions. He'd already identified the problems, the errors with optical configurations – time slip or drift.

He leaned back against the cold stone of the wall, aware of the frantic jitter in his foot, the constant flexing and unflexing of his fingers. Maybe he was losing the thread. He'd read so much – too much. Too many nights without sleep struggling to keep his thoughts focused, attempting to articulate his reasoning. Knowing it must mean something – it had to. The Great Pyramid of Giza centre of the world's landmass built upon the primeval mound, the reverence with which the ancient people held Sirius – so many connections.

Why couldn't Franklyn help him out instead of exhausting him with his constant requirements and demands to carry out more analysis on the missing capstone theory? It was important, but the work on optical configurations required more analysis too. If his theory on the errors he'd identified was correct it could be crucial in determining the timeframe for acceleration of the Universe. Yet Franklyn had failed to comment other than to require more in depth analysis. John couldn't help but be afraid he was losing track, stumbling into brick wall after brick wall, because he was being forced off the path. Maybe he hadn't even found it yet.

"John," Franklyn called from his office.

John pressed his palms against the stone. His stomach cramping, his mouth dry. Why had he asked Franklyn for a meeting when his brain felt as if it was dissolving? He moved forward reluctantly, entered the room. Franklyn sat at his desk facing his computer.

"I've looked at the note you sent me, John."

Still standing, John watched Franklyn scroll down the document. A note? It had taken him so long to write – over a hundred pages of text, ten pages of mathematical analysis and seven pages of diagrams. He ran his tongue across his lips. "I was hoping…"

"Scientists don't hope," Franklyn, cut in, swivelling his chair to face John as he spoke. "Hope is for the religious – the foolish."

John was aware of stepping back.

Franklyn's full upper lip rose slightly, revealing just the tips of his front teeth. He leaned back in his seat. The confident senior academic, relaxed. In charge as always, gesturing John toward a chair with no more than a slight movement of his chin.

John sat. His focus downward, fixed on the scuffed leather of his shoes, the spatters of mud on his frayed jeans, he couldn't look at Franklyn. He needed to compose himself before he spoke. The man's glare close to an assault, he wanted to avoid it till he was ready. Taking a deep breath as Julia had advised him, he slowly lifted his head.

"I think the figures tell us something, Dr Franklyn," he said, his eyes on the computer screen yet conscious of Franklyn's fixed stare upon him. "You asked me for more clarification and I've provided it. If I'm right the fact that some outer planets have only been discovered through the reflection of the light they produce or obscure and not the planet's mass as it relates to the rest of the solar system then that means there is a strong possibility that Sirius…"

Franklyn's laugh threw him off guard, invading the space around him. The old familiar sense of wooziness rushed in, tightening his throat; the urge to run as the panic rose, rapidly increasing the tension across his skull. He could feel the perspiration, the sudden dampness on his back, his forehead. He wanted to wipe away the clammy smear above his lip. He struggled to take a breath. Despite following the instructions Julia, the university counsellor, had given him, it caught in his chest.

"Breathe steady," she advised. "Keeping your thoughts focused, your vision directed on a single point, exploring its centre."

In her office it had seemed as if it might work. He'd even thought it might work in here, till Franklyn laughed.

Trying to swallow, and attempting to control the blurring in his vision, he glanced at Franklyn.

"I think," Franklyn said. All trace of laughter gone. His expression neutral, his hands flat against the desk, his profile caught in the light from the computer screen revealing nothing. "That you need to reconsider your position here, John," he extracted a nail file from the pencil holder as he spoke, began to clean under his nails. "I know we accepted you here on a scholarship because of what appeared to be your outstanding results." He paused, a smirk twisting his mouth. "Oh and the cosmology paper you'd supposedly written for your degree project, of course." He tapped the nail file against the palm of his hand.

John, feeling the sudden rush of anger sparked by the implied accusation, opened his mouth to speak.

Franklyn raised his hand. "However," he said.

John mentally scrambled to retrieve the words he'd intended to use in his own defence.

"Judging by the standard of your current work," Franklyn continued, "I'm questioning whether you are actually here on your own merit." He stopped, purposely examining his nails before beginning to file them.

John waited for the spasm in his diaphragm to release the breath caught in his chest. Was Franklyn accusing him of cheating? His mind swung backwards in time, his body experiencing every wave of fear and nausea as it had over fifteen years ago. The destroying of the work he'd spent so many hours on. The accusations that he was a liar and an attention seeker, the undeniable shame he'd felt. Even though he'd done nothing wrong. Berke the respected teacher – silent assassin of children in his care, John shut down the memory. He wanted to move forward, not back.

He turned to the present, aware suddenly of the darkening room, the day slipping imperceptibly away outside. He looked at Franklyn, who, checking his nails were to his satisfaction, returned the file to the pencil holder.

"Right, where was I?" Franklyn questioned, glancing at John, as if only dimly aware of his presence in the room.

John watched as Franklyn clicked the mouse. Closing the document he'd sent him.

"I'm not going to print it, John," Franklyn said as he highlighted the title in the file list, his hand lingering over the mouse before clicking for the drop-down menu and hitting the delete button. "I'm removing it." He turned. His face flushed the furrows on his forehead tight, his mouth a thin flat line. "Why? Why am I removing it? Because, John, quite simply, it's crap." He rolled his chair backwards and pushed himself out of his seat. "First class crap." He made his way to the door and opened it.

John stood, aware that the meeting was over, the space housing his brain generating a persistent dull pain.

"I think you need to know," Franklyn said, while checking his watch, "that self indulgence and flights of fancy carry no weight in this institution. The continuation of the scholarship we provided you with isn't a given." He took off his glasses, gestured toward the computer. "Your work lacks not only merit, but logic."

John stared at the blank screen Franklyn was now pointing at. Pixels, thousands and thousands of beams of light all crammed together almost interlinking, fired by a single click. He turned to Franklyn.

"How much did you read?" he said.

"Enough," said Franklyn, "to make a point of putting your current position here at Bloomfield on the agenda for the faculty meeting. We can't have you spouting to undergraduates in this institution, the kind of nonsense you're espousing in your papers."

Unaware of the point at which he'd actually mobilised his legs and removed himself from Franklyn's presence, John made his way out of the chapel building across the quadrangle and into the monk's corridor that led toward the car park. So the scholarship wasn't a given. Franklyn had said it more than once over the previous three years.

He kicked at a stone. It was as if Franklyn was holding him to ransom at every opportunity. Demanding more and more – constant calls for preparation of more papers Franklyn could put his name to. Providing what John knew were flat reiterations of the theories of other scholars and requiring that John tear them apart and rebuild in the likeness of Franklyn's own particular theoretical stance.

All of it, the whole purpose, so Franklyn could continue in his position at Bloomfield cultivating the academic field to grow his reputation and achieve his professorship. That's how it worked. Franklyn was good at accessing research funding which would enable him to pimp off other more able minds. Sometimes it seemed that the PhD researchers were so desperate for position and the possibility of long-term tenure at Bloomfield that some were willing to prostitute their own thinking.

He closed his eyes. The nausea returning, he couldn't, wouldn't do it. He'd held back from fulfilling Franklyn's requirements. They could withdraw the scholarship – throw him out. At this point he didn't care anymore. He'd thought this place would enlighten him. Instead it was threatening to force him back into the dark space he'd been determined to never willingly enter again.

He heard the sound of the sudden downpour beating against the tiled apex of the corridor and rushing along the cast iron gutters as he approached the exit. The rain predicted for earlier in the day had waited for him. He heaved open the arched door. The flagstones in the courtyard already slick with the rain as it ran in rivulets forming small spouts where it met the gaps in the broken kerb. He looked across to the yellow shelter, a flash of unexpected colour against the backdrop of the almost medieval stone archway, which led to the university's main gate. The shuttle bus would have long since left the campus.

He shouldn't have waited for Franklyn. The whole meeting had been futile. The words, the things he'd intended to say had shrivelled in his mouth. He'd let Franklyn humiliate him. He always let the bastard humiliate him. He'd even have to walk to the station now. He felt in his pocket for the train fare then remembered he'd needed to go to the cash point first.

He stopped. He was wearing his black bomber. His cash cards were in his only other jacket – his denim. The one now still on the back of his chair in his apartment with his cash cards buttoned safely in the top pocket. So? He was walking home – the full five miles. What did it matter? Maybe he needed the space, the quiet, the rain to wash him clean of Franklyn and the memory of his own inability to defend himself from the man. He needed to move. He ducked his head, began the journey.

# 2 ANGRY

"Have you ever argued with anyone, John?"

He scraped at a shred of ochre oil paint on the knee of his jeans. Why he'd given in to a mad urge to daub paint on canvas less than an hour before his appointment with Julia he didn't know. The result was a mess. But the canvas had drawn him, an escape into imagery to a space without words or numbers. He'd seen how the light from the window had caught the blue-cobalt, blended with green, of the background. Tried to recreate the impression of light illuminating the landscape. He'd failed.

Julia sighed. Reminded him of where he was. He looked up. Her face was relaxed; her blue eyes half closed, her mouth forming a tentative smile.

"Have you, John?"

He smiled back – his own smile reflexive. He shook his head – his hands involuntarily clasping the taught muscles around the long bones of his lower thighs.

"I guess, in my head I argue about everything." He pressed against his knees, softening the rigidity of his posture. "Everything I read. Everything I hear, everything I see. I always have."

"How about people?"

He noticed how her braid moved rhythmically across her shoulder as she spoke; thought about her question. Wondered why her questioning seemed so far off the mark as to the reason he was there.

"Do you argue with people, John?"

He couldn't think. Aware only vaguely that he challenged theoretical stances, provided analytical argument in the papers he produced. Did that count? Is that what she meant? He thought about his peers. He couldn't remember arguing with them, only arguing about something separate to both of them.

"Angry, then – can you remember being angry?"

He noticed her eyes had opened fully; averted his. He'd always been angry. Why was she asking him these questions? He'd only agreed to see her because she offered help with stress reduction techniques. He'd been advised that freezing on the spot when he tried to present a paper was not acceptable.

He knew it wasn't. But it didn't matter how much work he put in, how much effort. The moment he realised he was being assessed on his performance, rather than listened to for his ideas the breath died in his throat, visual acuity departed, the nausea rose. So much worse when Franklyn was there, Dr fucking Franklyn with his smirk and the way he shook his head as if to say "No, John, no John, you really shouldn't be wasting our time". Stupid but that's when he'd find sawdust in his mouth instead of words, a void where he should have had thoughts. He turned toward Julia who had moved forward ever so slightly on her chair.

"Yes," he told her.

She sat back.

He ran his fingers through his hair, sensed the throb of pulse against his temples. He could feel the anger now, wondered if Julia could see it.

He waited for her next question. There wasn't one. She just sat. As if she was allowing the silence to move around them – touching the walls, the floor, the ceiling. Fluid at first, then forming into a hard brittle mass hovering between them, building its own invisible power, almost unbearable, he couldn't stand it, smashing an imaginary fist through its centre, breaking it with his admission, "I'm so fucking angry, Julia," he said, his voice almost a whisper. "So fucking angry sometimes I think I'm going to explode."

Julia moved her head to one side. Unfazed. "Are you willing to work with the anger, John?"

He absorbed the softness of her voice. How could he work with something he couldn't even define, only attempt to control? "I apologise for my language," he said. "I've no idea where that came from."

"The fact...the truth is," she began, "unlike you, I know very little – probably nothing, about cosmology, geodetics, astronomy, black holes, exploding stars and outer space." She laughed.

He noticed for the first time she had a small dimple on one side of her face – the roundness of her cheeks fuller on the left as she expressed amusement.

"What I do know, John," she said, continuing, "is that suppressed anger affects not outer space but the inner man or woman...and has the same capacity to create or destruct as all of your cosmic energy forces."

"I don't know how much time I have..."

"John," she said. "None of us do."

He noticed the dimple again. Was she playing – pretending to misinterpret his meaning. "I mean..." He paused. "I don't know if I should be working harder toward finding the right kind of evidence for my ideas. When I presented the paper to Dr Franklyn..." He stopped. Focusing inward on the memory. "When I put together the thesis it seemed clear. I worked day and night ensuring clarity." He saw Julia smile. "It was just when I stood up on the rostrum in front of all the academics. I hardly managed to outline the summary. Dr Franklyn was shaking his head even before I began."

"And?" Julia's braid swung forward as she moved.

"I froze. Everything I felt – believed I understood seemed cloudy." He stared at his shoes. Imagined Julia thinking how stupid he was, wondered if her face was still relaxed – calm. "I had to stop. I stood there with every one of them, all the academics staring at me. I just waited till they all started talking amongst themselves – till they eventually filed out of the lecture room."

"Dr Franklyn too?"

"No, he waited – told me to collect my stuff. I told him I felt ill – virus or something, asked would he read the paper if I sent it to him?"

"That request resulting in the meeting you told me about – where he…"

"Told me the scholarship was not a given. Yes. It wasn't as if I didn't try all the techniques we'd talked about – you'd led me through. The breathing; the focus, it seemed like it might work. I'd completed a rewrite – everything. But he kept me waiting for so long…"

"He's done that before?"

"About every single time we've arranged a meeting. Sometimes he doesn't turn up at all."

"And that makes you feel?"

He looked around the room. The stripped pine bookcases lined with journals, the pieces of rock, some variegated with colour, some black that she used as bookends. The watercolour on the wall behind her with its softly muted colours depicting a sunrise over an expanse of water, he liked it, wasn't sure why.

"John," Julia called him back.

He looked across to where she sat. No barrier of a desk between them.

"I asked how does that make you feel?"

He stilled his gaze, searched for a lie that would suffice for a truth. Played with the jigsaw of words on his tongue, swallowed the stone that had formed in his throat and tasted the blood from where his teeth pressed down on the flesh of his lower lip.

"Feel," the word stretched out, long and empty. He didn't want to consider it, pushed the sense of it from him. It wouldn't go. He didn't want to talk about feelings. He wanted someone to help him gather the courage to act on what he knew. He felt as if his brain was dislodged. He needed to play for time in order for his emotions to subside till the word was no more than an echo of sound that couldn't hurt him. He didn't want to stay where he was.

9

"Like something, someone…" he said, unable to hold it at bay. Turning his head to find focus anywhere other than Julia's face. The cross point in the sash window then back to his hands still holding his knees, then back up at Julia. "Someone," he said, feeling something energising the base of his spine. He moved, unfurling his posture, pressing his hands down hard against the arms of the chair. "Like someone who should." He took a breath. "Like someone who should be getting out of here…" he rose to his feet as he spoke. "Thanks for your time," he said, before turning toward the door.

"John," she said.

He was already on his way.

# 3 MISSING

Tearing off his coat and scarf he made toward the window in the basement storage area, the place, which doubled as an office for the postgraduate researchers; nicknamed the Hot House. It had never made any sense to him why everywhere had to be heated like a sauna. This place was the worst, with all the hot water pipes for the upper floors criss-crossing the low ceiling.

When he'd been told he would share an office and heard what it was called, thoughts of a room – a place of ideas being nurtured to fruition with a view and a colleague who was as equally dedicated to quiet focussed study had been the image his mind had created. The reality had been this airless space, below ground almost, with only one window that could be partially opened. Four other researchers, including Greg, who he was hoping to avoid, shared the limited, chaotic and poorly lit space. The positives were that it provided additional area for the extensive documentation he was gathering. Was straight across from the library and enabled him occasionally to access the more extensive facilities of the Universities IT network and password controlled online sites.

He swiped the back of his hand across his forehead. Five minutes and he was already starting to cook. He'd only called to collect some of his files before heading to return some books to the library. He didn't have to attend any seminars or lectures or provide any individual student support till Friday. But if Franklyn had his way he wouldn't be required to attend anything or support anyone ever again. They'd pull in another PhD research student to help with the supervision of the undergraduate projects – one of the elements of the role he enjoyed most – Franklyn's supposed major area of concern.

He squeezed between the desks and sat down. Why did his theories seem so clear if Franklyn viewed everything presented to him as nonsense? He attempted to focus. He'd come for the file he needed. He'd probably be collecting the rest of his stuff sooner, rather than later, if Franklyn had spoken to the Faculty.

Rifling through the files he kept on, and around his workspace, he berated himself for his lack of organisation. But there was so little room. He was sure he'd left it here. He should have been able to walk in pick up what he wanted and get back out again. Preferably before Greg turned up, otherwise he'd never get out of the place. Once Greg started talking about his research that's all Greg did – talk about it. There didn't seem to be any papers being produced. Fewer to be rejected and humiliated over John guessed. How did Greg get away with it?

OK so Greg had some capacity in programming and database management on top of his degree, which meant he could offer a lot of technical support to some members of the Faculty. But in terms of his own research the only thing he seemed to produce was a constant torrent of talk and a continuing supply of ever multiplying coffee stained cups. They covered every spare space on Greg's desk, and his too by the look of it.

John picked up the cup that didn't belong on his desk. The cup didn't bear Greg's trademark black tar contents – his preferred strength of coffee – melded round the bottom of the cup.

John placed it next to Greg's PC. Reckoning it probably belonged to some poor unsuspecting graduate, or member of the academic administrative team who'd called in by mistake and been overwhelmed by Greg and his verbal addiction.

The lack of quiet meant that most, if not all, of John's own complex work was completed at home. Where he could think, but lack of space meant he'd stored a lot of his stuff here.

But he needed the presentation file. It contained all the data he'd been unable to present. The file held all his main calculations, some of the diagrams. Why wasn't it where he remembered leaving it? He'd only brought it back in here from his apartment so he could run through all his notes before he got behind the lectern three weeks ago. Why had he bothered? His mind, his memory, had clammed shut. One look at Franklyn's shaking head and a shutter had come down.

If he'd felt like a loner amongst the other researchers and academics before, he felt like a Pariah now. Several members of the academic team had looked straight through him when they'd seen him on campus. Signalling he was no longer part of the group.

He chewed on his lip, realising he probably never had been. Maybe it was just as well he hadn't attended the Cosmology Conference, the one he should have attended but wasn't invited to. At least he hadn't had to contend with the blank stares of the rest of the faculty members who'd heard of his failure. Or maybe they'd already heard from Dr Franklyn that the scholarship awarded by the university to John Begvious was likely to be withdrawn.

He looked through the bookcase. The file wasn't there. Kneeling down he pulled out some of the boxes stored beneath his desk. Nothing. Maybe he'd taken it home. He felt the familiar tension at the top of his skull, more a spasm than a headache. It was occurring more frequently now, whenever he tried to remember where he'd put things. That's why he rarely put anything away. The reason his apartment was such a mess. The reason his desk both above, and below had the things he needed easily accessible. He liked everything in view. So why couldn't he find what he was looking for?

He moved things about – checked the drawers. His diary was missing too. How much did he need it? It was hard to remember what was in there. Important dates, phone numbers, websites – meetings he'd attended. Had he even taken the file to the lecture hall? He put a hand to his head pressing hard against his left temple, which had started to contract, before grabbing his jacket, scarf and rucksack.

He was halfway to the door as Greg swung in. Greg – all twenty-one, solid muscular, stone of him. John's heart sank.

"Wondered where you'd got to, John." Greg manoeuvred his bulk forward keeping John's exit blocked. "As I was saying last week…" He waved his arm to indicate the past, causing the coffee from his cup to spill forward and splash down his leg as he gestured. He laughed. "Drink problem – never was a man who could hold it." He leaned forward to rub the stain, spilling more coffee as he did so. He looked up, "Thought you weren't due back in till the end of the week." He stood. "Funny, I was hoping to see you today – have a chat about my research." He rested his coffee on the filing cabinet by the door.

John groaned inwardly.

It was an hour later before Greg moved from the door to head back up to the main campus, for what John assumed from experience would be a long lunch break with one of the many female students Greg strung along. The guy was a magnet.

John felt sapped. He'd listened as best he could to the detailed account of the analysis Greg said he needed to carry out for the faculty team. Despite himself he'd offered to help Greg pull it together. Truth was it would probably take him less time to sort through, input, analyse and report on Greg's research than the time he spent listening to Greg procrastinating.

He considered whether he needed any more work to do. Did he really need any more on his plate? No, but for all Greg's inability to stop talking and do some work or let anyone else do theirs at least, for what it was worth, he treated John the way he treated everyone else. He seemed an OK guy. As well as the bulk of him taking up so much space Greg seemed to have an additional problem with fit. Greg didn't seem to fit at Bloomfield, John thought, anymore than he himself did.

With a rushed reminder, hastily tapped into his mobile to remember to check his emails later for Greg's outline and attachments, which he'd promised Greg he'd review, he ran up the stairs to the ground floor then through the side exit. Crossing over to the newly built library, a futuristic glass and metal building, incongruous amongst the sandstone block of the old, and located almost centre to the campus, he remembered the other papers he had in the file. The file that wasn't where he'd expected it to be. He hadn't even asked Greg had he seen it – hadn't had a chance. But he needed it. The rough data, the handwritten calculations and diagrams, his notes on Sirius A and Sirius B, the detail on the capstone, he hadn't typed them up yet but the notes were important, the diagrams and calculations too. All those ideas and thoughts that came to him late at night, scrawled down for future reference.

Sometimes he could research for hours without getting anywhere. Then suddenly a spark, as if he'd been looking through a Kaleidoscope, the pieces disparate – jumbled. Then he'd turn the cylinder – a slight movement of his head and a glimpse of the picture he was searching for would emerge. And somehow he'd know he wasn't crazy.

He stopped in his tracks before he even reached the looming shadow that the library building cast, over what had once been almost a suntrap of grassed area for student's to relax and catch up on their studies. Realising he'd been so keen for the chance to escape from Greg's verbal overload, he hadn't even checked his pigeonhole for mail – for the letter from Franklyn. The one he'd been expecting since their last meeting.

He turned. Started back toward the building he'd just left – the Hot House of an office. Sure that if past experience were anything to go by Franklyn would have made every effort to meet with the Faculty team by now. Keen to humiliate him further by discussing the worthiness of continuing the funding for the scholarship. If Franklyn had, and there was an agreement to get John out, Franklyn would waste no time putting it in writing. He'd never wanted him in full stop. John considered his options. He needed a way forward.

# 4 DEBRIS

"This place should be a certified danger zone, John."

He stared up at Sarah. Wished he'd locked the door.

"It's almost impossible to move, without risking the likelihood of sprawling over something," she said.

He stayed seated on the floor of his apartment. Exactly where he was when Sarah uninvited, arrived. She'd just pushed open the door, caught him staring into space like someone who'd lost the plot.

Despite his discomfort at being caught sitting like a pathetic heap he felt a rush of gladness that she was there. He averted, what he imagined was his own fraught gaze, away from her concerned one.

A quick survey of the room told him she was right. Files, documents, and boxes now littered every available surface of the apartment. The entire contents of his minimal cramped area in the Hot House office, which he'd removed in haste in a taxi, the day he'd discovered his file and diary were missing, only for both to mysteriously return in the space of his ten-minute absence. He'd only meant to go back and check his pigeonhole for mail.

Sarah cleared a space on the coffee table and sat down. "You weren't going to answer the phone were you?" She turned as the pile of documents she'd just displaced tottered and fell. The papers splaying like a Japanese fan. "Sorry," she said as she bent forward attempting to gather the pile together. "What you choose to do is none of my business, John. It's jus… well." She paused. "We, well I…not seeing you at the conference I was a bit concerned."

John wished there was somewhere other than the floor for him to sit.

"So what's going on?" she said.

"Stuff," he said, pushing himself up. Wishing for the second time he'd made sure the front door was locked when he'd come back in from picking up some food. But he hadn't. Instead he'd slithered down onto the only available square metre of space. Amidst what was probably the debris of both his past, and once intended future research prospects, attempting to play his guitar – badly. The way he seemed to do most things in his life.

There was just too much to sort out – his past, his future, where he was going next if the plug on his funding was pulled. He still hadn't heard if his allowance was to continue either.

"I may not be here," he said as he attempted to focus his thoughts. Aware of the look of puzzlement that crossed Sarah's face, he shrugged. "Not here – at Bloomfield – next semester. Would you like some coffee?"

"You're quitting?" she said.

He threaded his way across the room to the kitchen. For the first time in a fortnight seeing his living conditions as someone else may see them, the place a nightmare – an indisputable fire hazard. As well as the boxes and bags erupting their contents from every square foot of the room, were the finished and unfinished canvases. He quashed the urge to turn them against the wall.

"Why?" Sarah continued.

John felt himself pale. He didn't need this.

"No person in his or her right mind walks away from the kind of scholarship you've…"

He ran the tap. Drowning out the end of the sentence she was speaking. He wanted to tell her that maybe he wasn't in his right mind. Finding the file on his desk along with his diary when he'd returned to the Hot House to check his pigeonhole two weeks ago had sent him to some strange place.

Greg who had supposedly gone on his lunch just happened to be back in the room. He said he hadn't seen anyone come in. Said he'd wedged the door when he'd gone out for more coffee. Hadn't been able to figure why John was so uptight.

"You probably just missed it," he said. His back turned. Then he'd tried to get back on to the subject of his own research again, even though they'd been over it more than a thousand times, even though John had practically volunteered to do it for him. It was like a recording, a stuck track.

John remembered how he'd actually pushed past Greg to get out.

"I've emailed you the stuff…my research," Greg had shouted after him, totally unperturbed from the encounter.

John had needed air, something to silence the question that was running unanswered around his brain. Had he really not seen the file – was he losing it completely?

He'd felt a mad crazy panic. Was someone going through his work? Remembered other times he'd been unable to locate documents. When stuff, important papers, went missing from his desk, he'd thought… convinced himself, it was just his lack of organisation. The constant tiredness when he hadn't slept for days in a struggle to clarify and provide supportive evidence for everything he hypothesised before he delivered it to Franklyn.

He'd been halfway across the campus when he'd spotted one of the porter's transport trolleys lying idle. Before considering the reasonableness of what he was doing he'd hauled it back across the grassed area. Waited till he saw Greg exiting the building and crossing toward the cafeteria, the almost waist length ponytail, the guy was so proud of, freshly combed and cinched.

John made his move, pulling the trolley into the building and into the lift down to the Hot House. Loading almost all his files and papers onto it, before dragging the lot onto the old service elevator and up to the main floor, managing to get himself and his stuff out of the building like a bat out of hell before Greg returned from lunch to render him captive again. He'd paid the taxi driver extra to fill up the cab like a removal van, had gotten everything back to his apartment. Now all his possessions appeared to be mushrooming like fallout around him.

Then he'd started on the big search. Searching to see if there was anything missing, anything incriminating in the work he'd been doing. Anything Franklyn could use as leverage to convince the Faculty that he was a poor researcher or research supervisor or that he was indoctrinating the undergrads with his nonsensical theories.

He couldn't even tell if there was anything missing – couldn't remember how much of the stuff he was struggling to understand he'd written down or stored in his head. It was the trying so hard to get to grips with the ideas coming at him thick and fast. Something had to give. He sighed. Maybe it already had. He poured the boiling water onto the coffee.

Sarah had cleared more space when he returned with the drinks. He placed the mugs on the table before returning to his slumped position on the floor.

"I guess you're wondering what I'm doing here?" she said.

"Sort of." He forced a smile. "But it's good to see you whatever the reason." He sipped his coffee. "I just wish you hadn't caught me looking like someone who's lost it."

"Angus wondered why you never got back to him."

"Angus?" He experienced a sudden unexpected lift at the mention of his old school friend. "You've heard from Angus?"

"He's been trying to contact you – all of us. I met up with him at the conference."

"He was at the conference? I haven't heard from him." He paused. Tried hard to locate the memory of the last time they'd spoken. Remembered. "In fact the last contact I had was when he was horse riding, or planning to go horse riding across the Iranian desert…that's well over twelve – no eighteen months ago…"

"Yeah, the horse riding – he's done all sorts of stuff since then, John."

"He was with a team of others," John was trying to recall the detail. "A

17

group of gap year graduates or…I don't know. I'm sure I texted him at the time, Sarah. It wasn't as if there was an address or anything I…"

"You're right. It must have been over a year ago, at least. He said he'd emailed you here at the University. Even written an old fashioned letter, but nothing back from you."

"Emailed me?" John imagined the hundreds of emails choking up his PC.

His hands gripped his knees. "I can't…" He didn't finish; just felt a dim ache in his head. Had he even been misplacing letters and deleting emails? Binning mail because he didn't know what he was doing half the time.

Sarah picked up where she'd left off. "He contacted me because he thought you'd probably be at the conference…" She pulled out a band from her pocket and pulled her hair back, securing it behind her head. "You weren't there so I…"

"Where wasn't I?"

"The conference, I thought I'd already explained. Are you OK, John?"

"I don't understand, I…" he began

"John," Sarah said. "What's going on? You don't seem like yourself." She started to laugh then stopped. "What a totally meaningless expression," she said. "I mean who are you – who are we when we're not ourselves? You understand what I mean?"

"No, I mean, yes," John said, not sure if he did. He paused, considering, before continuing. "I was just confused about the conference and Angus. I haven't heard from him at all. How is he?"

"He's great, John. He's been in America for the past three months. He's been contacting everyone. You know the way he is. He got some teaching at Grettsberg…"

"Grettsberg, the observatory – the telescope?"

"Well, yes and…"

"How long has he been there?" He pushed himself up from the floor again, almost looming over Sarah. "Grettsberg. Has he said what it's like?"

"He said the university is fine he…"

"No, I mean the telescope, Sarah. Is it as good as they say it is? You must have interviewed some people… "

"John." Sarah waved a hand between them. "You haven't seen me for over six months and Angus for over – well almost two years and all you can talk about, all you're interested in is the telescope. How would I know what it's like? I came here to see if you were OK. For some reason you've decided on a big communication blackout. You're living…" She gestured round the room, "existing in some sort of bomb zone. You're gaunt. You're acting odd and you haven't even asked me how I am."

John wished there was some accessible space around him so he could pace. He was excited. But Sarah, "Dan," he said. "Have you two…" He tussled for words. He wasn't good at this sort of stuff – relationships. Sarah shook her head.

"Dan's fine, and we two haven't anything," Sarah said.

"So everything's OK – good?" John looked round the room trying to remember where in the conversation they where, the telescope, Angus, the telescope, the conference – Sarah, Sarah and Dan? There was something he hadn't asked. He looked at Sarah who was staring unblinking back at him. He remembered.

"Sarah," he said. "How are you?"

"John," she replied. "I'm fine. But something's telling me you're not."

# 5 GRETTSBERG

He picked up his emails. The one from Angus had arrived the day he'd taxied his belongings from Bloomfield. The day his laptop blatantly refused to communicate with him. He was thankful he had back up for the hard drive. The whole thing had just nuked on him. He'd needed a new motherboard. Luckily the insurance still covered the machine, but the entire contents of the hard drive had been wiped clean, including all the software. It had taken him two days to reinstall everything from the back up after the machine's prolonged stay in the service centre.

'Where the hell are you?' Angus questioned in the email.

Typical of Angus, almost two years he'd been galloping, sailing or hiking around the world for good causes. No one could keep up with him, and the so-called gap year that just got bigger and bigger, but the moment he stalled, he thought everyone should be exactly where he'd last seen them.

John didn't care. Angus was Angus. Angus and Arizona – he could barely believe it. Arizona, America. Sarah said Angus had secured some part time teaching gig at Grettsberg. Angus had confirmed it in his email. John sat back staring at the screen. Grettsberg. The home of the telescope – he could go. Angus had invited him.

He started typing. Explaining to Angus that the letter he'd sent must have gone astray. Telling Angus how great it was to hear from him and how much he was looking forward to meeting up. He didn't mention the Telescope. He wondered how much access Angus had to the observatory equipment. He read through his email before clicking the send button; then started scrolling through the rest of his contacts.

Greg's email was there with the attachment. John downloaded the zip file still wondering why he'd never received Angus's old fashioned written invitation, couldn't understand how the letter had never arrived. He checked his pigeonhole at the Hot House on a regular basis. There'd been nothing other than the usual journals he subscribed to arriving in the mail. The occasional note from an undergraduate panicking about their research project proposals – the kind of notes John always gave top priority to.

Thinking of letters, he wondered if Franklyn's letter would be waiting for him now – a bold print dismissal. Wondered whether he should call back in, check his mail, but the thought of seeing Greg whose research work he'd promised to look at, and completely forgotten about till he'd opened his emails after the two-week absence of his laptop made him feel bad. Maybe he'd have a look at Greg's stuff now. He downloaded the files. Began reading.

Two hours later he was still trying to work it out. The attachment Greg had emailed wasn't Greg's data at all. John realised it was one of his own files. The section on co-ordinates from the paper he knew he'd personally emailed to Franklyn. The paper Franklyn had deleted. The whole presentation had been altered though. It was formatted differently. John didn't remember doing that. Why had Greg changed it? Why did Greg have it?

Aware of the tightness across the top of his skull he checked through his emails in case there'd been some blip on the computer. Remembering the whole thing had been wiped clean so there was no way stuff from the hard drive could be attaching itself to Greg's emails. He needed to get out – walk. Put some distance between him and the stupid file. Was he going crazy or what?

# 6 THE FOOL

He'd been walking in circles round the block for over an hour. Luckily, the guy who lived on the corner who'd set himself up as the main neighbourhood watch captain knew him. Otherwise he'd likely have called the police, the innocent but crazed pacing John was doing clear evidence that he was acting as 'look out' for a burglary. He didn't need that. He didn't want to try and explain himself to the police when he still couldn't explain what was going on with his head.

No matter how many times he completed the route round the block, no matter how many ways he analysed the situation he came up blank. Greg having the co-ordinate files. Why? It wasn't even as if the files were important. He felt his mind pull to a halt. Of course the files weren't important. Why was he trying to work something out that probably didn't need working out? Anybody with any sense or understanding would have been able to produce the diagrams.

He stopped and leaned against the wall. He was losing it. He must be. Why had he been so convinced the file was his? Why – Because Greg had sent it to him? It was a straightforward simple deduction, failing to take into consideration the raft of other factors that could explain the anomaly.

He reached in his pocket for his key. He'd walked enough. There was no mystery or puzzle. Greg had probably just attached the wrong file. Everyone in the Egyptology department had probably pulled together the same diagrammatic framework. No big deal. Pretty obvious, from any simple mathematical analysis, that the points of the co-ordinates around the pyramid represented the points of the compass. The Great Pyramid of Giza was known as the central point of the Earth. It was nothing new. In fact, given he was supposedly a cosmologist in the making why had he digressed to linking parts of his research work to key elements of study outside of the area he was funded to engage with?

He rubbed his jaw. The digression, it probably explained why Franklyn had referred to his paper, the thesis as unadulterated crap. Or something crap. John couldn't remember now. It was probably full of regurgitated hypotheses, discounted postulations and theories that belonged within the framework of other disciplines. Maybe it was just as well – fortuitous, that he'd practically turned to stone on the rostrum, at the lectern. He'd have made an even bigger fool of himself if he'd opened his mouth, than the fool he'd made of himself by freezing like a statue.

He needed to find some way to untangle his thinking. Start fresh. At least he hadn't let Greg down with the research promise. Given that Greg hadn't sent him anything to work with. He didn't have to feel guilty about anything. He unlocked the door and headed up the stairs. He'd eat, play some guitar; let the paranoia unravel.

Halfway up the first flight he stopped. There was something else, too. If the work he'd been doing on the Great Pyramid of Giza, the missing capstone theory he'd been working on, didn't belong in the cosmology department why had Franklyn demanded he submit so much evidence to support it?

# 7 TWIST OF FATE

He had no memory of leaving Julia's office. Wondered how he'd managed to find his way back. He hadn't expected to feel as bad as he did – as if the blood had been slowly drained out of him. This must have been his fourth session with Julia. He'd imagined it would be like the previous three sessions. Uncomfortable, because talking about his own stuff had never been easy, but today he'd actually told her how he felt. Not just the physical symptoms he had when he stood up in front of an audience, but the other stuff. How had she got him there? His limbs felt like lead. Yet somehow his head felt like sponge.

He unlocked and pushed open the door to his apartment. He needed to eat, drink, but all he wanted to do was lie down. First he needed to open the windows. Get some air into the place.

He pulled up the blind and stared at the extensive view the letting agent had promised – the five storey high converted warehouse, which presented almost a solid wall of brick across the way ahead of him. That's how it had always been. The barrier of not knowing, the metaphorical brick wall that hid his past, and by so doing consequently obscured the view or his capacity to shape his future.

He kicked one of the half unpacked cardboard boxes that still littered the room. He'd promised Sarah he'd sort it out but hadn't. But he'd kept his promise to speak to someone. Julia had managed to fit him in with an earlier appointment than the one previously planned.

Julia, who he'd thought – no, Sarah had thought, when she'd pressured him to go see someone several months ago, that he'd be able to overcome his fear of public speaking. He hadn't. He'd just further recognised, or maybe simply admitted how bad he felt. He couldn't believe he'd actually told Julia all that stuff about Berke – Master Berke. What was Julia trying to do? Why did he have to talk about Berke – what did someone from the past have to do with the fact that Franklyn was going to get him thrown out of Bloomfield?

Yet it was still so much there. He'd walked back into that mental space so easily. Julia throwing him the key, he'd turned it without thinking.

He was there again now, a ten-year-old boy sitting quietly at his desk, fascinated by how the light from the window created variegated patterns across the metal-topped bench table of the science lab. Could still see Berke standing behind it, one half of his face in shadow, his hand clutched against the lapel of his Masters gown. Holding it forward like a cloak the way he always did.

"John's very interested in experiments. Aren't you, John?" he said whilst raising his eyebrows in question.

John remembered feeling the first flickers of acceptance. The corners of his mouth tugging almost, but not quite, into a grin, Berke was talking to him. Singling him out.

Maybe Berke had realized he was wrong to have accused him of cheating.

Berke smiled. "John has some very interesting ideas," he announced. Directing the statement to the other boys gathered in the classroom. "I've been working on some interesting ideas too."

Berke was smiling. John remembered continuing to sit quietly, his arms resting on the desk in front of him. He wasn't sure he liked Berke, but he liked interesting ideas and experiments especially if they involved light and energy and parallax like Einstein had been working on. It was the main reason he continued to turn up for some of the extra curricular sessions with the masters.

The Masters – teachers really, took turns to deliver short sessions in the evenings after day school. It was part of the ethos of the school, the Headmaster, Mr Gould, told both old hands and newcomers at the start of each new autumn term. He explained with pride how all the boys had the opportunity to pursue their interests in the evenings within the confines of the school and its grounds.

"We want all our boys to develop into fully rounded characters," he said. Then waited, allowing the hesitant tinkles of laughter that he knew his words would promote before continuing. "Not necessarily the Friar Tuck type of roundness – though goodness knows all our boys eat enough in the dining hall to be staking a claim to his name, and his girth in the future." More laughter followed. "No, what we, all of us here at Holmwood Hill, want for you all is that you pursue as many interests as possible, the arts, science, music and, of course sport. We mustn't forget sport. We here have a formidable record against our opponents at Chirkwood." He beamed, "A record I'd like to keep."

John liked Mr Gould. Was grateful that he'd arranged for him to be accommodated by the Headmaster and his wife during the school breaks. An arrangement that ensured no charges of special treatment if individual pupils were to both study, and be lodged at Holmwood, outside of term time. In retrospect John realised it was the only time he'd been glad he didn't really do sports. If he had he'd have been caught between his alliances to both Holmwood and Chirkwood, whenever he was out on the pitch.

He hadn't been the only boy who needed to be accommodated during the school breaks, even if he was the only boy who had no family to return to at any time.

Sometimes Haziq was accommodated due to the fact that his scientist father and mother always travelled together as part of the international research projects his father was involved in.

Angus joining them one summer-break because his parents had needed to leave for America to deal with a massive lawsuit involving copyright of one of the Snow Leopard's songs. That was the summer Dan had been accommodated too.

When Berke had called him to the front of the class to assist in the experiment John remembered thinking how he'd be able to tell the others. Angus, Haziq and Dan liked experiments. Haziq had shown them all the journals, his father's name written in bold at the head of the page. His eyes flashing with pride and excitement, his skin flushing darker round his angled cheekbones when declaring his father's professorship.

Berke informed the class that what was about to take place was a very special experiment. "An experiment where it is important to remain very quiet," he advised. "You have to close your eyes and keep them closed," he said. "Close your eyes now, John."

John obeyed.

"This is an experiment about the ability to remain inside yourself in the dark while faint electrical pressure is applied."

The palms of John's hands were suddenly damp, his shoulder blades drawing back involuntarily. He wanted to open his eyes and go back to his desk, but wanted Berke and the watching class to see his willingness to participate even more.

"I'm just going to put some cotton wool in your ears before we begin," said Berke.

John remained still as Berke did so. Stood waiting, holding his breath till the first pressure was applied. He exhaled. It didn't hurt. It was just a faint feeling of pressure, as Berke said it would be. It didn't feel like an electrical impulse, but then he didn't know what an electrical impulse would feel like.

It was hard to stay still. The darkness strange, couldn't really feel the edges of his body anymore, as if he was vibrating – small circular movements. He was being turned round he was sure. Maybe it was the electricity that was making him dizzy. He could hear muffled sounds despite the cotton wool in his ears. He was being lifted upwards. Wondered if he was levitating then felt the metal of the lab bench cold against the backs of his bare knees. He was being forced into a sitting position on the bench then the hands left him and the skin on his forehead prickled as the pressure was applied again and then again. The cotton wool was removed from his ears.

"Stand up with your eyes closed," Berke ordered.

Struggling to keep his balance, John complied with the request as the laughter exploded around him. He opened his eyes. Most of the boys in front of him were doubled up with laughter, hands across their mouths trying to stifle the sound.

Berke stood to one side. "Experiment completed," he said. "Anyone who willingly agrees to be kept in the dark is an idiot."

The laughter continued.

John lowered his head, the need for the toilet cramping his stomach. He saw the points on his body where he'd believed the electrical pressure had been applied. There'd been none. He was covered in labels. Each one daubed with an insult. He raised his hand to his forehead. Shaking as he peeled the paper from his skin. John Begvious, his name, was written in cursive script across the first label. Idiot was written in capitals on the second.

He remembered how heavy shame was. He hadn't been able to lift his head. He didn't want Berke or the other boys in the class looking at him, just wanted the waves of humiliation to stop clamping his chest and his gut. Was thankful that Angus, Dan and Haziq, the few he considered his friends were not there to witness him shaking and crying in front of an audience of laughing boys, and a Master whose expression had fleetingly appeared as one of utter satisfaction.

The air from outside the window cooled the heat in his head. He was back in the present, the brick walls of the warehouse still facing him. Nothing much had changed since Berke's experiment. No matter how hard he tried to slam the door on his memories so little had changed. He was still in the dark even if not of his own making or his own volition. John Begvious – a man without any links to his past.

He turned away from the window and reached for his guitar before finding a space on the floor. He picked out the first few notes then began to strum the chords of 'Simple Twist of Fate'. That's what life threw at you. Maybe his parents only found each other for long enough to bring him into being then were lost to each other completely long before he was even born.

# 8 WEIRD

"This is some load of stuff." Dan cast his eyes around the room.

John touched one of the neatly piled cardboard containers he and Sarah had done their best to organise. She'd even advised that he label each box outlining its contents so that he'd be able to find everything he wanted when he returned. John wasn't so sure. He'd formed almost a mental map of the location of things he needed, despite the fact that they appeared haphazardly strewn around the apartment, or heaped in questionable order under and around his desk in the Hot House, as many of the files and documents now surrounding him, had been.

As if reading his thoughts Sarah spoke. "All important," she said. "John needs it all. For when he resumes work on his PhD, don't you, John?"

John shook his head, not quite sure if he was agreeing or otherwise. He was still fighting the urge to unpack and call the whole plan off.

"John," said Sarah.

He knew she was waiting for an answer. She'd been trying to get some confirmation that his PhD was on hold, rather than expunged from his plans for the future since she first turned up unexpectedly over a fortnight ago.

"I've really no idea what I need," he heard himself saying, hedging Sarah's call for some assurance on his academic intentions. "But I can't take it with me if I'm going away for three months."

"The important stuff's backed up on hard drive?" Dan asked.

John chewed his lip. Scared that maybe Dan wasn't as confident as Sarah was of the safety of the storage facility where he'd agreed to store all his stuff. "Well, yes," he began. "You reckon the facility…"

"You need to have it somewhere safe if you're going to sublet the apartment," said Sarah. "How d'you think I'd feel if the place got burgled and…"

"She didn't have enough space for all her own junk," Dan added before Sarah could finish.

Sarah shot Dan a look. John tried to imagine what a relationship must be like.

"Thing is," said Sarah. "I'll keep everything in order till you get back."

"I…" said John.

"It's so…some kind of weird," said Sarah. "How things work out. Who'd have thought you'd get an invite to see Angus just when I needed a place to stay." She ran a hand along the wall. "I'll be perfectly placed for my job at the television studio, but there's no way I could live, even for three months, surrounded by these murky green walls. Is it OK if I paint the place?"

"Sure," said John. "Anything you want. Will you have enough space? Do I need to shift any furniture or anything?"

"Enough for the tools of my trade, I only need as much gear as the next man – or woman." She turned to John. "It's cost me a fortune – cameras, digital processing software, recording equipment, mikes. When I started out I thought they'd all be provided for." She blew air. "But if I'm trying to make a name with freelance commissions. I've got to have my own equipment, anyway."

"It means a lot, you two helping me out, here." John gestured round the room. "I wouldn't have known where to begin…"

"John," Sarah raised her arm "You're helping me out."

"Is true," said Dan as he tested the weight of one of the boxes. "Don't sweat." He smiled. "And I can shoot over at weekends. Or any other time I decide I can't live without her."

John headed toward the kitchen. He'd make coffee or check if there was anything he'd missed.

"Angus thinks it's 'Far Out' that you're going out there," Sarah said as Dan headed downstairs to the van. "What a guy. The way he talks. Sometimes I think he got caught in some kind of generation mix up. Have you booked a date yet?"

John bent to pick up a stray piece of paper, examining it for importance before realising it was a flyer that had come loose from one of the boxes he'd collected for packing his things.

"I don't think it's really sunk in yet," he said as he moved some books around in a box then stopped and stared. "I still can't believe I'm going." He took a deep breath. "It's all moved so fast. You turning up here after the interview, you didn't even tell me that's why you were up here."

"I didn't – didn't want to mention it when you seemed so low." She made as if to move a chair. "You know, breezing in and telling you my good news when you looked as if you'd thrown in the towel." She smiled. "Not awfully good practice."

"I wouldn't have minded. I know how hard you've been working – this TV thing – good opportunity?"

"Think so. If things work out who knows? The reporting I did on the conference swung it for me, I think. But never mind that; let's talk about your trip. I was asking have you got a date?"

He picked up the flyer again, squashed it in his hand and threw it across the room in the direction of the still resident paper bin.

"John," Sarah said.

"I haven't exactly booked a ticket yet," he said hurriedly as he extracted some of the books he'd been moving around in the box that had already been packed and was waiting supposedly ready to be carried down to the van,

"John," Sarah said motioning with her head that he should put the items back in the box.

John shrugged then complied. "I'm going though," he said. "I can't wait to see…"

"Please don't say the telescope, John…"

John shook his head. "I wouldn't dare, Sarah. I didn't even mention it in my emails to Angus but I can't wait." He picked up a box. "I guess I should get some of this stuff downstairs and in the van."

# 9 PYRAMID SECRETS

"Wow," said Sarah, after Dan had finally driven off and they'd returned upstairs. "You actually have floor space. This is not a bad apartment. You could easily, hey John, what's wrong? You look really pale."

John sat down. He wasn't sure if the wooziness he was feeling in his head was a result of running up and down the stairs too many times, or the severing of the attachment bond to all the material results of his work dating back years.

"I just feel a bit weird – all my stuff going off in the van," he said. "Or maybe I've some kind of a blood pressure problem because I'm unfit." He started to rub the muscles above his knees. "It's kind of spooky letting it all go like that – almost as if all the evidence of me – my existence is tied up in the paperwork I've created." He stared up at Sarah, "What if it all goes missing?"

"John," Sarah said.

"Didn't you want to go with Dan?"

"No space, no point," said Sarah. "The guys at the facility will help him unload. I wanted to catch up, where you're up to with things, your research?"

"I've got some theories. Just theories," said John.

"Everything begins as an idea?"

"Sort of," John said, wondering why he hadn't made it a hundred percent clear to Sarah that he may be getting booted off the scholarship.

"But you're working on…"

"Cosmology," he said wondering if he could claim to be working on anything. "You know I've been working on the stabilising forces of the Universe."

"So what was the Egypt thread you were telling me about?"

John couldn't remember talking about Egypt.

"The Great Pyramid, stuff, the capstone…"

"I talked to you. I can't remember. When?"

"I'll make us some coffee," Sarah said. She walked toward the kitchen. "You told me all about the links. The links it has, well the links the ancient people believed it had with the planet Sirius."

She stopped and turned to John. "It's just I've heard some very

31

interesting hypotheses about the measurements associated with the Great Pyramid. At the conference – the fundamental dimensions idea. You familiar?"

"The pyramid code," said John. "The truth is out there somewhere."

"You think the code theory is a good one then?"

"Sort of," he said as she turned and disappeared through the door. "The measurements must be telling us something." He slid a hand through his hair. He couldn't remember having the conversation Sarah was talking about. He listened to the sound of running water, the clink of crockery; the vague hum of traffic outside. Why couldn't he remember things?

"The pyramid layout," Sarah said returning with the drinks. She placed them on the coffee table. "There are all kinds of theories and ideas about how it was built – its structure and shape. What's your take, John?"

He sat down on the now almost clear sofa. At least he didn't have to sit on the floor any more. "Well," he said, not quite sure why Sarah was interrogating him. "Some researchers have suggested that a massive ramp was built to enable the huge blocks to be put into place – but others have argued that you couldn't construct such a ramp, and there's no evidence of where the material from the ramp was removed to, once the pyramid was built – you probably know all this though."

"Some," said Sarah, using her free hand to check the safety of a folding chair that had been unearthed during the sorting and packing, before she sat on it. "I heard some of that, is there any real evidence for either stance?"

"If you look at the basic building blocks of matter," said John. "Theoretical physics – squares and pyramids and stuff…"

"It would have taken years to build," Sarah said. "That seems to be the general consensus of the commentators and researchers I've been reading up on."

"It may have," said John, turning an imaginary pyramid around in his mind as if its shape could reveal its truth. "I didn't know you were that interested," he added. "It's been estimated that there are over two million blocks used in its construction. That's more material than used in all the cathedrals across Europe. So whoever…"

"There are all sorts of theories about its purpose," said Sarah, reaching for her coffee. "I grew up believing what I was told – it was a tomb, no question…"

"Yet no burial artefacts have ever been found in the pyramid to confirm that theory," John stated, the often obscured fact, before continuing. "And while the building of the pyramid itself has been attributed to Khufu, the evidence…"

"D'you think it was, John?"

"Built by Khufu?" He pondered. "There's an amazing amount of speculation. No clear-cut view. It's not easy, Sarah. Evidence is a bit like the science of statistics. Findings can be presented in a way that supports the view, or thesis a person is trying to promote."

He swallowed a mouthful of coffee, wondered for a moment if he was guilty of exactly the same thing. If he was, it wasn't consciously. But then given some of the unexpected twists and turns of his thoughts and emotions during the counselling sessions with Julia maybe it wasn't always easy, or sometimes even possible to locate the root or the driving energy that shaped decisions, directed behaviour or fuelled the terror that could render a person speechless in front of their peers and assessors.

"Your own research turned up anything compelling to support the competing stances?" Sarah said. "I'm only asking because I'm trying to get a handle on things in case I need to write something up." She smiled. "This new job, it could take me anywhere in terms of the programmes we'll be producing. I gave them such a broad overview at interview I could find myself hooked up on the Egyptology theme."

"You could?" said John.

"So where are you at so far?"

"I've been working on lots of different things."

"Spreading yourself far and wide." Sarah laughed. "Why change the habit of a lifetime?"

John wasn't sure if she recognised he was going off track. Had some idea of the fact he was straying beyond the bounds of his own discipline, was testing him. He didn't know whether to care.

"I've been trying different theoretical models for the geometry of the pyramid for some time," he said. "But I keep coming up with inaccuracies in the pyramid's currently perceived size – so I've recalculated and established that for a perfect fit for something called the golden rule…"

"Golden rule?"

"The Golden rule," he said. "The pyramid would have to have a height greater than the present measured height from the Giza Plato which is over four hundred and thirty five foot. The size of a forty storey building."

"For what, John?" She sat forward. "You may as well educate me, seeing as I'm here and I need to know these things for when I get the opportunity to freelance on the science conferences or even contribute to the programme making."

"I'd say over twice the height we believe it to be."

"You're losing me…" Her mobile buzzed. She answered. It was Dan.

Glad that the conversation had swung away from his area of research John swallowed a mouthful of coffee. Sarah didn't need to know about the energy mass transfer calculations he'd been working on to establish how much energy would need to be exerted to build the pyramid if it was twice its current height. Sometimes he wasn't even sure why he was working on it himself.

She clicked off the phone. "Dan has just finished stashing your stuff. He'll be heading back soon," she said. "Quick or what?" She stood up. "So when d'you reckon on me, moving in? I start at the TV Studio beginning of July."

He sipped his coffee. Conscious of how quickly things had changed. Glanced around the apartment, which now that it was mostly clear except for a few key things already looked as if he'd left. He still wasn't sure what he was going to do with his guitar and paints, the portable easel, the canvasses. His laptop was definitely going with him. He thought of all his files, all the things he liked to have around him. Dan was probably turning the key in the storage facility right now. What if he lost the key?

"John," Sarah asked again. "When do you think I'll be able to move in?"

"I'm…" He stalled, wasn't really sure he had the courage to leave – even if it was all practically set in stone.

"I'll need a date."

He hadn't realised he was holding his breath till he suddenly exhaled, the air hissing through his teeth. "How about two weeks?" he heard himself saying. There, he'd said it. He'd put a deadline on what he had to do before he flew out to see Angus.

"It'll be great, John," said Sarah looking suddenly concerned. "It's a good decision."

He wondered why it seemed so easy for people to read his mind. Did his face register all his internal struggles? He finished his drink and picked up the mugs setting them on the tray.

"I'll miss working with some of the young undergraduates," he said. "I've always liked the way some of their minds are geared for the exploration rather than…"

"The journeys end," said Sarah.

He nodded. Despite wanting to move away from the subject of his research his mind was tracking the elements of the conversation.

"I've tried hard to keep focused on the facts," he said as he picked up the tray. He turned to Sarah. "But the same numbers keep coming up what ever way I look at things. Telling me that the agreed original calculations are inaccurate."

"The height," said Sarah. "You think there's some error there – that's what Franklyn has a problem with?"

"I've kept to as many of the facts in my papers as is possible. But if I tell you what I really think…"

"I won't laugh," she said before starting to. She stopped herself. "I'm only laughing because I get scared when you look so serious, John. I don't think the stuff with Franklyn is one bit funny. The guy is a grade 'A' jerk…"

"Sorry," he said. "My fault for speaking my thoughts." He moved toward the kitchen.

"So what's the golden rule? Speak your thoughts. I'm interested. I am."

He stopped, placed the tray down. "I've a theory…" He moved the tray with his fingertip, "That the Great Pyramid is actually a sun temple. But not in the accepted mundane academic sense, more a spiritual temple of the spiritual sun – in fact the first temple built." He paused, staring at the floor, amazed to see so much available space around his feet.

"And Franklyn?" Sarah spoke.

"I haven't told him the half of it, not yet." He raised his head. "But I've given him enough so he can work it out for himself if he wants to explore the possibilities."

"Spiritual temple," said Sarah. "That's not so far off the mark of some of the material I've been reading." She pulled the band from her hair. "Some call it modern heretics," she said. "Claiming that the design of a structure as fantastic as the Great Pyramid…"

"Wasn't even built on the physical plane," said John before she could even finish. He'd been thinking long and hard about that possibility too.

# 10 RETROSPECT

Sitting in the cafeteria outside the station John realised his coffee was probably now cold. He still couldn't believe he'd actually booked a plane ticket to Arizona. He hated flying. It terrified him. He'd only ever been persuaded to fly all those years ago because it meant he would be able to spend time with Angus and his parents.

He'd never forgotten the day Angus had lifted him out of the empty space he thought he'd inhabit forever.

"I've told the folks 'bout you being sick," Angus explained as he searched through the cupboard beside John's bed. "You ever have anything hidden in here that a boy can find and eat? I'm starved."
John rifled through the drawer at the top and produced a cellophane packet of three biscuits that had come sometime with his afternoon tea. "Here," he said, throwing them toward Angus who caught them, opened them and had all three biscuits in his mouth before John even returned his arm to his side, but just the simple act of sitting up, searching for, finding and throwing the packet tired him.

The pneumonia was beaten but he still felt exhausted. The nurse had tried to encourage him to get up and about but every effort was a trial. He hardly remembered leaving the room where Berke had ridiculed him. Didn't remember getting back to the dormitory. All he remembered was the Matron in sickbay, the nurse, the difficulty in breathing, the pain in his chest and Berke's face and the laughter surrounding him. His bed in the infirmary was a safe space. As much as he was trying his body didn't want to leave it.

Angus finished chewing and took a swig of water from a glass. "So, I told them about you being here in the infirmary for weeks."

He'd watched as Angus took another swig of his water.

"Ma said, maybe you'd like to come stay with us." Angus wiped a few crumbs from his lap to the floor.

John swallowed the sudden rush of saliva in his mouth, felt as if his heavy body was suddenly full of air – sure he must be levitating.

"Ma and Pa," said Angus. "Even if they did wait till middle age before they had me, they're still OK for a couple of old people - cool. The house in Wales is really isolated – acres of land. We'll be doing something in

Spain to do with Pa's music for part of the break you can come to that too…Hey, John – are you OK?" Angus suddenly stood up. "Do I need to get the nurse? You've gone all red. You're breathing funny."

He'd watched Angus's back as he ran off to get the nurse, tasted the salt of unexpected tears trickling into his mouth, wiped them away with his hand.

Now more than fifteen years later history was repeating itself: Angus, again throwing him a line to hold on to. He thought about the ticket to Arizona. Questioned whether he was using it as a 'get out' card, in the event that Franklyn had the scholarship withdrawn. Sarah intimated, that if it were her, she'd fight any proposals Franklyn made. John wasn't sure he wanted to. From day one he'd felt he was fighting a losing battle with the man. For almost three years he'd struggled to meet Franklyn's requirements but he'd drawn the line at following Franklyn's directives to falsify data or use less robust means of analysis so that Franklyn's own theories could be supported.

In retrospect he realised challenging Franklyn's methods was a mistake. The problem was he'd thought that was all he was challenging – the methodology or lack of it. But maybe Franklyn had taken it personally, the reason he savaged or ridiculed everything John had presented to him.

But Franklyn's response had served as some strange torturous motivator. John could almost, but not quite, laugh at himself for the depth and breadth of analysis he'd undertaken in order to demonstrate his worthiness. It weighed like a rock on his chest. The way he'd come to define himself. Every piece of work, every paper he'd produced since as far back as he could remember was like an offering. He could see that now. His way of shouting without utterance 'Hey look how hard I've worked. Surely I'm worthy. Please accept me.' He'd lost count of the times in the past months that he'd asked himself the question he still couldn't answer - 'Worthy of what?'

He looked down at the coffee he kept forgetting to drink. Wishing his mind would stop drawing him off on strange tangents associated with the past. He'd booked the ticket. That was good. It meant he was moving forward not remaining static. Once an object or person was initiated into motion it could become self-perpetuating. Like a ball rolling down a hill, once started it was difficult to stop. He pressed his fingers against his temple. Maybe he was getting confused with the law of cause and effect. Whatever it was it was preferable to stagnation and waiting for Franklyn's metaphoric Sword of Damocles to fall.

Making the decision was the catalyst for change. He'd already, with Sarah and Dan's help, organised the sublet of his apartment. Boxed and stored all his documentation – well most of it. Dan had, thankfully, returned with the key to the storage facility safe. He lifted his cup made the effort to swallow the coffee he'd paid for.

He stood. He now had to check out his mail in the pigeonhole at the Hot House office. Download any files from the hard drive on his PC there, and pack up anything else he needed out of the space. Even if Franklyn wasn't successful in evicting him from the university, he still wanted to make sure there was nothing he'd left behind when making his frantic escape from the place. He'd need to respond to any of the undergrads who, may have been panicking about late submission of projects too. Then he'd be able to rest relatively easy knowing they could enjoy their summer freedoms. He just hoped Greg wouldn't be hovering around. Although knowing Greg he'd be making the most of the post exam lull and absence of academics to while away his time elsewhere.

Heading toward the campus from the station road, he wondered if Angus would be able to get him access to the telescope at Grettsberg. Angus hadn't made it clear what his teaching role was. But surely... He remembered Sarah's admonishments. She'd practically ordered him to keep his interests under his hat. He'd try but he didn't hold out much hope.

Reaching the main campus it was, as he'd expected, practically devoid of human life. Once the panic of exams was over there was always an exodus of students. The sudden disappearance of most of those on the academic staff usually followed as they hauled off with the scripts to mark.

The place was almost serene with its sandstone buildings and cobbled paths leading to flag stoned courtyards and grassed seating areas hung over with sycamore trees. The old convent area was still much in evidence with the cross that loomed large embedded into the fascia of the building which once housed the Sisters, but now was home to several IT suites and the Astrophysics labs. The stone grotto now covered in moss and some sort of creeping ivy that couldn't quite obscure the beatific statue image of Mary the Immaculate, a centrepiece to the grounds and a resting perch for the birds who populated the garden.

Crossing the grassed area, he did what he always did: touched the cold stone of the grotto. He liked that the spiritual, religious and scientific had managed somehow to collide here at Bloomfield.

Entering the foyer area he used his swipe card to gain access to the main building. Aware of the quiet as he made his way down the steps to the basement area he breathed a sigh of relief. He could probably do what he needed to do without interruption.

Peering through the glass of the Hot House door before he typed in the code he felt a sudden tightening at the back of his head. His PC didn't appear to be on his desk. He pressed in the security code and opened the door – the blast of heat causing him to shrug off his jacket even before he entered. His PC was gone.

He looked around. Sometimes people moved things because they needed more space. Fact was he hadn't been in here for several weeks. Since the day he'd taxied his stuff out. Walking over to his desk was a waste of time. The computer wasn't going to materialise as he approached. Backing out he grabbed his jacket from where he'd thrown it. Were there any rules about removing a persons personal PC and what did he have stored on the hard drive anyway?

The nausea he'd felt the day his file had gone missing was starting to creep up into his throat again. He stepped back into the hallway and pulled the door shut. Once outside he turned left, moving to the far corridor, where the pigeonholes were located along with a range of metal office cabinets and cupboards, that because of lack of space could not be accommodated in the Hot House or any of the other basement rooms used by the Faculty. He needed to collect any mail then maybe speak at the main university office about his missing PC. Place a request for forwarding any future correspondence to his new address. The only trouble was that he didn't really have a forwarding address – yet.

The mail area was in its usual state of disarray. It seemed that most of those whose correspondence arrived here had a propensity to tear it open and litter the area with the contents of the envelopes. Pushing the discarded flyers and unwanted missives to one side he scanned the boxes. He always had trouble locating his own.

Whoever set the system up, had, for some unknown reason, decided against an alphabetic letter system based on surname and instead had opted for a numeric code based on the faculty each individual belonged to, followed by the initials of the person to whom the pigeonhole was designated.

Expecting an almost empty box, given the absence of mail on his last visit, John inadvertently moved his eyes back and forward and up and down around the now packed full space below his faculty code number and name. It took him several minutes to realise that it was his mailbox that was full. He reached for the letters just as he heard someone coming through the security door. He didn't want to speak to anyone – least of all Greg. Reaching for a stray carrier bag hung on a hook at the edge of the table he swept his mail inside and stepped to the side of the filing and stationary cabinets.

Half aware that what he was doing would seem ridiculous to any casual observer, he edged along the wall in order to gain a better view of the corridor hallway that led to the Hot House. If Greg went inside he'd just move quickly past the door, up the stairs and out.

The poor lighting in the area made it difficult to see the faces of the two people walking toward him then stopping at the Hot House door. But despite the fact he couldn't see them it was clear who they were. Greg was carrying a PC and Franklyn was keying in the code to open the door.

"OK, Greg," said Franklyn as Greg disappeared inside. "I've enough for now." Franklyn was about to turn when Greg must have said something. "Just put it back on his desk. If he comes back – I don't want him to know it's been away."

# 11 SNEAK

"I just can't get with the fact that you were hiding behind filing cabinets, John. Sneaking along darkened corridors..."

"You weren't there, Dan," Sarah said.

"I just wasn't expecting to see Franklyn and Greg acting like... acting like..."

"Partners in crime?" Dan suggested as he picked up his beer.

John stared at the table. He hadn't even told them about the letters yet. The stack of backdated mail he'd picked up from the university. He should never have used the place as his forwarding address. He'd just never felt comfortable with the system at the apartment where the mail for all the tenants was just posted through the door to lay on the floor till someone picked it up.

"You said on the phone that there was something else."

Sarah's voice cut through his thoughts. Catching her darting a glance at Dan he wondered how the poor guy put up with having to shelve his plans in order to try and sort out someone else's confusion and mess.

He chewed the corner of his lip. Attempted an apology, "I'm really sorry to have dragged you both out here because of my lack of ability to function like a normal human being," he said.

"Hey," Sarah said reaching for his arm.

"Who's normal round here?" said Dan.

"It's just – well, the backdated mail from Angus was there," John said, wondering how that was supposed to clarify anything.

"Well that's good," said Sarah smiling. "Now you know I was telling you the truth about him trying to contact you..."

"It looked as if it'd been opened..."

"Well maybe," said Sarah pulling back her hair, "it had to be opened because it went astray." She let her hair fall loose again. "They have to do that to look for a forwarding address if they're going to return the mail. I mean..."

"The senders address, was on the back of the letters, Sarah." John cast his eyes back to the table picking up his beer staring at it then returning it to the table.

"So there was no reason for anyone to open the mail?" Dan leaned forward before continuing. "I'd definitely be questioning that, John. It's an offence to open someone else's mail."

"Dan, Sarah," John said. "I know I'm going to sound, well it's a bit…" He stalled again, wondering how to articulate what he was thinking. Sarah had already suggested he wasn't too good when she'd turned up unexpectedly a few weeks ago. She'd even encouraged him to make an emergency appointment to speak with someone and he had. He'd made and kept the appointment with Julia. He'd even agreed to see Julia again to work with the anger.

"John," Sarah waved her hand in front of his face. "You were starting to tell us something then you just glazed over. Are you OK?"

There it was again. Was he OK? Did wondering if the Grettsberg address on the back of Angus's letters implied the reason they were opened indicate that he most definitely wasn't OK? He turned the question round and over in his mind before answering. "Probably not," he replied. "But I'm doing as you suggested and getting some help."

"Was there anything missing from the hard drive of your PC?"

Dan's question reminded him how this had all started. If Sarah hadn't rang to check how he was and query if he'd booked his ticket he wouldn't have told her about any of it. He'd garbled about the missing files, the missing PC, asked her to check that Dan was sure about the security of the storage facility where they'd both advised him to store his documents and papers along with all the other stuff he wouldn't need if he were in Arizona.

"What about the other letters? You said there was a stack of mail," Sarah said.

He looked from her then to Dan. He wasn't sure he could tell them about the other letter yet. He'd intended to. It was the first thing he'd wanted to tell Sarah when he answered her call. But what if it was nothing? What if the requested meeting with the solicitor was just to confirm what he'd known for a long time – that there was nothing for him to know? He answered Dan's question first.

"I can't tell if anything is missing. I just don't understand why they wanted to access my stuff." He massaged the muscles above his knees before continuing.

"I've always backed up my files when I remembered. But there are so many times I forget." He turned to Sarah. He struggled briefly with the decision. Why shouldn't she know? She was the nearest to a sister he'd ever have and Dan, like Angus, almost a brother – family. He turned his glass in circles on the table. His eyes focused on the centre of his glass, the movement of the liquid within it.

"There was a letter from Cody and Barlow." He looked up, making eye contact first with Sarah, then with Dan. "The solicitors who've handled my allowance all these years," he clarified before picking up his beer. He didn't drink. "I've been waiting to hear from them for over a year. Maybe now as I'm coming up to twenty five it's going to stop – the allowance." It was the easy answer to explain away his concerns, far easier than telling Sarah and Dan how desperate he was for it to be more than that.

Sarah frowned. "You've not been in touch to speak with them?"

He wondered if he should tell her just how scared he was. He'd read and reread the letter a hundred times to try and locate some hidden message – some between the lines clue in communication. He hadn't found one.

"If you need any legal advice," Dan offered. "I, or maybe someone I know, should be able to help out. Just give a shout and I'll try and sort something." He paused. "If it's an end to your allowance and Franklyn achieves what you say he's threatened you'll need to be thinking about where…"

"Where you go from here," Sarah said.

"Arizona," said John, determined to follow through on his plan no matter what. Unless of course there was some way back to where he began, wherever that was, but after almost twenty-five years of silence even in his most optimistic moments he knew it was hardly likely. He sat up straighter. He needed to give Sarah and Dan some space to stop worrying about him. "Arizona," he said again. "The ticket's paid for. My bag's almost packed."

# 12 THE LETTER

He was out of himself, yet at the very centre of his being, couldn't work out whether to hold on or let go of the power – the charge. The electricity of connection was prickling his skin, surging the blood through his veins till it hammered in his chest, his own rapid heartbeat echoing in his ears and blasting through the housing of his skull. She'd held these artefacts – maybe even fashioned this tiny charm with her own hands. Was it possible that wherever she was now she could feel the sense of his joy? Could she watch the track – the journey, of the tears on his face?

He was glad he was alone. Here in the small conference room with its bookshelves lined with ledgers from another age safely protected behind glass. The basement room window high up on the wall where it abutted the pavement, enabling him to see only the moving legs of passers by scurrying on to their appointments and plans while he sat unnoticed, the threads of the past weaving an image around his heart and soul of the woman who'd given birth to him.

He opened his hand again. They lay there still. The gifts from his mother, the silver cross, the tiny charm of the otter – if that was what it was, and the stone with the painted symbol. He looked again at the letter on the mahogany table in front of him, began to read it for the fifth time.

*Dear John*

*I hope this letter finds you well and does not hurt, shock, or disappoint. I would wish only good things for you. My name is Thomas Begvious. No, I am not your natural father. I have only shared with you my name, as I am the man who found you.*

*I am your benefactor, the man who has, through my own good fortune, been enabled to provide you with financial support throughout your formative years. Finding you altered the course of my life. I hope my distant support has enabled you to gain both the knowledge and understanding which I pray will provide a guide for your life too.*

*Although I have no doubt you have imagined the background to your* birth many times I can only tell you the little that I know for certain with the rest being the information I have gleaned and believe to be true from my researches.

My discovery of you as a baby who had only recently been delivered to this world was set against the backdrop of a city night from which I had sought escape. In those times back then I lived an unusual life. Seeking peace in strange and sometimes dark places. I had stumbled and veered from the path I had intended to follow. The light I had searched for had been swallowed by the darkness of a night that promised no dawn. I heard only echoes of the questions I had asked. Not answers. Somewhere on that plane of sound I heard your cries.

I searched and found you. You were beneath the bridge that spanned the railway track, safe from the railway line in a hidden recess of the embankment. You were protected from the cold by cardboard boxes and well swaddled with clothes and blankets. The leather pouch, which contained all the things, which you now have in your possession, was concealed and strapped inside your wrappings. It was sometime later that I was to discover their existence.

When I lifted you from your protected place I experienced great happiness that you were alive and seemingly well. You cried with great gusto as I rushed toward the road to flag down a passing car to take you to the safety and care of a hospital. I hoped this was an indicator of strong lungs and a desire to connect with the world rather than a desire to leave it.

The weeks that followed my discovery of you were filled with interventions from the authorities to try to support you with care and also to locate the whereabouts of the woman or girl to whom you belonged. They were not successful in their search. However the small artefacts and scroll inside the leather pouch, which were with you when you were found, indicated that it is possible and maybe probable that your mother shared a connection with the Hopi Indians.

Although unable to provide you with the physical care you so much needed, I was, after many months of legal wrangling and much support from solicitors, given the right to become your legal guardian and benefactor. I was also given the opportunity to provide you with my family name and also to choose your Christian name. I chose the name of John, which has a special *meaning. I hope you find the meaning of your name to always be true in your life.*

*I spent many years searching for your birth mother in the first decade following the gift to me of finding you. Indeed, I invested vast amounts of time and money hiring private detectives to trace the records of those who had given birth within the time frame of your delivery, especially those with even the most fragile link to the Hopi. When the searches of both the authorities and my own revealed little I came to believe that maybe your mother had travelled some long distance before disembarking from the train and walking some ways to the lonely embankment before leaving you safe to be found. Both the police and the authorities confirmed that you had not been alone long. You were fed and mostly clean and warm. Over the years I have many times wondered if your mother was witness to my discovery of you and only when she saw that I carried you safely to the road to seek help from a passing driver did she continue on her journey.*

*During these searches, I also focused on the belongings, which had been secured safely in the pouch that was strapped to your body. The tiny charm I discovered was handmade and representative of the Otter Child, the silver cross seemed old and impossible to trace or link to the Hopi but has long been a protective talisman. The small stone with the symbol is unmistakably linked to the Hopi and known as the Hopi Clan Rock. The leather parchment was rolled and secured. Again some of the symbols indicate the Hopi connection. You will see that as well as the symbols there is an inscription made unexpectedly in pen. The inscription surrounds a date and time which I believe may well be your true date and time of birth. Translation of the words around the date proved difficult but I believe that the essence of their meaning is a promise to 'Watch over you'. Wherever your mother may be I am sure she will keep this promise even if only in her heart and or spirit. I hope you will keep her promise as given to you in your own heart also.*

*As someone who has studied many religions, sciences and esoteric practices including Astrology I believe it may be pertinent to suggest you have an Astrologer draw your chart from the date and time given. You could then explore if the most significant events in your life as you remember them coincide with the transiting and progression of the planets in your chart. In this way you may know for sure – if you believe in such things – that your mother did provide you with the accurate time and date of your birth. You may ask if she did this for a reason. As much as I may have wished to visit your chart myself I believe it is only for you to so do if it is your wish.*

*All things, I believe, have meaning. The gift of finding you, as I have explained, altered the course of my life. I returned to the libraries of my past – those vast places where knowledge and records are stored. They illuminate me. I hope you find they illuminate you too.*

*Be sure to know that whilst I will not intervene in your life, which I hope and pray is a good one, you are at all times welcome to contact me if you should at any time require support of any kind. Be assured that your allowance will continue.*

*Yours in spirit*

Thomas Begvious.

Staring at the letter, the strong, yet cursive script, his namesake's signature, John experienced a sense of distance from himself. As if he was somewhere else in the room hovering beyond and outside of his skin, watching his head enlarge with the knowledge that everything he'd thought may be true was not. Feeling the ache of unwilling acceptance pressing against his chest and attempting to swallow the disappointment, which snared the muscles of his throat, he reached for the parchment.

So long, for all his life – some part of every day, he'd allowed his mind to travel backward to the time when he was born, always pursuing all elements of possibility, believing that somewhere, she, his mother, would be waiting for him. Now it seemed that in truth she'd been running from him. Running so fast and so far there was no trace – no track to find or follow.

He stood up from the table, more to see if he could than to move beyond the space he inhabited. While his head seemed to be expanding his legs seemed unable to support his weight. The ground beneath his feet felt so much less solid than he remembered it, the parchment still in his hands, its texture more like fine worn leather than paper. She'd held these things. He kept his balance. His left hand still closed around the gifts that she'd left for him, conscious that the room seemed to be moving. Not spinning, but shifting in angle like a sinking ship whose prow has already dipped beneath the waves.

He sank down deeper, the wooden backrest of the chair a rigid reminder that somehow he was no longer standing. He unrolled the parchment again. Stared at the symbols then closed his eyes. Committing the images within him in order that his heart could decipher the message and promise, his mother had bequeathed.

# 13 IT'S TIME

He hadn't intended to see Julia again after his discovery, but somehow once again he found himself in the confines, yet space, of her counselling room and once again she'd waited for him to talk.

He'd wanted to tell her about vast immeasurable swirling within him. The gifts his mother had left with the child he once was. But instead he was talking about his theories.

He'd talked about the lack of clear evidence for when the pyramid was built. The guesswork used in the absence of markings – anything and everything that didn't relate to him.

"I think what you're telling me is very interesting, John," she said, her voice soft, body angling toward him as she spoke.

"But, as I've told you before," she continued. "I have no background in your area of research, so it's impossible for me to know whether Dr Franklyn is right or wrong in challenging your theories and hypotheses, or whether they are pertinent to the discipline you are being funded to research."

He recognised what she was saying as fact. He'd asked himself the same questions.

"Have you explored the ways in which you can support your hypotheses?" Julia added before sitting back in her chair.

He felt uncomfortably aware that she seemed to be leaving little space for him to answer her questions, wondered if she was finding it less easy to manage the counselling interaction, wondered if maybe he'd decided not to let her.

"Well one way is to confirm that the pyramid is twice the height as previously considered." It wasn't really the response she was probably looking for but it was all he could talk about. "Twice as high as everyone's been thinking it is," he added. "That would throw most of the stuff written about it out the window," he ran a hand across his mouth before continuing, "Including how long it took to build…"

"John…" Julia attempted unsuccessfully to cut in.

"It's clear to me." He stared at the palms of his hands for a moment. "Clear – well almost clear – that we, or they, have been looking in the wrong place for indicators, for markings for evidence. That's why there's so much confusion, so much argument, why there's no clear direction…" He stalled, leaning forward and rubbing his knees. "But the facts of the matter are beyond the height or depth of the Great Pyramid. It's more about its location relative to everything else and its potential for…"

"John…"

He continued on. "Any markings, any evidence has been, and still is hidden," he said. "My guess is that the Giza Plato desert has covered the greater portion of the pyramid and that the actual base level is much lower – far deeper than anyone has ever realised. They're all looking at the wrong level for any kind of inscription."

"And you think it's a sun temple?"

He experienced a sudden blanching of his skin, moved his chair backwards. Why did he let this happen? He was running off at the mouth. Trying to convince Julia that he had some kind of right to expound theories outside of accepted academic thinking. He chaffed his hands together trying to chase away the chill, stared at the knuckles of his fingers – his bony wrists.

"Is the fact that you think it is a sun temple, and Dr Franklyn doesn't, lead to your anger, John?"

Julia's voice reminded him of why he was sitting there. He was supposed to be dealing – or learning to deal, with his fear of speaking in public and with the anger he'd refused to acknowledge.

He lifted his head but kept the focus of his eyes above and to the left of her face.

"I'm sorry," he said. Guessing she was probably thinking that he needed to see someone else. Someone who dealt with – treated – more serious maladjustments. If he wanted to convince her of the need for a referral he was doing a good job.

"John…"

He could see her head moving as she spoke, was unable to make full eye contact. He didn't want to read what she was probably thinking.

"Are you going to tell me why you think the pyramid is a sun temple, or do you want to ask me who painted the water colour on the wall behind my head?"

He picked up the thread of humour in her voice, turned his head, his eyes meeting hers before he had time to look away.

"You wanted me to talk about my anger and all I can talk about are my theories…"

"They're important to you, John. I'm feeling you'd maybe like other people to understand what's important to you. Are you angry that they maybe don't try to do that?"

He noticed how she expressed that soft smile again. The smile that made him forget what he was talking about. The faint indentation of a dimple in her cheek was there again. She didn't seem to be looking at him as if he was completely crazy. He took a breath.

"It's more than that," he said. "I want someone to recognise that what I've been working on is important – not just important to me, but important."

He watched as Julia waited, a heartbeat of silence, before speaking.

"Important in what way, John?"

"You've heard of all the different predictions that have been made over time?"

"Some," she said. "In my line of work though I try to focus on the here and now and how we can make it better."

"Like yesterday's gone, tomorrow may never come?" he asked.

Julia nodded.

He paused before continuing. "I think that's a line in a song."

"A good one," she laughed as she spoke.

He felt his own face relax.

"So, are you going to tell me?" she said.

He wondered if he should. He looked at her half closed eyes, her readiness to listen. "Well," he began. "Some years ago a theory was proposed that the great pyramid was a representation of the Earth." He sat forward, his eyes in direct contact with Julia's. "But there's more going on than that. I've been working stuff out for some time. The mathematics of the entire structure, the geometry of shape and sound, it's known that specific numbers give rise to specific geometries, harmonies and proportions. I've so far worked out…" He stopped. Started again, "What I'm saying here is: it has a square base and triangular sides." He glanced at his feet. Wished the floor would swallow him up. He was talking like a five-year old. He looked back up. "I know that much is obvious to everyone so please don't laugh." He waited and watched. Sure in his mind that Julia was fighting a fierce battle to keep her face straight.

"OK," he said. Satisfied Julia was willing to at least conceal any amusement she may have been feeling even if the swell of her cheek threatened to reveal the small dimple that had started to fascinate him.

He pulled his gaze away. "The base," he said, "contains the idea of the four corners of the Earth." He gestured. "Even though we know the Earth's not square – You follow?"

Julia nodded.

"So, the thinking is that the square represents the Earth and mankind – whereas the sides of the pyramid represent the journey from the Earth to the highest point in existence. I also read somewhere…" He paused, aware of his hands moving to express what he was saying. "Fact is," he said.

"There are so many fantastic theoretical viewpoints outside of the standard academic theories. What am I trying to tell you?" He squeezed his jaw. "That's right," he said, speaking to his own internal monitor. "What I'm trying to say is that when the sun shines the pyramid casts a giant shadow – I'm interested in the reasoning…well not so much the reasoning but the purpose of the shadow as much as I'm interested in the idea of resonance."

He sat back conscious that he was losing the train of thought he'd begun with. Agitated by the million and one things he wanted to say but didn't have enough time to say them all.

Julia appeared calm. He glanced at the clock she had hung on the wall. How could he possibly explain his thinking in the ten minutes he had left of his session? A session where he was supposed to be exploring his anger and explaining the fact that he was leaving for Arizona. A session where he thought he might tell her he almost knew where he came from, who he might be. Instead once again his thinking was hostage to his theories. He glanced again at Julia. "I know I'm not explaining myself very well and there isn't much time…"

"All of eight minutes," she said. "So maybe you best cut to the chase."

He massaged the muscles above his knees before forming an apex with his thumbs and fingers. "The highest point," he said, "is directly in line with the Sirius system. I believe there is a resonant connection – link – between what is happening here and in the cosmos. It's all tied in with the geometry of resonance. It's taken scientists too long to discover what an ancient people have known for centuries – you ever heard of the…" He stopped and stared again at his hands. He wanted to add that the ancient peoples he was talking about were the Dogon. But he also wanted to talk about the Hopi. The ancient tribe to whom it now seemed he was inextricably linked and yet it still seemed so fragile – private.

He raised his head again. His eyes averted to the window. "There are other planets out there which impact on the harmony and resonance of the Earth we…"

"It's time, John," Julia said motioning to the clock.

He stared at the circular face of the timepiece, noted the speed of the second finger; considered the orbits of the planet Earth, the arpeggio of time ticking away. "I know," he said rising to his feet. "It's time." He tried to summon the courage he needed. He saw a flicker, something he wasn't sure of in Julia's eyes. Reached out a hand, "Thank you," he said. "You've been a great help."

# 14 STRANGE

Staring at his half filled suitcase and the few remnants of his existence scattered around the apartment he realised he still didn't know if he could take his painting equipment and his guitar to Arizona. Did he need them – were they just props he used to give himself some definition as a person? Did people carry these things around the world? He seemed to know so little about ordinary things. Wondered when and how he'd be able to catch up with everyone else.

He didn't want to leave his guitar. His first real, meaningful present, from someone outside of his institutionalised life, a Martin Guitar, autographed by Paul Yeager, the Snow Leopards' lead guitarist and singer, the wild man of rock – Angus's father. He touched its Rosewood frame, inhaled its intoxicating scent. How quickly his life had changed.

That first planned holiday with the Yeager's when he'd been packing his things. A hoard of boys had gathered round his bed. Demonstrating for the first time, an interest in him – even those who'd watched and laughed during Berke's experiment.

"There'll be girls everywhere," said one.

"Drugs, drink, wild parties," shouted another.

Their words and claims started to bind together in a rat-tat of sound punctuated by laughter. The air infused with their testosterone-fuelled sweat as they crowded around him. Wanting to know why he was going? Demanding he get them an invitation next time.

He'd placed his hands over his ears to block out the sound of the different voices, forming one indiscernible noise, competing for his attention.

"You'll need to do more than that," shouted the boy who'd started it all as he grabbed for a tennis racquet, began playing air guitar, creating a screeching riff of noise, "to drown out the sounds of the Wild Man of Rock." The entire dormitory of boys started to leap about.

John's heart had crashed in his chest. The case he'd been packing lay overturned on the floor. Beads of sweat were running down between his shoulder blades. For the first time since Angus had invited him he wasn't sure if he really wanted to go.

If those boys had only known the truth, Paul Yeager – Wild Man of

Rock, looked like a gardener or farmer when he'd picked them up from the station. The van, an open backed truck, half filled with bags of compost and an upturned wheelbarrow. Paul Yeager ruddy and weathered from the sun. The hair tied back and almost hidden inside the hood of his jacket.

"Old Man," Angus shouted, before running toward him. "This is John."

Biting back the claw of loneliness that stabbed at his stomach, John watched as Paul Yeager's arms went round Angus and hefted him over his shoulder before staggering forward.

"Man, am I pleased to meet you," Paul Yeager said, holding out a hand.

John met it with his.

"You've been teaching my boy to paint."

John darted a glance at Angus. Wondering how the few times he'd worked with Angus could be described as teaching by this soft voiced man who towered above him.

"Maybe you could teach me, too," Paul Yeager said.

John laughed. Realised Paul Yeager still had hold of his hand. He laughed again at the thought of teaching this huge man to wield a paintbrush instead of an electric guitar.

"I'll teach you to play a few riffs in return if that's what you need, Man."

John was aware of his head moving in agreement as they climbed in the truck – set off on the road.

"We'll need to clean out the horses first, maybe help Ma." Paul Yeager turned slightly, winked. "Angus's mother – Ma, she's got to get her seeds planted before nightfall." He veered the truck around a tight bend in the road, which had now become a track. "New moon tonight," he said as he bumped and swerved around the dips and holes that indicated a well worn track, "always promises the best chance of success if you plant or start a new project when the moon is on your side." He laughed. Angus did too.

"Ma's mad," Angus said. "She'll probably want to cast your horoscope. Give us some chakra clearing exercises." He motioned with his arms. "To dispel the negative energies built up during the school term."

Paul Yeager laughed even louder. Angus joined in. John tried a smile.

"All you have to do is tell her what time and date you were born," said Angus jabbing John with his elbow.

John stopped smiling. How could he tell them? Back then he didn't know.

But now, fifteen years later, he knew. That's if the dates and times on the leathered parchment were what Thomas Begvious, his benefactor, thought they were.

Why did knowing make such a difference? He picked at the strings of the guitar. His mother. He'd wanted to know her. Find her. Not just know when he'd entered the world. Yet somehow the confirmation, if that's what the date and time indicated, felt like proof of something.

He began to play the soft haunting tune of the song he'd always believed captured the sense of his beginnings. He sang the first few verses, his voice breaking on some of the words, halting, unable to express some of the sentiments captured in the lyrics, his fingers unwilling to complete the task of playing.

He thought of Julia. Why hadn't he told her about the meeting at the solicitors? He'd intended to. Planned to tell her all about the letter, the gifts and the promise from his mother – he hadn't. He hadn't even told Sarah and Dan or emailed Angus. He'd simply sent a text saying the meeting had gone OK. His allowance was not being withdrawn.

There seemed no way of explaining. No words to gather and form in the shape of sentences. He put down the guitar. The words of the song trapped in his chest. He'd imagined so many scenarios of how he'd come to be. Two people lost to each other before they knew they'd created him, or two young people ill equipped to care for a child whose parents or grandparents had arranged for the child to be taken care of rather than impact on some planned future. Imagined a girl so young she'd been forced to hand him over for adoption, but his own imaginary older, more affluent, already married father, had stepped in and forbade the action setting up an allowance to support the child to adulthood. He'd even considered that maybe mother and child had been torn apart because of the cultural, religious or racial differences in the union. He'd thought so many things trying to make sense of who he was.

He touched his face. Considered how strange, or maybe not strange at all, that he had never in his wildest imaginings considered a link with the North American Indians. Why had he never questioned the fact that he was born in America, yet raised in England? Why had he almost forgotten those origins? He knew he was slightly olive skinned; had the type of face that could have indicated distant Latin origins, but he was devoid of any cultural background other than the culture of academia.

He realised how quiet the room was, while the space where his heart should be was no more than an ache. How could it be that he'd never felt the true sense of himself – still couldn't feel it now?

# 15 FIRED-UP

Smashing his knuckles repeatedly into his open hand he paced the room. He needed to call someone – but whom? He'd already taken too much of Sarah and Dan's time. There had to be someone at the University, some sort of an advocate, but he was getting no response from his emails other than the 'out of office' reply. Half of the staff had already disappeared on holiday.

He tried to wet his dry lips with his equally dry tongue before reaching for his bottle of water. He'd already consumed enough water to drown himself in a desperate attempt to stop the sensation that was snaking across his arms and his chest. But he had no experience of this. How did he defend himself? If he'd known Franklyn's threats to speak to the Faculty had included this accusation he'd have found a way to protect himself. But, Franklyn's concerns were supposedly about the robustness of the research, the weakness of ideas, his worthiness to continue with the scholarship given he may be influencing students, not an out and out accusation of plagiarism – a charge of copying the work of another and presenting it as his own. He'd never done that.

He punched his palm some more, his pacing more erratic than before. Had he inadvertently used something without proper referencing of the source? They must have sent him a letter first, surely? But he hadn't been back to the Hot House since he'd picked up all the backdated mail. The email said he had ten days to provide a response to the charge that Franklyn had laid at his door. As he'd failed to respond within the timeframe the complaint against him had now been progressed by the Faculty and referred to the Research Council.

Franklyn hadn't wasted any time. But why hadn't anyone contacted him or emailed him before today? He was leaving for Arizona in the early hours of the morning. How could he respond? How was he supposed to defend himself? It was madness. His work had been suspended, the email said. The research he'd been carrying out was not to be used in any way till after the hearing. He was now not allowed to submit any papers to journals or discuss his findings with anyone.

He sat down, fired up his laptop again. He needed to tell them it was all some sort of a mistake. Franklyn had said he was deleting the last papers

John had presented him with. John could see him now, the day in Franklyn's office still fresh in his mind. The image of Franklyn's hand hovering over the delete button, "I'm not going to print it, John," Franklyn had said. John remembered it all clearly. The way Franklyn had highlighted the title, lingering for a moment before clicking the delete button. "I'm removing it," he'd said. He'd definitely said he was removing it, removing it because it was crap. Yet now he was saying it was fucking plagiarised crap. John clicked on his emails and read the so-called charge before pressing the connect button on his mobile to link him through to Franklyn's office.

It took only seconds for the ringing to stop and be replaced by the answer-phone message. John listened. "This is Dr Franklyn's Office. Dr Franklyn will be unavailable till the tenth of September. If you need to leave a message please do so after the tone or contact the Faculty office."

After more than two hours of trying to speak with someone he gave up. The whole academic community had vanished. He'd repeated his query to at least six different people at the research council office. None could advise. He thought he'd touched lucky when one of the operators a guy with a faint but unmistakeable Irish accent had suggested he search the research council website for information on policy, procedure and disciplinary action in plagiarism cases.

"From what you're telling me there may be something, some procedure that hasn't been followed correctly," he said. "If that turns out to be the case any action that's been initiated could be invalidated. But you didn't hear that from me. Other than that, there's nothing I can do to help," he'd said. "But I wish you luck."

Not sure whether it was the inflection of Irish brogue that made the guy seem so genuine as if he really did wish him luck, or whether the guy just liked sending out a good vibe John had no idea but he thanked the guy profusely before ending the call and starting the search of the website.

After clocking up many more hours spent searching and reading the Research Council website he wanted to lie down. Like the guy on the phone had said, in cases involving claims of academic plagiarism there did seem to be a specific procedure that had to be followed, but unpicking and understanding the finer points of the agreed process wasn't easy. From what he was reading Franklyn seemed to have moved very fast to start the disciplinary process against him. The timescales on the website didn't seem to fit with the speed at which the process had gotten underway.

But then, he reasoned, maybe the process had been initiated as quickly as it had because of the time of year. Academics were notorious for vacating the premises once the exams were over and the papers marked. Reappearing again only briefly for Graduation.

Heading to the kitchen in search of some painkillers in order to deal with the pain that was spreading across the side of his head he considered how he would word the appeal he needed to write. Recognising the scattered meaningless disorder of his ideas as his minds tired refusal to harness his thoughts he filled the kettle and clicked it on before spooning coffee from a jar. He'd forgotten to buy milk and sugar so many times that he was almost beginning to think he preferred his coffee black. He laughed without heart to himself. He enjoyed black coffee almost as much as he enjoyed feeling half starved because he forgot to buy food. The headache was beginning to worsen – a dull deep pulsating pain.

He opened the draw, which normally contained all manner of detritus, including headache medication, before remembering he'd been clearing everything out to make the place habitable for Sarah. He was out of everything he needed. Typical. He watched as the light on the kettle flicked on indicating the water was boiling before pouring it into his cup. Maybe the caffeine would sort out his headache on its own. Then it was back to the Hot House to search for mail. If the Research Council website was correct. Franklyn would have had to provide written notice of the action with the standard documentation on the process and rights of appeal. If he hadn't done that then maybe the whole complaint would be void. Maybe…

# 16 BAGGAGE

"As if we'd just let you go without saying goodbye," Sarah said.

"The place looks twice the size," said Dan, while doing a quick check around the apartment. "Tempted to stay? Some of those canvases of yours could look pretty good against a neutral backdrop."

John shook his head. "No," he said. Though inside he wasn't sure how he felt. "I may not be looking forward to the flight, but I'm looking forward to carrying my case across the tarmac to the terminal and being somewhere I never thought I'd get the chance to go." He said the word 'again' in his mind. It seemed so strange to be thinking that in some ways he was going home.

"No need to stroll across the tarmac these days," said Sarah. "When did you last fly?"

John tried to block out the question. He was doing his best not to think about the actual reality of being airborne. Instead he was trying to focus his thinking to a point where he'd arrived. "I don't?" he said, as he knelt on his case in order to zip it up. He glanced up at Sarah, "how come I got so lucky?" he said.

"Lucky?" asked Dan absentmindedly as he climbed onto a chair to check the top of a bookcase.

"Lucky?" Sarah echoed.

John stood up. "To have people around me," he said.

"No more than seventy pounds, remember," advised Dan pointing at the case. "Otherwise you'll have to pay surcharges on top of what you'll probably need to pay for the guitar if they won't let you take it through the gate. Remember you don't ask you just stroll through. If you ask they'll definitely say no. It's how things work."

"See," said John. "That's how lucky I am. You take on my apartment, help me out at every turn and even turn up tonight to drive me to the airport." He paused testing his case for apparent weight. "And know all the things I don't know and should."

Sarah moved across the room joining Dan in his last minute check of the apartment by opening and closing various doors.

"I'm not good at talk," he said. "But your support now and in the past has always, and does mean a lot to me. Thanks."

# 17 PLAGIARISM

It was only as they were packing the boot that John realised just how little in the way of personal possessions he actually had when all the documentation associated with his years of research was no longer present. Even with the guitar, laptop and case, where he'd found space to pack his painting gear, there was still a decent gap in the luggage area of Dan's hatchback.

He stared; conscious of how little there was associated with him and his life.

"Might as well get in the car," Sarah said.

He did. They were on the road and heading toward the airport before he shook off the feeling, the sense of smallness. The late hour meant there was little traffic other than the occasional maniac speeder who flashed passed them, thankfully without hitch. Sarah drove while Dan fell into a deep sleep in the seat beside her.

"I really don't like to ask this," Sarah said, casting a glance in the rear view mirror to catch his eye. "You know with you off to America, and a long overdue good time and holiday with Angus, but have you heard anything from the university? Your texts and emails haven't been giving much away."

He played at readjusting his seatbelt.

"Tell me it's none of my business and I'll back off," she said. "But I – Dan, too, know how much effort you've put into your work, know how much your research means." She paused, changing lanes in response to an overhead warning of road works up ahead. "So if there is anything we can do to help, we will."

John considered. He didn't want to burden either of them more than he already had. But somewhere inside there was a sense of discomfort that he was closing them out of his life by not sharing the recent revelations about his past and the possible incriminating actions Franklyn was taking to impact on his future.

"It's just," he began to speak then faltered. Sarah remained silent. He found himself thinking of Julia and the silences in the counselling sessions. He'd emailed her earlier in the day to thank her for her being there; let her know of his plans. She'd probably be very glad he was putting such a distance between them after his mad and convoluted ravings about his theories at their last session. "It's just," he began again, "a bit difficult at the moment. There's stuff I'd like to talk – tell you about, but I'm kind of confused about where it's all going." He gripped the muscles above his knees. "Franklyn…well he's accusing me of plagiarism…"

"Plagiarism – You? Ha!" Sarah swerved as she turned toward him. "Frick," she said turning back and straightening the steering wheel.

"What?" muttered Dan.

"Go back to sleep," said Sarah.

John saw how she touched Dan's hand.

"He's exhausted," she said. Law seems such a cool option till you discover how much of your life it demands."

"You shouldn't have come, Sarah, I…"

"You didn't ask us to, John. He's already had a few hours sleep before we set off. That's why I'm driving."

"He works hard," John said.

"He does," Sarah acknowledged. "I'm going to make him take some time off. Have a holiday." She laughed quietly. "Who knows we might follow you over to Arizona if Angus has the space to put us up. I've always fancied a tour of the Grand Canyon. Or maybe you'll hit on something big and I can cover the story!" She switched lanes to give some space to another car speeding up from behind. "Anyway, this 'crock of' that Franklyn's proposing – plagiarism. You're the last person on earth who'd copy or cheat. What's he playing at?"

He readjusted his seatbelt as he sat back. "I really don't know." He paused "I've never falsified or fabricated any data. I've never, to my knowledge, appropriated anyone else's ideas, processes or results without giving appropriate credit. I've always used the correct citations and referencing conventions."

"So you're in the clear?"

"It doesn't mean I'm not uneasy." He took a breath. "I spoke with a guy from the Research Council today. Well I spoke with lots of people today but one guy out of many was actually helpful. He advised me to scour the website on disciplinary actions. I did."

"And?"

"There seems to be some sort of process that has to be followed from the university. Some opportunities and rights of appeal, I'm not certain but it seems as if the proper procedure hasn't been followed."

"Doesn't surprise me – from what you've told me, what little you've told me about Franklyn, the man is a worm." She paused, dropping into the left hand lane in the direction of the slip road. "So you're going to appeal?"

John shrugged in his seat. "I would if I could speak to someone but the whole academic outfit – department is…" He stopped, flexed his shoulders tried to loosen the tension. "Franklyn isn't back till September, making me wonder all the more about my files and PC. Was he looking for evidence against me?"

"John," said Sarah. "There isn't any, unless of course he's as low as he seems and plans to fabricate something."

"I guess that's what I'm afraid of," he said.

# 18 THE KEY

He couldn't believe he was actually strapped into his seat, the plane ready for take off. The terror he was feeling, the almost numbness of his body and spasm in his shoulders a reminder of why he kept his feet firmly on the ground if he could. Heights were bad enough but he'd been working on that over the years. The rock climbing Angus had introduced him to, being a way of testing himself periodically. Being enclosed was the worst. Once in the air he couldn't say he'd like to get off. He was trapped. How come everyone else looked so normal? He'd managed the short flight to Spain with Angus and his parents several times over the years while he was growing up. Though terrified, the Yeager's managed to help him keep a lid on it.

The Yeager's, so different to the people he'd expected them to be. The fantasies of the boys at school had been just that – fantasies. The supposed rock star's mansion in Wales turned out to be a partially renovated farmhouse, without even a television. There were no drugs and very little alcohol. But the music – it played all day. Not just rock but classical, folk, blues – jazz too. Manda even played the flute and the harp when she wasn't planting seeds or weaving fabrics.

"Harmonies," Paul Yeager spoke in that soft unassuming voice that defied his stage presence. "It's not just sound, John. Music resonates with some sacred place," he'd carefully placed John's fingers on the strings of the guitar he'd gifted to him.

John inhaled, focusing his energy on the unexpectedly difficult process of keeping his recalcitrant fingers in the required position. It looked so easy when you watched someone, yet required such precise skill.

Paul Yeager had been right. There was something intangible and almost sacred captured in the vibration of sound. John knew he'd never quite mastered the guitar the way he'd wished to, he'd managed to play a few tunes and discover not only the love of music, but also the mathematics of music. Acoustics were part of the mathematics of framing and carrying notes to their highest and most melodic points. He'd listened to the choirs in the chapel at school. Hard to explain but the sound had the capacity to lift some essence within the internal structure of the self, enabling expansion beyond the physical.

He remembered studying the apex of the chapel roof. Later exploring the architecture of cathedrals. The idea of spires had drawn him, vaulted ceilings. Pyramids had been a natural progression – the fascination with the meaning and purpose of shape. Shapes weren't random. Someone somewhere knew, or had known about the purpose of form.

He thought about the Egyptian Key of Life – the Ankh. It wasn't shaped like a key at all. Its shape represented something – some way of gaining entry. To what – where? In the Egyptian book of Hermetica, the text was clear that 'Specific numbers gave rise to specific harmonies and proportions'. What did the Ankh have to do with harmonies? He was getting tangled again. But the mathematics of sound was it what the Hermetica was talking about?

"Would you like a drink, sir?"

Torn abruptly from his thoughts, he turned. The air hostess smiled.

"A drink?" He realised that if refreshments were being offered they were airborne.

"You can take off your seat belt if you like," she said.

"Sure," said John in an imitation of how Angus would probably respond. "A coffee would be nice."

He'd drunk the coffee. Cream and sugar making it taste almost like a desert after his usual diet of black. He glanced up at the screen. Saw Tom Cruise in close up before the scene switched to the outside of a building, the old cinematography trick for switching scenes while maintaining levels of continuity. He'd forgotten they showed films as part of the flight experience.

He checked his watch. Where had he been for the past half hour? The terror was gone. He'd been lost in his thoughts again. His fear at take-off followed by the sudden mental or emotional escape into his past meant he hadn't even heard a word, was barely aware of his surroundings. The hostess probably thought he'd been asleep. He hadn't been. He'd somehow amazingly just closed his eyes and forgotten where he was and that he was terrified of being there. Almost forgotten that he could allow his thoughts to run free too, being so focused on Franklyn's required acceptance of his work had made his thinking rigid. Robust and scientific but there was so little flow. The ability to synchronise a range of information, data and any other available evidence was the key which led to leaps in understanding – discovery. He'd been denied that.

Franklyn had demanded that he continually backtrack to establish a framework for the theories instead of allowing or encouraging him to use what he'd already defined as the building blocks of a thesis to expound on what those things meant.

There were still too many unanswered questions. He rested his head on the back of the seat. He had to go with what he already knew. What he believed to be true. Even at this stage and despite Franklyn's attempts to paralyse his research, there was still enough compelling evidence to bring about a paradigm shift. He touched the leather pouch he had inside his jacket. Thought of the gifts it held within. He had to go on. He had no choice.

# 19 SIRIUS

The man who came toward him looked familiar. But it wasn't until Angus was less than two metres away that John recognised the smile. The teeth forever slightly crooked.

He felt his own teeth reveal themselves as his face opened up into a genuine and delighted grin. Angus looked so different but the eyes and the smile were the same. John allowed himself to be crushed in a hug.

"Man," Angus said, "where've you been?"

John hugged him back and laughed.

"You look exactly the same as you did last time I saw you, you dude." Angus stepped back. "You've still got hair." He pointed at John's head then rubbed his own bald one before shaking it in dismay. "Tell me," he said as he once again threw his arm around John, "tell me that Dan, my other old friend, at least is marginally follicly challenged."

John laughed again, shook his head in response. The guy may look different but he was still most definitely the guy he remembered. "Good to see you, Angus," he said. Despite the fleeting concern about Angus's baldness and gaunt appearance, it was. It was more than good to see Angus again. He hadn't realised how much he'd missed him.

"So," said Angus as they put the airport behind them and drove toward the main highway. "How are things going with the research – you cracked the mysteries of the Universe yet?"

John kept his eyes on the enfolding vista ahead of him. He couldn't discern whether the light-headedness he was feeling was excitement, fear, or simple anxiety at what lay ahead. Maybe it was all three. Or maybe even the physiological effects of aircraft coffee.

"I'm making progress," he said. "And you – how come you're here at Grettsberg?"

"Long story," said Angus. "But given you've asked I'll tell you. I decided it was time to get back to where I sort of began. Like you, well probably because of you, Man." He turned his head momentarily in John's direction, "I'm still kinda interested in the whole cosmic meaning of things." He paused before accelerating to overtake another vehicle. "The more I travelled, the more I saw." He laughed. "Kinda obvious, I know. But some of the treks, the expeditions for charity…" He pressed a button

65

on the dashboard.

The sound of the Eagles singing 'Peaceful Easy Feeling' swelled out from the speakers. John felt the beat. Angus knew how to make things come alive. The scenery so much unexpected flatness as counterpoint to the mountains that fringed the outlying areas, so much distance, so unlike his imagined view of how it would be, suddenly began to vibrate with the music. He felt the pulse of excitement in his skin. He was here in Arizona, the Eagles song a perfect cue to begin his journey. He flashed a glance at Angus whose eyes were fixed on the road ahead.

It felt good they were moving toward a destination. He was glad of the air conditioning too. A heat haze was shimmering off the tarmac of the road, the sky a drape of blue no hint of cloud, just the burning sun high in the sky. He considered the size of the yellow orb — the Sun. It was massive. Yet Sirius was about twice its size and twenty five times more luminous. Her rising — to the ancients she was always female — marking the flooding of the Nile in Ancient Egypt, her brightness a result of intrinsic luminosity making her the perfect star for navigation in the Pacific Ocean — a stellar compass.

He knew the star, Sirius, could be seen from almost every inhabited region of the Earth's surface. It could even be observed in daylight under the right conditions and was known under many names — the deer hunter, the leader, Loki's torch; the celestial wolf. The Giza Sphinx being erected to face toward her as she rose over the horizon at sunrise during the summer solstice. The key mysteries associated with the architecture of the Giza Plateau inextricably linked with the astronomical influence of her placing in the sky. Sirius had played such a part in myth, legend, and religion yet nobody was taking her power or potential seriously. Yet mathematically and astronomically the signs were clearly there.

He touched the leather pouch inside his jacket. In his wildest dreams he'd never imagined a connection to the Hopi Indians with their myths, legends and prophecies. The Blue Star Katchina Prophecy had lingered in his mind. A man called Waters had written about it. The academic demands for scientific proof, the sometimes mind numbing attention to what 'was' instead of what 'could' be coupled with his own determination to approach the study of cosmology in a robust methodological manner had been squeezing the life out of his fascination with alternative views and hypotheses outside of the mainstream. Franklyn's threat of disciplinary action and withdrawal of the scholarship had changed all that.

He'd scoured his own internal memory bank. The Hopi believed that 'The fourth World' was approaching its demise, believed that there were signs of imminent destruction. The images on the leathered parchment mirrored those symbols he'd become familiar with. The message seemed clear. The translation of the Hopi prophecies somehow indicating what the science he was studying was telling him too. The Earth was under threat.

"Cosmic meaning of things?" he said. Questioning the words Angus had spoken earlier before he'd boosted the acoustics.

"Yeah," said Angus. "The whole charity trip was easy for me."

John noticed how Angus ran his tongue back and forth along his bottom lip after he spoke.

"Well, not physically easy. You probably noticed I don't look too good," said Angus averting his head slightly in John's direction. "I managed to pick up something nasty." He coughed. "Thought it was going to be some kinda early 'Goodnight Vienna' – you know – the curtain call. The Old Man and Ma thought so too."

John shivered. Aware of the potential for loss, Angus, his first friend, "But you're OK now?" he said.

Angus let out a long whistling sigh. "Getting there," he answered. "Turns out I contracted some evil bug. I've been on all sorts of medication. Good news is I'm clear now. But it beat the hell out of me before it quit the scene."

They both were silent, the landscape opening out before them, the mountains shimmering in the distance almost an image from a dream.

He wondered how Angus would react when, or maybe if, he told him about the appointment at the solicitor's office. The outline of his past the mysterious Thomas Begvious had provided. The gifts his mother had left him with. But something, he wasn't quite sure what, was making him hold back. He didn't want to tell Angus about the revelations about his past yet, didn't want to drag the focus of the conversation back to himself when Angus, strangely for Angus, seemed like he wanted to talk about things beyond the immediate space in time he was operating in.

"This is some place, Angus," he said instead, conscious he'd slipped into the old Angus mode of phraseology. He couldn't help it. Paul Yeager along with his roadies and soundmen had a lot to answer for.

Angus nodded.

John struggled with the silence that followed before being the first to break it. "Angus," he said. "How come no-one let me know you were ill? Sarah and Dan – did they know?" He didn't wait for Angus to answer. "I just thought you were having an incredible time. Thought that's why I didn't hear back from you. I contacted you – text I think – when you were riding across the Iranian or Jordanian desert."

"Jordanian," said Angus without taking his eyes off the road. "I probably never received anything or if I did I was too out of it to remember. But hey, Man, I'm mending now. I may look like I'm ready to bite the dust but I've already managed to put on over twenty-six kilos. The hair went due to some kinda shock to my system. But what the…I got real low, though, Man."

He watched as Angus's profile darkened.

"I never understood when people talked about being depressed." He whistled. "Boy, do I know now." He changed gears, prepared to accelerate. "I'm outa there now. Guess that's why I didn't contact anyone." He reached forward again. "Wait till you hear this," he said as he switched tracks. "The Old Man…"

John felt the sudden rush as Paul Yeager's electric blues-rock guitar riff erupted through the sound system. For a moment he spun back in time, remembering the real wild man of rock, his gentle ways.

"Guess what?" said Angus.

"What," John queried, aware that the mood had become lighter, the vibration more upbeat.

"He's still got it," Angus said.

"What," said John, guessing Angus meant the power to pull a crowd – grab top space in the album charts, he knew Paul Yeager was still doing those things.

"The hair," said Angus. "He's still got the fucking hair, Man."

# 20 FREEDOM

He placed his hands against the glass and stared. The expanse opened up before him, the distance almost infinite, the land blending into sky.

Ascending to the heights of Canyon Pass in the car, Angus had wound down the windows with the flick of a switch and told him to "Taste, the air."

John did. It was sweet.

"Rarefied, hey?" Angus said, his voice buoyant.

The way John remembered it had always seemed to be.

"Frank Sinatra, I never could figure what he was singing about," Angus continued.

John shrugged. Tried to grasp the sense of what Angus was talking about.

"Come Fly With Me, the song. Frank Sinatra – remember?" Angus clicked off the track; sang the song through as John continued to try and capture the uncompromised views on his mental canvas.

Now they were here, perched above the landscape with an unspoiled high Sonoran Desert canyon panorama in every direction.

"Something else, eh?" Angus came up and stood beside him.

"I didn't expect this," said John, his eyes still fixed on the horizon. "I thought maybe a small apartment. But this place…"

"The folks own it." Angus reached to the side of the glass doors pressing a switch. They slid open. "That's what I meant when I said the treks – the expeditions for charity were easy for me." He stepped outside.

"I was just doin it for fun." He waved his arm as if brushing something away. "But there were others who were doing it because it was a good thing to do. It cost them in terms of jobs, relationships." He paused. "They were doing it for the memories of people they loved." He sat down at a wooden table flanked by chairs that surrounded a now empty pool. "Getting sick made me realise it was time I grew up and stopped being the kid of rich folks."

John stayed where he was. Felt as if he was in an elevator that had just stopped suddenly.

"You're just Angus," he said. He knew the Yeager's were rich. But they lived such simple lives when he stayed with them it was something

69

easy to forget. Now, looking around him at the plot of land the house was built upon and the view it commanded he realised he'd only ever known them for who they were not what they owned. "Your parents," he said. "They've always seemed so…"

"Cool," said Angus. "They are. They commit themselves to causes where their presence, money or music can help. I've lost count of the things they've achieved for others on the back of Pa's fame."

"They never talk about it." John sat down at the table, still mesmerised by the space, the sense of freedom.

"They keep most of what they do anonymous. So in some ways I did all the charity work – the expeditions and stuff. So they'd be proud of me."

"They always were – are," John said.

"Yeah," said Angus, several moments later, as if he'd been carefully analysing the comment. "I just kinda don't know why." He stretched. "Drink and food, hey? I'm starved you must be too. Juanita, Ma's little friend who helps out from time to time made us a stash." He headed inside.

John stood up and followed him.

"I should show you round some," said Angus. "But I think we should eat first." He glanced over to the doors where John's guitar and luggage rested against the wall. "I am some bad host, Man. I haven't even shown you where you're sleeping. C'mon through here…" He started to move then stopped. "Let's get your stuff."

John followed the instruction.

"Man," said Angus as he picked up the guitar. "Is this?"

"The Martin guitar, your dad gave me."

"You gonna blow my mind with some sweet sounds, Man?"

John heard the sound of his own laughter. "Wish I could," he said.

Angus smiled. "Me too Man," he said. "Though I can play a bit now, no riffs, just some finger picking." He frowned. "No, cancel that. Strumming is about as good as I get." He laughed. "But it's bad. James Taylor would kill me if he heard what I do to some of his numbers. How bout you – still into Dylan?"

John nodded.

"Who wouldn't be?" said Angus turning and striding away. The guitar case firmly gripped in his hand, "the man's pure magician."

He was still standing where Angus had left him, aware that he couldn't quite accustom himself to the unexpected surroundings, unsure of the rules that operated with this new, not altogether carefree Angus. It was hard, picking up on a friendship after such a long absence of contact – maybe even harder than he'd expected it to be.

Angus stopped, motioned with his head. "It's through here," he said. "Follow."

By the time he'd taken the shower, Angus said he had time for before they ate, he was beginning to feel more orientated.

The room was spacious, with windows that stretched its length. From where he was sitting, on the huge antique pine double bed, it appeared as if he was hovering in mid air.

"Check the springs, Man," Angus had said.

John had.

"Shipped over," Angus said. "Ma, she has to have some history around her. We've got half of the rustic furniture ever made in the UK here, but these," he pointed to the rugs, "are Native American. She's helped set up some exports – all the profits go back into the communities who produce the work."

John ran his hand along the throw on the bed, pressed his feet into the rug on the floor. He'd wanted to ask Angus about the people who produced the fantastically vibrant textiles, wanted to ask if Manda had contact with the Hopi. He hadn't.

# 21 BLUE STAR

"Grabbed my interest, Man, I needed a job too," said Angus as they headed toward the university in the truck. "The target asteroid is about a third of a mile in diameter, discovered in 1999. Every six years it nears the Earth. It'll be 2017 before ground based telescopes can see it again. I've managed to get myself on the team. Small fry person but who cares. I've arranged for you to meet the main guy before he does the usual academic leave taking number. It gets so hot here during the summer months anyone with any sense or any place to go, splits."

"They're studying the 'Yarkovsky' effect – investigating how to alter the course or deflect potentially earth-impacting asteroids," Said John, working hard to keep his building excitement confined. His cards close to his chest. He didn't want Angus to think he was only here for the telescopes or an opportunity to engage with the group who were trying to buy time on a network of telescopes operating across the world and beyond it – in Chile, Puerto Rica the Canary Islands. Here, right here in Arizona and out there. John glanced at the scorching blue sky, out there in space too. He was here because Angus had asked him to be. The rest was an unmissable and fantastic opportunity to get closer to the people who were carrying out ground breaking research into the potential hazardous threats posed by near Earth asteroids should they strike the planet – the world they knew. And an opportunity to search for the answers to the mystery surrounding his birth and the mother lost to him before his life had barely begun.

It seemed a lifetime ago that he'd climbed on the plane, yet the fact was it was three single days ago, just over seventy-two hours. Angus had swung in mood from his old positive confident self. The guy who believed anything and everything was possible to someone who unexpectedly nosedived emotionally. John wondered if the illness had affected him in some way deeper than the physical.

"Haziq is here too."

"Haziq?" For a moment John's mind was blank before the image of the sculpted face, beaming with pride, edged into his visual thought space. "Haziq?" He sat forward. "Haziq, who stayed with us – his father, wasn't he…"

"Involved in radiological research," said Angus, eyes on the road.

"He's working at the Uni?" John felt the pull of the past, the potential of the future.

"He's on the team," said Angus. "The Osirix Ress project. He's doing background work, data analysis mostly geological data. They're hoping to bring a sample of the asteroid back to Earth to measure and analyse."

John nodded, unwilling to explain he knew all the finer details. He knew the B-type asteroid, which was carbonaceous and related to unusual outer main-belt asteroids that acted like comets by outgassing volatiles, had been spotted by one of the top men at the Lunar and Planetary Observatory. There'd been nothing in the scientific literature about it but plenty on the Internet. Astronomers had been observing it for a long time. They already had radar images, visible and near infrared observations, which confirmed it was a B-type (bluish) asteroid. They'd got a pretty good light curve and a rotation period but the rotation period they'd specified was wrong. John remembered how he'd grasped at the evidence of the error. Using it to demonstrate how easily errors could occur in order to lend support to his hypothesis on the limitations of the reconfiguring of optical observations because of technical anomalies. Franklyn had brushed the evidence aside. Ignored the paper John had submitted to him on the subject.

The error seemed even more relevant now than it did then. Discovering the Hopi connection, the sudden frantic dead of night Internet search after the visit to the solicitors, the search for information on his background – his roots; it had almost blown his mind wide open. There'd been all sorts of crazy stuff. The Internet – a minefield for the unwary. Whole sites dedicated to the threat of Armageddon. But there amidst all the falsified evidence, the over-the-top claims that had little or no substance, appeared the writings on the Blue Star Katchina Prophecy. It wasn't the first time he'd read about the Hopi prophecy but somehow it was the first time he'd made the link. The imagery had opened up – the flash, flash, flash, of comprehension, creating an almost indelible imprint that illuminated his calculations.

The scientific community had demonstrated they were capable of error through operating independently of each other, within their respective disciplines. Technical anomalies were sometimes overlooked, or the evidence of them not shared. The Osirix Ress work, proof of that. His own analysis and research showed that the academics had gotten other things wrong too. If his own calculations were right, not only was the Great Pyramid of Giza key in some way to the diminishing magnetic forces of the Earth, but Sirius, which appeared to be represented as the Hopi's prophesised Blue Star Katchina, was going to be unmasked. Posing a greater threat to the Earth far sooner than current modern scientific calculations and thinking were capable of even speculating.

He knew that his painstaking work on the telescopes, the virtually imperceptible drift, meant that the calculations being used for distance in terms of the ability and time it took for light to travel were wrong. He needed to find out how wrong. It was easier to feel safe when the technical equipment suggested that the reception of light indicated that a volatile mass was many years away from any contact with the Earth. What if those indications and predictions were wrong? He needed to talk to these people out here. Maybe unlike Franklyn they'd listen.

"You're too quiet – worried about the roads out here, Man?" Angus sounded amused. "I know you were never too keen on heights – but be sure you know I follow the guidance of the Eagles out here."

John let go of his thoughts, shook his head, not sure if Angus was about to switch psychological gears and start speaking of spiritual matters as he had the previous night. The sudden unexpected shift he'd made from talking about planning a walk in the mountains to the beliefs of the peoples the land had been stolen from.

"Guidance of the Eagles?" John said. "You like to follow the guidance of the Eagles – as part of North American culture?"

"Oh, Man," said Angus pressing a button on the dashboard. "I am so glad you're here." The sound system burst into life. The Eagles track was playing again. "Like these guys, Man, like the song...I Take It Easy." He sang the last few words.

John started to laugh before joining in to sing along as the sun rose ever higher in the afternoon sky.

# 22 MID STRIDE

The campus was as quiet as the one back home, the layout a mixture of modern and old. John attempted to make the cognitive adjustments to the mental framework he'd developed to enable him to find his way around at Bloomfield. This place was bigger, the site more spread out. There were less hard angles and more slopes. The pathway to what he assumed was the main building curving upwards. He was doing his best to make general comments to Angus as they crossed the main quad, but his mind was fizzling. Thoughts were firing and sparking – synthesizing. All the theories he'd developed, the discoveries he'd made, and been ignored or penalised for, along with some he'd yet to share, were being reignited. Maybe this was the place he was meant to be.

It was here, they'd developed the HiRISE camera, a UA-designed camera expected to capture the highest-resolution images of Sirius ever seen. The journey of the Orbiter was 300 million miles. The project expected to be in its Primary Science Phase in the month of October. Currently operating on the surface of Mars was the Lander known as the Phoenix Scout Mission, led by one of the top Scientists from Grettsberg. The mission's purpose to improve knowledge of the Martian Arctic. How amazing was that?

He glanced again at the buildings ahead. He felt like a kid again. The kid he was before Berke. The weight of Franklyn suddenly lifted. Knew that the people here weren't trying to make names for themselves on the back of other people's theories. Most of them could already claim successful and notable involvement with NASA missions.

He stopped and took a breath. They had the Steward Observatory here, too. Operating the 12-Meter Telescope on Kressa Peak and the Submillimeter Telescope on Mount Graham. Surely there would be someone he could talk to who would at least give his findings some consideration? If they didn't and they thought, like Franklyn did, that he was shooting in the dark, at least they couldn't throw him out of the place, or withdraw his scholarship funding because he wasn't registered here. But maybe...

"I'll introduce you to a few guys on the team."

Angus's voice, reminded him he was still on the outside of the building not engaged with those carrying out the research. "The team," he said, wondering if he could ever be part of it. Then he remembered. "Haziq," he said. "Is he here, too? You said he was working on the geological data."

Angus stopped mid stride before reaching out and grabbing his arm. "There's something I didn't tell you earlier," he said, "because I'm aware I keep on taking the mood down a notch or two, Man."

John waited while Angus appeared to struggle with his thinking. Was he going to tell him he couldn't speak with the people here – Haziq included – or was he going to hit him with something else?

"If you'd rather I kept a low profile," he said. "Stayed in the background, that's OK with me." It was a lie. It wasn't OK, but Angus was his friend, and despite his need to get to the right people he realised he didn't want to jeopardise the reconnection. He'd find another way.

"No," Angus shook his head. "It's just Haziq has had some big set back in his life. I wouldn't want you to take his attitude wrong, Man. He's well…"

"I understand about setbacks," John said. "My own research, I've had…"

"It's not his research, Man."

He heard the edge in Angus's voice. As if research was a minor matter. "Health," said John. "He's been ill too?"

"Nah," Angus's voice had dropped to little more than a whisper. "His parents, they…they…well, they're dead."

John felt as if the light had suddenly gone out on the day. Remembered Haziq totally besotted and adoring of his mother and father He'd been so proud.

"Bomb," said Angus.

"How – I mean why?"

"Wrong place, wrong time, Man."

John clutched air. All the excitement and plans he'd been working on dissolving in the flow of grief he felt for Haziq.

"C'mon," Angus nudged his arm. "Just wanted to prepare you, Man…"

# 23 ECLECTIC

They walked the rest of the way in silence. John wanting to ask questions about Haziq, Haziq's parents, how it happened. There was little point. Knowing the facts didn't change things – wouldn't make things any easier for Haziq.

But how had Haziq come to be here - had Angus invited him, too? It didn't matter.

Everything was changing or had already changed. He'd imagined everyone else's life continuing in the same positive way he remembered, thought that only he had problems with grief and loss and the struggle to stay sane. Imagined that the Franklyn issue, the whole disciplinary and withdrawal of funding threat, was some big gargantuan deal, he tried to shake off the heaviness in his bones, wished he could spit out the sourness of shame in his mouth.

"Is there any way – anything I can do to help?" he asked, as they entered the main building.

"We can only try, Man," said Angus, before loping up the stairs ahead of him.

He followed.

"Hey," said Angus as they walked through the doors he'd just used a security code to open, "we find living beings here."

John watched as a tall slim man with silver grey hair, a triangular jaw and a deep tan stood up and took off his glasses.

"John, Brett Fielding, Brett, John," Angus said introducing them.

Brett held out his hand. The smile was fleeting. John shook the hand which gripped his own.

"Good to meet you," said Brett.

John realised that despite the grey hair Brett was younger than he first appeared, probably only in his late twenties or early thirties. "You too," John answered, searching his mental library for who Brett could be.

"Angus, showing you around?" Brett Fielding paused. "Delete that question," he said before John could respond. "Of course he is."

"Well," said John.

"There's a lot to see," said Brett. "Angus tells us you're a cosmology genius."

John couldn't help but notice, that despite the fact the smile had returned, the expression in Brett's eyes was less friendly.

"Something of an eclectic too, Astronomy, Astrophysics…" Brett continued.

"I'm interested and work hard, that's all." John said, feeling it was an immature response. Maybe it was the way the guy towered over him. John guessed he must have been at least Six four. But so was Paul Yeager, but something about Paul Yeager made it difficult to ever feel small in his presence.

"There are some great minds here," said Brett.

"Fantastic equipment too," said Angus.

"It helps," Brett said, as he put his glasses back on and returned to his seat. "But without the correct thinking behind the scenes, the equipment wouldn't be much use."

"Brett scopes most of the work before it gets to planning stage," said Angus.

John's memory clicked. How could he have forgotten? It must have been the shock of hearing the terrible news of Haziq's loss. "Brett Fielding," he said "Highest-resolution images of Sirius ever seen."

Brett smiled, this time his eyes did too. "Background man," he said. "But it all went to plan – highest resolutions ever seen."

Once the introductions were over they found a place outside in the shade. It was still too hot. John wondered if they'd be better inside – at least there was air conditioning. His head was spinning. Angus had introduced him to no more than five people but he was already exhausted. They probably thought he was some kind of oddball. He'd hardly engaged with the social niceties that people expected. He'd either found himself either unable to speak, or blurting out the details he knew about the projects they were working on before clamming up again.

"I didn't do too well, did I?" He popped the ring on the coke Angus had just passed to him. The cafeteria had been shut. Luckily Angus had coins for the coke machine. The iciness of the can felt good in his hands.

Angus laughed. Pinged open his coke. "Life isn't a contest, Man." He took a swig of his drink. "I'd think you made those guys feel pretty good, knowing as much about both them and their work as you obviously do." He rolled the coke can across his forehead. "Can't understand why you weren't at the conference. I was only over there on a seventy hour round trip courtesy of the department – a blast, a real blast, Man – some thinking going on out there. Thought I'd catch you…"

"I wasn't invited," John said.

"How come?" Angus narrowed his eyes.

John wasn't sure whether it was the brightness of the sun or a sudden mood change. "Sarah not tell you?" he asked keeping his gaze firmly fixed on his hands.

"Sarah told me she'd contact you when I emailed her to say I'd finally gotten round to communicating. But you weren't answering." Angus took a swig of his drink. "She's kinda like an honorary sister." He laughed. "Real mad at me for not keeping in touch. Guess I let her think my lack of contact was because I'd been having a wild time." He gestured to John, drawing an imaginary loop over his head. "Man thing – kinda stupid but what the…"

John nodded.

"So what's going on, Man?"

While part of him wanted to tell Angus, wanted some feedback on whether what he was doing was right, after hearing about Haziq, his own concerns seemed minor. But he guessed Angus would find out anyway. He took a swig of coke, before telling the story.

"I saw the guy, at the conference," said Angus after hearing the fairly abbreviated version John had given him of Franklyn's actions "He seemed cool – real confident guy. Talked about the German astronomer Friedrich – Friedrich…"

"Bessel, eighteen forty-four…" said John.

"In one," said Angus. "My memory sucks. The brain still works – real sharp at times, but the memory." He pressed a finger against his nose.

John waited, giving Angus time to collect the thoughts he was having trouble finding. Giving himself time to stifle the bad feeling that was creeping round his gut.

Angus continued. "Talked about how the Friedrich guy deduced from changes in the proper motion of Sirius that it had an unseen companion."

"Yes," said John, wondering why Franklyn had chosen to talk about the proper motion of planets. It was a subject area he'd consistently tried to close John down on, but demanded more extensive evidence for, continually pressurising him to provide more mathematical analysis to support his hypotheses.

"It was almost two decades before it could be observed by telescopic means," John explained. "Alvin Graham Clark, American telescope-maker and astronomer, eighteen sixty-two." He paused before continuing. "The previously unseen companion was identified during testing of the largest refracting telescope in existence at the time…"

"Yeees." Angus altered his position so that the sun was no longer directly in his face.

John accommodated the move. "The telescopes you have here," he said, despite his determination not to mention his interest too soon. "When can I have a look at them?"

## 24 THE DEN

He fired up his laptop. Angus had helped him rig up an office in the so-called Den of the ranch house. He had his papers spread all over the room. It was starting to appear like the apartment.

"No sweat," Angus said, when John apologised. "Place is for living and working in, Man."

Now as he'd seen some of the other houses located in the area he realised that this place, fantastic as it was, was a place for 'living in'. The floors were easily swept or mopped, no over concern about strolling in and out with boots on. Juanita whom he'd only met once was paid a wage to just check things out and air the place if it was left empty for any period of time. It already felt as much a home to him as the Yeager's farmhouse in Wales.

"Cost less than a quarter of what the farmhouse would sell for," Angus told him. "They rented it at first. Then bought it as a 'head clearing space' for when the Old Man had to do business over here. Then Ma started to get interested in the whole social and community side of things."

John thought about the flare of unexpected anger he'd felt when Angus had told him about the displacement of the people – the Hopi, to whom, if Thomas Begvious was right, he shared some kind of history. He could see how Manda would have wanted to engage with a people whose culture and esteem was being decimated by ill thought out bureaucratic social systems that moved them from a way of being that was natural and close to their own original roots to one where they had no sense of continuity of self or culture.

He still hadn't told Angus about what he'd found out. It was still too raw in his heart. The thought of the girl who was his mother and why she had abandoned him continued to sneak into his mind at so many different points of the day and woke him in the night, the rush of emotion wiping out all thoughts of the Earth, the cosmos, what he had to do.

He clicked on his emails. There was still nothing from Franklyn, the university or the research council. The emails he'd sent were probably at the bottom of the pile of the mailboxes of all those he'd contacted. It would probably be September, the start of the new semester, before he received a response from anyone.

He clicked open Sarah's email. Sarah the honorary sister, Dan's girl from as far back as he could remember.

Her email outlined everything was fine. The new job demanding, but she was meeting lots of people who could open other doors within the media. She'd settled in the apartment. Dan was much less tired. She'd sold two of her freelance articles to a major newspaper. She'd typed the major in bold capitals. John dashed of a reply, sending congratulations. He'd have to tell Angus. He clicked his mailbox shut and opened up the document he'd been working on.

He did a quick mental switch. It was important that he clarified his thinking. He needed to have his pitch ready for when he found the right people to deliver it to. It was clear that the evidence from not only his research, but those of many others too, identified that the Universe was expanding at an accelerating rate. It was also becoming increasingly evident that there appeared to be an unknown form of energy associated with the vacuum of space. The cosmologists were calling it the "missing energy" of the Universe. The argument being, that if both current theory and new observations were correct, the energy must be acting as a repulsive force to counteract gravity's restraining influence and thus speed up cosmic expansion.

He realised that for some reason his hands were shaking. Was he scared or excited? He didn't know. The physiology was the same. He reached into the pouch he kept inside his backpack and retrieved the leathered parchment. He knew now what some of the symbols meant. The plus and the minus signs and the circle were representations of the symbols on the Hopi Rock. They represented positive, negative and neutral forces in a magnetic field. He considered the signs, ran his hand across the cloth. He'd come to think of it as cloth now. His cloth, like a comfort blanket a kid may refuse to be without. That's what it had become. He kept it close to him at all times.

Casting his eyes back to his PC he read the document on the screen. He'd referenced the material he was using to support his position, the elements of his thesis, which suggested a missing energy, which had led to the catastrophes of antiquity and were now gaining force again. He read it now.

*'Increasing evidence, based on distant supernova explosions, suggest that the Universe is not decelerating, as expected, but flying apart faster than ever before. The missing energy, scientists propose, exerts a negative pressure, which by the rules of Einstein's theory of general relativity leads to a negative gravitational force on the Universe.*

*Supernova astronomers have made a strong case for an accelerating Universe and thus for something like the missing energy. These astronomers have provided for the first time observationally consistent evidence that there is some form of vacuum energy.'*

It was the plus and minus signs on the Hopi Rock. He felt sure. The idea of the alternate forces the + representing the plus energy and the − representing the minus energy and the circle representing the Earth. He'd considered the extent to which the symbols could be interpreted as related to the pole shift hypothesis. The idea that the sudden shifting of the magnetic poles of the Earth had led to cataclysmic events, yet no form of the hypothesis had ever been accepted by the scientific community, although he was only too aware that even if that were the case it didn't exclude the possibility of evidence emerging to support Hapgood's theory.

He sat back. He'd already considered that the symbols could be related to the known phenomena of geomagnetic reversal where the Earth's magnetic fields of magnetic north and magnetic south were interchanged over periods of one to ten thousand years. Why would the Hopi rock symbol be representing such a gradual change? He knew that the plus and minus symbols represented positive, negative and neutral forces in a magnetic field. The belief being that where the energies crossed was an opening, a vortex into the next dimension.

Now he'd read the Blue Star Katchina Prophecy with the film of academia peeled from his eyes it made his own theories come alive. Prophecy, legend and parable often contained essential truths. He knew that. The esoteric texts he'd studied in the long hours alone at boarding school had revealed that much to him. The understanding, and scientific clarification of which, had led to Berke's humiliation of him. Now it was clearer. Far clearer.

The Hopi Prophecy talked of the emergence of the Blue Star Katchina making its appearance in the heavens and the Fifth World emerging. The belief was that the Blue Star would dance in the plaza and remove its mask − a dwelling place in the heavens that would fall with a great crash. The prophecy. It was confirming what he'd been able to see happening through his research. Now he needed to understand the energy within the vortex − the hidden force that sustained balance.

He again felt the softness of the leathered parchment. There was a part of him, somewhere far back in his skull, the base of his brain, the limbic system, the emotional instinctive nature of himself that was telling him in every cell of his being that the truth, the confirmation of the truth was being laid before him.

Attempted to steady his shaking hand. Closing his eyes attempting to steady the tremor resulting from the sense of something uncoiling like a serpent at the base of his spine. Wondered if he was going crazy, questioned whether he would ever have made the same connections if the leather pouch, the parchment − his cloth, and the tiny artefacts had not been gifted to him? He didn't know. How could he?

But after so many years studying the rotation and movement of stars and planets, his intense interest in the Sirius system, which had led him inadvertently to study the importance of its heliacal position to the ancients, and its seeming profound connection to the Great Pyramid, the Sphinx – maybe the entire architecture of the Giza Plateau, the connections were surely far beyond the randomness of chance.

He stood up. Thankful that for all its rustic charm the place had air conditioning. It was already too hot outside. There was no way of cooling off. Angus had never gotten around to filling the small plunge pool. His illness, the bug he'd contracted, had been associated with some sort of amoebic dysentery outbreak and he was almost afraid of the possible organisms that could develop in a poorly maintained area of water.

"Ma's never liked the idea of chlorination," he said by way of an apology that they were living in probably the only place in the area without a facility for swimming. "You know how she was about chemicals and stuff. Apparently there are all sorts of possible carcinogens. Even the oxygenated pools depend on bleach of some sort. She's talked of hay as a natural form of oxygenation but I'm not taking any chances."

John sat down again. At least it was easy to breathe. Although, the way his thoughts were firing, he kept forgetting to. The reality of what was coming together was pretty much making him hold his breath. If he were to explain it in simple terms would anyone listen?

Sirius itself was the brightest star in the sky. Its name derived from the Ancient Greek Seirios, which meant glowing or scorcher. It wasn't alone it was part of a system – a binary system. A white main sequence star Sirius A and a faint white dwarf companion Sirius B. Bessel had deduced the existence of Sirius B long before a telescope had been designed to observe it. That's what, according to Angus, and Angus had no cause to lie, Franklyn had been talking about at the conference.

He wondered if Franklyn had gone so far as to discuss the tribe who'd known of the existence of the Sirius system even before Bessel had deduced its existence, or science had been able to use telescopic means to detect its presence. It was Key to the Dogon culture and belief system. Its position in the heavens revered. The Hopi talked of the Blue Star dancing in the plaza before removing her mask. Sirius. They had to be talking about Sirius. If you followed an imaginary line through the three stars that made up Orion's belt she'd be there. Radiating that unmistakeable bluish light – Sirius the Blue Star.

Realising that if his calculations were right the 'dancing' in the plaza was due to the changes in the magnetic fields then the fact was that Sirius would no longer be maintained in orbit. Already her wavy motion, due to the unstable gravitational pull of the dwarf star Sirius B, was observable. As that pull diminished or disappeared, he or she, as the Ancients called her, would be spinning out of control in the heavens – the Hopi's plaza in the sky. The mask, they were talking about was Sirius B. Sirius B was the mask – the covering that obscured the reality, the orbital irregularities of which had already been observed, leading astronomers to postulate on another small companion star. The theory had been discounted yet the orbital irregularities had increased.

The third star either existed or the evidence of an accelerating Universe had to be recognised. The Supernova astronomers had already provided the first observationally consistent evidence that there was some form of vacuum energy. If no third star existed to account for the orbital irregularities of Sirius, then the vacuum of energy was the only alternative hypothesis. Which meant, as he'd already predicted, Sirius was already beginning to dance.

Finding the reason for the missing energy, and establishing how the vacuum could be filled, still seemed beyond the scope of his thinking, yet it could be the only way to stabilise and increase the magnetic energies, which could stabilise the Earth, and deflect the catastrophe of diminishing forces propelling Sirius into direct collision.

He'd focused so much on the centrality of the capstone theory, Franklyn had demanded he did, but there was something missing. Something fundamental was missing. Staring at the computer screen he tried to will his mind to keep functioning – to solve the massive puzzle the cosmos had created.

# 25 DESERT

The day was ablaze. He'd never walked so far in the heat they were experiencing. Yet his body felt strangely rested, his mind at peace. They were on the second trail of the journey – a trek through the wilderness areas of the Sonoran desert.

They'd completed the Brittlebush trail by starting just before dawn; walking through the less intense heat of the earlier part of the day and heading toward where it intersected with The Margie's Cove Trail, a nine mile route through the heart of the sixty-three thousand two hundred acre North Maricopa Mountain Wilderness. The area was different to the walks of his youth in the Snowdonia Mountains of Wales. The heat especially different, yet the vistas, so starkly defined, bearing so little likeness yet still comparable in the sense of mental space they enabled.

They'd seen desert mule deer, desert bighorn sheep and numerous varieties of lizards and birds neither he nor Angus could identify. Now that night had fallen and both he, and Angus, had settled in their sleeping bags, John thought about the Coyote, wondered if they'd hear its call.

He'd been reluctant to embark on the exploration. Desperate to stay in front of his PC, working on the ever growing files of documents containing his calculations. Angus had sprung the idea – the plan – on him. He'd panicked. Despite the fact what he was producing regarding his theories was becoming increasingly meaningless he didn't want to stop.

"We've got a temperature drop, Man," Angus announced after returning from a 'catch up' meeting at the university. "We could take a break in the mountains."

He saw how excited Angus was, watched as Angus started to search through cupboards throwing out boots and bags.

"You can't stay in this place for the entirety," Angus said. "You need a break, Man. You're starting to look dark around the eyes."

Now they were here, the quiet settling around them, the skies above the possible plaza of the Hopi prophecy – an invitation of infinity.

"Can send you crazy, Man," Angus's voice was low.

John turned, thought Angus had long been asleep. "The sky," he said.

"Trying to work out how it all became," said Angus, moving slightly to accommodate the rearranging of the rolled up coat he was using as a pillow.

"You too?" said John.

"That's why I dragged you out here." He continued to tussle with the coat. "All them papers, Man. The diagrams, the numbers you're working on. I thought I'd drag you away so you'd get some rest."

"You were right," said John. "It's restful here." It was. "But you can't get away from it can you?"

"No, Man." Angus laughed. "No matter where you go it's up there."

John continued staring at the sky. So many things he couldn't get away from. The hike, the long hours of steady movement broken only by the sounds of scurrying animals and the birds' overhead had calmed him, but the sense of urgency to clarify his thinking on the mathematics of his hypotheses had not retreated. Angus was right he had started to appear hollow looking. He'd seen it himself.

He was exhausted. In some ways even more exhausted than when he was struggling to gain some sense of acknowledgement and comprehension of his findings from Franklyn. He'd wanted to move forward then. To have his findings recognised and replicated, so he could be sure. Now as he was free to synthesize both his own findings and the findings of others the work he was carrying out had gathered speed. Yet he felt as if he was fighting his way through a wind tunnel. He was moving but remaining static. He needed someone to listen. He needed to stop the world – literally. Everything was moving except him – moving out of control.

Yet from where he lay the sky seemed so still. Even without the help of a telescope he could see the shimmering white curve, the cosmic river of white diamonds – stars – that formed the Milky Way. He'd read that the ancient Egyptians believed that the Giza Plateau was a reflection of the heavens. The Nile, the earthly river, a representation of the heavenly river of light that formed the celestial spectacle held within the deepening violet of the vast expanse of sky that he was now lying beneath. Orion's Belt reflected on the earthly plane by the Great Pyramid Khufu and its companions Khafre and Menkaure.

'As above so below', it was written in the texts. A message clarifying the intention, or understanding of the people, who'd populated Egypt, that place of historic abundance and knowledge. 'As above so below' John understood that the literal representation was capturing some essence of the material world as a mirror image of above – but why? The question hadn't been fully answered. Yet it was as if the clues had been laid out. The challenge to resolve the extraordinary puzzle they presented a reminder of how small a space modern man occupied in the great scheme of things. Again he thought of the Ankh – the Egyptian Key of Life. Maybe there was something, some barricaded truth, some hidden rusted mythical lock it could open.

Instinctively he reached inside the rucksack beside him. The leather pouch warm to his touch.

"Angus," he hardly recognised the sound of his own voice, felt as if the night, the sky, the rough terrain of the desert were a backdrop to a stage he'd finally found the courage to stand and speak from. "I found," he began, "I think I know who I am. Where I came from…"

Angus made no response, his breathing the regular and steady rhythm of a man in sleep. John turned on his side, away from the image of infinity above. He'd almost told someone, but where to begin? How did you explain a lifetime of loss when you'd never known what or who it was that was missing from your life? He closed his eyes. Thomas Begvious, the man who found him had searched for answers. He'd given over everything he'd found. As sleep slowly closed his eyes, John wasn't sure whether it was enough.

# 26 LIGHTENING BURST

"Home to twenty-two Native American Tribes," Angus said as they stowed the sleeping bags into their backpacks. "Ma, could tell you much more than I can. She's researched and explored the cultural differences and needs of the people so that she can advocate for their rights from their perspective, not hers."

John wanted to ask more but Angus had already started to clear up around them before they moved on. John followed suit, checking his bag, ensuring there was nothing that had rolled out of sight as they'd made a basic camp the night before. They still had enough water to cover the distance on the route that would take them back to the truck. The heat of the day was yet to build. The sooner they set off the less likely they would use up their resources before getting back to where they'd parked before they'd set out.

"We take the hills to the south and over the saddle between the peaks." Angus pointed up toward the burnished slope in the land, which looked almost red, curving into an orange dip in the centre. "Let's go."

Less than an hour later they both needed to stop for breath as the trek rose upwards, traversing a sharp-edged, yet crumbly rock slope that would take them to the top of the pass. They drank the first daily ration of water while sitting on the boulders that framed and punctuated the incline. The light had now changed dramatically. The sky taking on an almost preternatural lilac flush, the landscape appearing drier, more golden, less red. Greyish and flat in places interspersed with the green of vegetation. John wasn't sure why but he suddenly felt a desire to be back on the road. "Are we still on the planned route?" he said, aware his question sounded more abrupt than intended.

Angus closed his water bottle, re-stashed it in his backpack. "I'm good with maps, Man," he said, retrieving the map from its side pocket holder and opening it up. "We just follow this path." He turned the map. "Across and down, then follow through here and pick up the main route." He pointed at one of many lines slicing its way through land area depicted on the map. "Here – see. Then we're back on track and follow this path back to the area where we originally set off. Home and dry." He rolled up the map and returned it to its pocket.

John squeezed the flesh of his jaw, tried not to consider the distance ahead.

The trek over proved to be slower going than at first appeared. The descent from the saddle shaped viewpoint, rockier and strewn with large boulders wedged into what was a narrow wash.

John noticed Angus checking the sky every few yards downwards as they manoeuvred around or climbed over the rocks. Despite the heat Angus was moving quickly his breathing becoming laboured.

John felt his own lungs rebelling when Angus took a sudden turn, which took them upwards, his legs weak with the increased exertion required by the steep and unexpected incline. They'd barely reached the top when Angus almost collapsed. The day turned dark. John felt the snap of change in the air.

Within seconds the lightning burst. The sky and the path they'd moved so speedily from, awash.

# 27 THE PAST

"I didn't realise why you were moving so fast," even as John said the words the sky seemed to be unrolling a sheet of blue, expunging the evidence of the freak storm.

"Weather forecast was clear, Man." Angus pulled a towel from his rucksack, rubbing it across his face before throwing it to John. "One of the benefits of hairlessness." He laughed as he monitored the sweeping dark clouds dissipating in the distance. "It's heading away from us," he said, his eyes taking in the spread of land. "If we keep heading across this way." He pointed. "Not the intended path but we should be able to pick up the main route."

Two hours later they were still hiking, Angus periodically checking the map. The temperature rising. John longing for the mountains and treks of their youth, where he at least had some idea of familiar landmarks - a sense of where they were going; how they would get there.

"I need to eat, Man," Angus slowed as he spoke.

Again John noticed the greyish pallor that didn't relate to the heat or strain of the hike. He watched as Angus slipped his rucksack and sat in the nearest thing that could be described as shade. A spot no more than a graceful curve in the flow of the land with a tilted canopy of foliage, overhung by some rocks higher up the slope. John gratefully shrugged off his own bag, allowing himself the luxury of a rest, his back toward the sun and the almost cool of the curtain of leaves.

He watched as Angus tore open the flap of his bag and delved inside, pulling out the vacuum-sealed sprouted wheat loaf and the ring pull tins, one of pâté and one of jam that was to form their lunch. Then rooted in his own bag for the camping cutlery he'd stored there. The single all-inclusive utensil that still pleased him as much as it did on his first camping trip, he passed it to Angus along with the plastic dishes he'd unhooked from the side compartment of his bag.

"It's the heat," he said as he placed the items on the dusty ground before lifting the bread and small cans from Angus's lap. "Just rest a bit. I'll sort out the food."

He prepared the lunch, which they both consumed in silence, increasingly conscious that Angus appeared to have turned his awareness inward, just as he had also.

"Keep on thinking I'm over it," Angus said.

John repacked the remains of the food they'd just eaten.

"Then, whoosh something hits me. Sorry, Man."

"You were moving pretty fast when that storm started to move in," John said as he fastened his bag. "How often do the weather forecasters get their predictions wrong out here?" Seeing Angus's previously grey face almost returned to its usual colour set in a questioning frown, realised the implication of his words. He hastily backtracked.

"I'm only asking because of my concerns about the unpredictability of a world climate that becomes increasingly volatile due to the diminishing magnetic forces of the Earth and the instability of sudden solar storms…"

Angus started to laugh.

John experienced the familiar self-consciousness freezing the words he was about to say.

"John, Man," Angus said. He started to heave himself up. "I was expecting a lecture on the packing of extra waterproofs. That's all."

John watched as the grin relaxed, revealing a more sombre expression. "They need to get it right up here though," Angus said. He gestured to the point in the retreating distance where they'd been before he'd picked up speed and changed stride on the pre-planned route. "There's no way out if you get caught in the flood between some of the clefts in the rock down there. The water, it builds and moves too fast." He turned. "You gonna cut me in on the background to some of the theories that you're working on, Man? I'm finding it hard to keep up."

John gazed up at the sky. Considered how much he'd told Angus already. So much about how he felt about what was happening out there beyond himself yet nothing about what was happening within himself, the confusion, the longing, the anger – the joy. He set the now filled backpack on the ground beside him, experienced the hesitancy of intended disclosure, the half breath of anxiety. "Angus," he said. "Can I tell you something else?"

Angus wrapped a hand around the strap of his bag, moving it toward him, "Sure, Man," he said.

John told him. Told him everything he knew about his past – his mother, the Hopi connection and the man Thomas Begvious, the secret benefactor – the silent force in the background of his life.

# 28 SCEPTICISM

Brett Fielding moved the papers around on the conference table in front of him.

John waited. He'd said what he wanted to say.

Angus kept his focus on the window.

John was aware that it was probably the first time Angus had heard him talk at such great length and with such intense conviction. It seemed he wasn't going to interrupt.

"The mathematics, the calculations of what you're presenting here, are difficult to take in," said Brett, raising his hand before pressing the pen he was holding momentarily against his lips. "You want some sort of support to progress these findings or what you believe to be accurate hypotheses on the orbit and oscillation of the two defining stars of the Sirius system?"

The tone of Brett Fielding's voice suggested scepticism. John felt as if he was back in Franklyn's office fighting for the right to be taken seriously, experiencing the same dryness in his throat, as the tight band of tension across his neck and shoulders spread upwards to his temples. He inhaled, not quite inflating his diaphragm. "I just need…" He stalled, began again, "I'd find it helpful…would appreciate the opportunity to speak with the team who are observing the oscillations. Discuss whether what the calculations are proposing to me is as accurate as I believe."

Angus made as if to stand up but didn't. John glanced at him. Wondered if Angus thought he was pushing too hard. These were the people Angus worked with. John didn't want to cause problems but now felt he had little choice.

Brett Fielding gathered the papers together, stacked them in a neat pile. "You'll need to email this to me," he said while massaging the small of his back with his left hand. "I can speak with some senior members of the team, but I can't promise anything."

John felt some of the tension in his muscles retract.

"I'm going to have to present this as something we're working on." Fielding pointed at the papers now neatly stacked in front of him. "I can't say you've just turned up to challenge current theory and thinking."

John nodded in agreement. If he could get inside the Observatory and talk to the team in there, or even observe what was happening first hand rather than through computer simulations it would help. He'd already started to question his own sanity. The third star that astronomers and cosmologists had claimed was no more than a background object was; he was convinced, far more than that. It was a vortex of vacuum energy.

He considered his original thesis on planetary orbits. How the discovery of not only mass, but also reflected light, could enable the identification of hidden stars and planets within a solar system. Sirius had long been assumed as one star because of its luminosity. The Dogon tribe had known the light was concealing the hidden Sirius B, though no one knew how, or why, they'd acquired such knowledge. Bessel had known too, because of the motion of the supposed single star. The development of the telescope had proven both the Dogon and Bessel, right.

Science knew it was possible to be right on the basis of the mathematics, the use of the appropriate equation. They now knew for fact that Sirius was actually a binary system of two stars. Bessel, like the Dogon, had pre-empted the development of powerful telescopic instrumentation to know and predict what was happening in the Universe. John was convinced he had too.

"I really hadn't grasped what you were saying, Man," Angus said as they made their way back to the truck. "I mean I knew it was big, that you'd pulled together data from several different disciplines." He reached for the keys in his pocket. "But you're talking of the possibility of some sort of apocalypse." He pressed the remote on the key fob. "How did you come up with all – I mean, how did you have the time? I…"

"Never had anything else…" John felt his words ricochet off the roof of the truck. He wanted to catch them as they bounced away from him. Stuff them in his pocket. Cancel them. He hadn't meant it to sound the way it did. It sounded the way it was. He'd spent most of his life filling in great big fat expanses of nothingness. Interminable chapters of endless time spent analysing and calculating the space in the Universe above and around him beyond the Earth – doing anything and everything to escape the space he couldn't fill inside him. He opened the door and climbed in.

Angus hauled himself into the driver's seat.

They were on the main major stretch of road leading out towards the desert before Angus spoke again.

"D'you really think we're all toast, Man?"

John considered. Given all he'd said to Fielding, or maybe in retrospect the little he'd actually conveyed in the meeting, he needed to explain where he was going with everything. "If I'm right," he said. "And despite the fact I've been knocked down intellectually by Franklyn and others, I think I am. Then it's about trying to identify a solution." He pressed his temple. "The problem I've been having is that no one would –

will, listen to me." He darted a glance in Angus's direction. "People either think – well I don't know what they think…but the evidence is stacking up so high I feel duty bound…" He stared ahead through the windscreen of the truck, aware that he'd trailed off mid sentence.

Angus said nothing. They drove on without speaking. The faint sound of the ropes they'd used on the trek still tied to the truck, hitting the metal of the rear door, clicking rhythmically like a metronome.

John's thoughts sped backwards. The metronome. The mathematics of sound, he'd seen the shapes of sound recorded by laser. The very first Paul Yeager and the Snow Leopards' concert he'd attended.

Both he and Angus had managed to hook up with the team working on the laser projected sound system. They'd watched how sound erupted and moved in different ways, discovered that images of its movement could be reproduced in colour and light. The whole thing had escalated his interest into acoustics and the specific harmonies and proportions spoken of in the Hermetica, which some believed held the secret of an evolutionary code – a code which illustrated the manifestation of life as a continual flow toward higher spiritual levels. John remembered how Schwaller had alluded to the idea, or the belief in his work also. Schwaller recognised that consciousness; the development of modern consciousness had led humankind away from something essential, something of central importance.

The more he thought about it the clearer it became. The Giza Plateau housed not only the most carefully almost divinely constructed astronomical architecture known to mankind which was intrinsically linked to the rising and falling of the light of the Sirius system, Orion's Belt, the seasons of the Earth and the precession of the equinoxes, but also something else.

That something else, it was something he kept on coming back to. Struggling with. Other researchers and commentators had explored the work of astronomers and studied the ancient texts in order to illustrate the correlation between the three belt stars of the Orion constellation and the ground plan of the three pyramids of Giza. It had already been determined that the monuments at Giza worked together in a synchronistical manner – like some fantastic celestial clock. The question had already been asked as to why the ancients had sought to create an image, a reflection of the skies, or maybe a reflection of the heavens at Giza – so many were still trying to find the answer. But had anyone yet asked why the ancients had sought to build the most incredible acoustic chambers for the framing and magnification of sound? He needed to find out.

# 29 LIFE'S WORK

He could feel himself drifting backwards. As if his unconscious was pulling him someplace. He resisted. Projected his vision and focus on the sweep of tarmac that lay before them, the taillights of cars in the distance starting to ignite, the night drawing in. He hadn't realised how long they'd actually spent talking with Brett Fielding. He turned toward Angus.

"Thinking," Angus said. "You OK with Fielding taking your work and sharing your ideas, Man?"

John noticed Angus's profile no longer seemed gaunt. He must have been slowly but steadily gaining the lost weight. The moods had regulated too. "You think I shouldn't be?" he asked. Aware that it wouldn't be the first time he'd trusted someone whose morals were questionable. Greg back at Bloomfield had seemed so upfront. The guy had been a pain at times with his verbal profligacy but he'd trusted him. Just thinking about Greg's easy duplicity, his smiling exchange with Franklyn when they'd returned the computer to the Hot House made his skin crawl. He still felt nauseous at the thought. "You don't think…" he started to speak.

Angus shook his head before turning momentarily. "It's not my life's work, Man. But he's telling the truth. No-ones going to take the time out from the projects they're working on to analyse your data. It just doesn't work that way."

John gripped the muscles above his knees. "I didn't expect it to," he said.

"There are all sorts of funding issues associated with the work that's carried out. Everything has to be scoped to identify project needs and costs before a project plan is drawn up and submitted to the appropriate funding bodies. Fielding is often heavily involved in that side of things. I guess you already know all this."

John nodded. He knew from his own work and involvement within the university at home that money was rarely handed out indiscriminately.

Angus continued. "It also has to tie in with work that's currently being peer reviewed." He paused, checked his rear-view mirror before continuing, "How do you think what they do here can help, Man?"

Considering the question as Angus took the slip road toward the lower slopes of the rise that led upwards to the ranch house, he realised he wasn't sure of the answer. Even if he could get the attention of senior people working in the field, would they be able to see what he could see? Franklyn hadn't been able to. "I'm hoping," he said. "In fact I'm more than hoping. I'm praying that there's someone on the team whose vision isn't blurred…"

"By academic and funding constraints," said Angus, before he could finish, ending with an empty sounding laugh.

"You know?" said John.

"Sure I do, Man. It's an age-old game. Toe the line and don't rock the boat if you want to keep the job."

# 30 THE QUEST

It was dark outside by the time they'd eaten and caught up on the day's emails. Several of which were from Sarah and Dan. The first suggesting the possibility of some time off, followed by an email that said they'd cancelled the idea. Followed by a third that said due to a case Dan was working on, it would probably be late September before they could consider a break.

"Fancy a sit by an empty pool?" asked Angus. "I think one beer outside on this balmy evening is unlikely to have the temperance society bolting up here to try and reform us."

John laughed, felt some of the stress of the day dissipate.

Angus disappeared to the kitchen. Returned with half of a six-pack, which he carried outside, John followed.

"So," said Angus, after he'd swallowed half of a can of beer. "I think we need a plan." He tapped his can up and down on the table in front of him. "If Haziq was here he may have been able to help, though he can be distant a lot of the time." He turned to John. "The guy was always a bit like that. But now it's as if he goes into lockdown."

"I would have…"John thought about what he was going to say. He was going to say he would have liked to see Haziq, though in truth he was scared of seeing him. He wanted to see the boy, or the young man he remembered, but what would he talk about? Haziq had mostly talked about his parents. Now they were gone.

"What exactly is he working on?" he said instead. Then honestly, "I'm not sure I'd know what to say to him now."

Angus shrugged in response; drank some more of his beer before answering.

"I kinda felt the same at first, I'd talk about – well just about anything and everything that didn't include his parents. Then I realised something…"

John swigged his own beer before asking. "What?"

"I realised," said Angus. "That anything and everything includes the people we love. There really aren't any demarcation lines, Man." He laughed. "So now I include his parents, I make reference to them, in the conversations." He took another swig of his beer. "I say things like – What would your father have made of that?" He paused again. "Or I'll say 'remember when your mother said or did, or when you told me, she,' I'll find something that includes them and somehow it works."

"He's Haziq again, the Haziq he was before?"

"Almost," said Angus. "As near as I guess he ever can be."

"When do you think he'll be back?"

Angus rolled the beer can round in his hands before responding.

"It was a surprise to me that he'd gone at all," he said. "I don't see as much of him as I'd like to – you know, Man. I mean as much as I should. It, well it can be hard." He put down his empty can and picked up the remaining beer. "Like to share," he said as he cracked it open.

John shook his head. One beer was enough if he wanted to keep his head clear and he did.

Angus took a long swig. "Would anyone believe this?" he said. "Two young guys sitting here with the world spread out before them with only a single beer left to share."

"It's all yours," said John.

"Sure," said Angus. "So should I email Haziq again? I mean, I know he observes his own religious festivals so maybe this wouldn't be a good time for him to be getting heavily involved…"

"D'you think he'd be willing?" John asked, aware that given what had happened Haziq may not want involvement.

Angus considered the question.

"Well," he said. "Haziq is a smart guy. A smart guy, who's become a very sad guy. If what you're willing to share – your theories and ideas – can spark his interest – challenge his thinking, then getting involved may be the best thing for him." He paused for a moment. "He's probably just as likely as me to prefer involvement to the alternative scenario. What sane guy doesn't crave some mission or quest outside the rigidity of accepted academia?"

"You don't think I may be crazy?" John voiced the fear that continued to snake into his mind on a regular basis.

Angus chuckled. "We're all crazy, Man. Gotta be to survive. But maybe we need to plan how we're gonna pitch your script to the right people." He finished off the beer in one long gurgle. "Fielding may be able to get us access and meetings with the key people here at Kressa Peak but if what your calculations are telling you turns out to be true we're going to need more than Brett Fielding's card to get us through the door we need to be knocking on."

# 31 WHITE DWARF

John thought about what Angus had said long after they'd turned in for the night. He knew lying awake wasn't the best way to keep his mind functioning. Guessed that the continued lack of sleep was contributing to his feelings of sudden unexpected panic and creeping paranoia. For the moment there was little more he could do. He'd pretty much laid it out for Fielding.

There was no argument that white dwarf stars, of which Sirius B was one, were considered to be in their final evolutionary state. It was agreed that stars whose mass was not high enough to become a neutron star became white dwarfs, in terms of mass that, as they'd discussed with Fielding, accounted for almost ninety-eight percent of the stars in the entire galaxy. Once the hydrogen-fusing lifetime of these stars ended they expanded to become what was known as a red giant.

The red giant fused helium to carbon and oxygen in its core by the triple-alpha process. Without sufficient mass to generate the core temperatures required to fuse carbon, an inert mass of carbon and oxygen would build up at its centre. After shedding its outer layers only the white dwarf core would be left. There was a chain of processes, which led to the core materials, of which the white dwarf was composed, being rendered incapable of fusion reactions. A point was reached where no matter how bright it appeared, no matter how much reflected luminosity emanated from its orbital location, it reached a point where it had no source of energy, no source of heat generated fusion to protect it or prevent gravitational collapse.

Once that happened, and he'd calculated that it was already happening, it could no longer be supported by electron degeneracy pressure. When that happened the so-called white dwarf became a celestial time bomb – waiting in the heavens to explode – the Hopi dwelling place falling from the sky. Leaving Sirius unmasked and dancing in the Plaza.

Dancing, thought John, toward the Earth. He prayed that he was wrong before praying that if he were not, someone would believe him.

# 32 GUT FEELING

The sky was slowly swallowing the light as the sun dipped toward the curve of the mountains in the distance. An immense palette of shifting colour, a moving a rainbow of hues, interspersed by shafts of light as the high pressure air current shifted the currently forming and building high cloud in its wake.

Beyond the initial introductions, John knew he had to keep quiet when they got there. Fielding had been adamant.

"I've explained you're a visiting PhD student accompanying us as part of the required programme of work related i.e., employability experience now required of PhD students and postdoctoral researchers," he'd advised. "They'll be OK, they are OK with that. It's something we, well all universities now, devote time and funding too." He retrieved a document from his inside pocket. "But you're expected to sign one of these."

John had dutifully signed. He'd read the document swiftly first. It was an agreement that he would not take any photographs, documents, photocopies of documents or use any form of recording device.

It was also required that the content of any discussions would remain confidential and not be used in any way without the full agreement and reference to the personnel on site and the university by whom they were funded. Angus had signed one too.

Now they were on their way. Fielding had taken the front seat next to Angus who had volunteered to drive. John had taken a seat in the back. They were all tired. Talk between them had drifted and petered out. Fielding had dozed off within minutes off them hitting the highway.

The day had been exceptionally hot even for the higher elevations of Flagstaff where they'd had to drive in order to pick up Fielding from the airport. His plane had been delayed then diverted from Tucson due to an unexpected dust storm. While waiting for Fielding's arrival, John had willingly been guided by Angus on a tour of the place, though the heat had steadily gotten to them both.

By the time Fielding called on his mobile to tell them he'd landed and was ready to be picked up it had been time to eat. They'd collected Fielding from the airport before calling in to a local diner in order to prepare for the drive and the night ahead.

"Nostalgic, hey?" Angus said as they strolled from the truck across the tarmac. The fifties-themed neon sign was already lit. "The Old Man loves some of these places," he said, "the 'Route 66' ambience."

Fielding nodded.

"Won't eat a bite though," Angus added as he pushed open the door, "too many years with Ma – the health police."

After an omelette and salad each for John and Fielding, and a turkey burger for Angus they'd cleaned up and headed back to the truck. Angus driving, John now relaxed in the back.

He'd imagined the journey as no more than a route to gain access to the magnificence of the observatories – the telescopes. Was unprepared for the sense of exhilaration he was experiencing at the sweeping wide angled views of nature that revealed themselves unexpectedly on the sudden turn of a hairpin bend as they climbed skywards toward the peak of what he now knew was believed by the Native American peoples to be a sacred mountain – their sacred mountain.

He'd always been so focused on the mathematics of space, the science of the sky, the geology of the land, the architecture of sound and even the structure of time. How much had he missed?

He thought about the leathered pouch safely concealed in his bag. Discovering the possibility of a blood link with the Hopi people had made his eyes open wider. He was seeing and feeling far more than he'd ever seen. The colours, the hues, and both the light and shadow around him. Merging with the sense of things, instead of trying to recreate them as he had in his paintings.

He ran a hand across his eyes, wondered if he'd been viewing the things around him through a broken or clouded lens. Now the images were beginning to sharpen. The view from the space he now was looking from no longer a mass of indiscriminate pieces without shape. The letter from Thomas Begvious, the gifts from his mother, repairing, reshaping and cleansing the lens he now saw through – opening up the tunnel of his vision. Now at every turn of he saw something he'd never expected to see.

Despite the chill he was glad Angus had rolled down the windows of the truck to allow the cooler fresher mountain air to take over from the air conditioning of the day. The natural airflow, though far colder than he'd expected, was soothing. Each distance they travelled to the next curve around the rocks in the direction of Kressa Peak was contributing to a building effervescence of excitement inside his chest. He wanted to laugh out loud – felt like an Initiate on the verge of some momentous rite.

It was crazy to feel so elated. He didn't have to wait all these years for an agreement with Fielding. He could have come here any time. As a visitor – a tourist but this was better. Even if, as Angus had advised, that despite the need for signing agreements, there were likely to be other people at the summit visiting as part of a college or university trip, or simply tourists keen to capture the landmark monument on film.

They were on the final rise toward the peak, an altitude of sixty seven hundred feet above sea level, on land leased from the tribe known as the Desert People when the first observatory came into view. The white curved dome seemingly jutting outwards and upwards precariously from the ledge of rock where it was mounted. From the perspective and angle of view from the road the perceiver could almost imagine that it hovered in space elevated only by the air streams from below. An optical illusion John knew. Created by the falling light and the sense of expectation he was finding hard to contain.

"OK back there?" Angus asked. The first words he'd spoken since they'd set off on the road.

John wasn't sure whether it was because Angus wanted to keep discussion in front of, and with, Fielding, to a minimum for some particular reason or whether he thought it safer to concentrate on the driving demands.

"Fine – good," he said, again conscious of the fact that he was making a habit of using the same type of phraseology as Angus did or once had. He wished he could stop. He remembered doing it as a kid too. He often found himself picking up other people's speech patterns or repeating what they'd said to see how it sounded. He'd read about it years later how kids sometimes did it. He tried to remember what it was called. Was it echoic or echolic speech?

The thought slipped from his mind as they pulled into the parking area before following the arrow and sign that indicated parking for observatory personnel. Fielding, almost on cue, started to stir. John cast his eyes rapidly around the surrounding area, picking up the shapes of several of the twenty-four telescope observatories located on the site, twenty-two optical, and two radio telescopes.

Angus pulled into a lot, just as a square framed heavily built man in khakis and boots headed toward them.

"I've got the passes," said Fielding as he undid his seat belt and started to climb from the truck.

John started to follow.

"Wait," Fielding used his hand as a halt as he spoke.

John did as he was told.

"He likes to be the one in charge," Angus muttered, almost under his breath, as Fielding strode across the gravel to meet the man making his way toward them.

"That's OK," said John, although somewhere in his gut it wasn't.

# 33 ELEVATED

"You realise of course that we do our work here at night?"

Carlos Ogilvy spoke with only the faintest hint of an accent, which John couldn't quite discern. The name wasn't familiar, yet John was confident he'd done as much background research on the observatory personnel as was possible. He liked to know who people were as well as understand the area and scope of their work. It was a way of not only understanding and respecting the work people did, but also the people who did the work. Still it was often the case that visiting astronomers could take charge of certain projects. Both he and Angus nodded in response to the question.

"Here," said Carlos Ogilvy, "we sleep all day and work through the night. I trust you have slept well and eaten too."

Again he and Angus nodded like two schoolboys. It was ridiculous, thought John. Agreeing and acting out the pretence. As if they wouldn't know about the fact that the night sky was the one to observe, that observatory personnel slept in what could only be described as light and sound tight boxes to enable sleep during normal waking hours. That was why, despite the fact that computer technology meant that much of the work of astronomy could now be carried out at a distance, most astronomers preferred to locate on site. It wasn't only more romantic to be located where the actual equipment was operating it was also more sensible, because procedures and working practices reduced distraction to a minimum during daytime hours.

He saw Angus wink at him, swallowed the unexpected irritation that had dampened the high he'd been riding on. He was almost forgetting that he was here as a visiting PhD student, not someone who needed to get the backup from experts to be granted a hearing in the inner sanctum of the higher echelons of the church of science.

"You may wish to spend some time in the visitor centre," said Fielding.

John flinched. It was practically a dismissal.

"There are some interesting exhibits inside the centre, some good short films and an interesting space exploratory gift shop. You should still have time to view some of the public telescopes – view the sun and see the sunspot activity…"

"Dr Fielding…" John tried to interrupt.

"Great idea," Angus cut in, grabbing John's arm as he did so.

John could hear his own heart beating. He wasn't sure what was happening. What was Fielding up to?

"Back in an hour," said Angus, as he threw an arm around John's shoulders and led him back across the gravel.

"I thought we…" John could hear the tremor is his own voice.

"That you were going to walk in here and act like the fucking genius you are, Man." Angus asked as he released his hold.

John felt his shoulders slump.

"As far as the Ogilvy guy is concerned we're getting the same treatment as any student or graduate intern…"

"But…" said John.

"But, nothing, Man." Angus guided him forward. "This is just the first stage of a possible way in, Fielding's going to organise something so we can be part of the night shift…"

"Was this a mistake?"

"What kind of a mistake, Man?"

"I don't know. Maybe I should be banging on someone's door demanding." John paused. Asking his internal self whose door, in reality, would he be banging on? He turned to Angus. "I'm sorry," he said. "I'm acting like a…" He stopped himself from saying Jerk. "It's just that everything is starting to make more and more sense. It's as if everything is falling into place. Everything seems to be speeding up in my head, the figures the detail – all of it. It's almost fighting to get out of me. Everything – I don't feel as if I'm in a position to be waiting around playing games."

"John, Man," said Angus. "You're not in a position to do anything else."

After forcing themselves to view the tourist areas, Angus checked his watch and suggested they set of back to the Personnel Compound.

"You calmer, now, Man?"

John laughed. There was no humour in it. "I was just so high on the way up here," he said.

"The mountain does that, Man." Angus stopped, looked around him. "Not just the air, it's…"

"The energy," said John.

Angus nodded.

When they passed through initial security, to re-enter the building signed for 'Site Personnel Only', Ogilvy and Fielding hardly acknowledged their return other than to make brief introductions when the technical team arrived for the night shift. John knew how these places worked. Despite the hierarchy that placed the astronomers at the head of operations, always it was the engineers and computer scientists who controlled and managed the equipment – the telescopes.

Astronomers were in the minority. Their job was to direct the observations – to know what they were looking for. But, John considered, even now still conscious of the possible arrogance of his thoughts, those at the top of the hierarchy could sometimes lose sight of the bigger picture. Or fail to recognise that technology wasn't moving fast enough to capture the true picture of the heavens at all.

"It costs a minimum of five thousand dollars a night…"

John glanced toward Carlos Ogilvy. He hadn't even realised the guy had been talking, had to pull himself back from this continual slipping away into his own thoughts.

"It can be a long night," Ogilvy continued. "But we have limitless coffee."

There was vaguely suppressed laughter. John wondered why people always did that. Laugh when people in charge, those at the top, said something with a deliberate wry smile. As if on cue, all those of supposed lesser status would laugh. Even Fielding was smiling, as if the comment about coffee was actually funny.

"Right," said Ogilvy. "We'll head through to the control room first before we actually view the telescope."

John hung back at the end of the line as they all trooped after Ogilvy and Fielding.

Ogilvy kept talking pretty much continually as the group moved along the corridor toward the control room. He talked about the number of telescopes on site. How the radio telescopes were now affected by the impact of the increasing use of mobile phones and satellite systems. Explained how both mobile and other radio wave signals were a form of pollution to radio telescopes, as much if not more, than light was to optical telescopes.

He talked about the light ordinance in nearby Tucson, which was part of a policy to protect the observatories from light pollution. John wanted to ask why, if they recognised the problems that the modern world had brought to the science of astronomy, why hadn't they recognised that over time the impact of those pollutions would have influenced the measurements they were taking? There were just too many reasons why mistakes were being made.

He ticked off a mental list of the disciplines working in the field. There were many. Even Astronomy wasn't a seamless singular endeavour. The technology of the construction of the equipment, the engineering, the science, the reading of the observations, it had become increasingly complex and diverse. The information was no longer gathered by a single person sitting alone in the dark and cold of the night, physically manipulating the angle of observation and keeping the guide star on the cross hair in a clear and unpolluted sky. Now computer scientists – the observing technicians, controlled all the moving parts of the telescope. Everything had to be set up in a mad flurry of activity before they hit 'go' on the computer. Then they would all sit and wait while the accumulation of one photon after another took place till the directed observation was complete. Then they would begin again. It was all about light gathering – the ability to capture light and reconstruct that light to form images. But the telescope was continually moving in an arc toward the west following the rise of the sun in the sky from east to west.

"So this is the control room?"

John walked into the back of Angus as Ogilvy spoke, Angus steadying himself by grabbing the back of a chair, which almost tipped over. Both Ogilvy and Fielding stared at Angus.

"Everything all right?" said Fielding with a pointed stare.

"I…" said Angus.

"My fault," said John, before Angus tried to explain himself. He was doing it again – disappearing into an inner world losing a sense of his surroundings. "I was a little disorientated. I'm sorry."

Ogilvy grinned, showing teeth that would make an orthodontist proud.

"Excited, eh?" He looked genuinely amused.

"Very," said John, keen to project the image of the eager student, Fielding had introduced him as.

"Good," said Ogilvy. "Excitement will keep you awake just as well as the coffee will." The others laughed.

By two o'clock in the morning John understood the meaning behind the laughter. The coffee. It was the foulest tasting liquid he'd ever consumed. There was no way it could ever have been drunk black. Even with extra sugar and milk it was the nearest thing to poison he'd ever ingested. Angus had merely grimaced after the first sip before tossing the rest down his throat.

Ogilvy had shown them the main observatory room – a large hexagonal space that housed the incredible piece of stargazing machinery – the telescope. To the uninitiated observer it could appear as simply a large hulking contraption, which moved about clumsily. To John it was as sleek, and as almost perfect, as anything he'd ever seen.

He touched the cool metal of its side as Ogilvy talked about the highly curved primary mirror and how the shutters would open to reveal the internal one. He listened as Ogilvy talked about the spectrograph and how it divided light up by wavelength. How instead of the image of a sparkling point in the sky, the spectrograph provided an image of a straight line.

He'd shown how the room itself opened up to the night not only the roof, but the walls as well opened as the shutters drew back to create the airflow that was necessary to keep the images stable.

John fought and successfully resisted the urge to question the accuracy of the mirrors, which he knew being made of glass had the intrinsic problem associated with barely imperceptible flow when the mirror was tilted. Resulting in the slight downward fall of the constituents of the glass, making it almost impossible to completely capture and reproduce the optical shape that was being reflected in light upon it. It was part of the conundrum he'd struggled with in the laboratory and the observatory at school as a teenager. Adaptive optics had enabled a massive leap in the capturing of light that could be transformed into images. Providing the kind of pictures of the Universe that previously could only have been recorded in the unpolluted sky beyond and outside of the Earth's atmosphere.

Yet no one seemed to be making the connection he had. Sirius determined to be 6.8 light years away according to the pictures. The images they'd previously recorded through the reflection of light through the almost imperceptible flow of the mirrored lens. At 6.8 light years away all they had were images of Sirius in the past because it took that long for the reflected light to reach the Earth for recording purposes. They were working with outdated data. No one had put forward a theory, or hypothesis to challenge that thinking, except him.

He pulled back to the present. Ogilvy taking pains to explain the detail of the process they'd be taking part in. John gave his full attention as Ogilvy continued to talk. Ogilvy didn't at any point ask if there were any questions, but made the effort of drawing in the technicians at various points, giving them the opportunity to explain their roles. Despite the fact that John knew pretty much everything he needed to know about the process, he made the effort to listen intently when the others were speaking.

As the night wore on, Fielding had stayed pretty much with Ogilvy and the technical team in terms of following the dialogue that Ogilvy had set up. It was now almost three-thirty in the morning and Fielding still hadn't attempted to digress to discuss the calculations John had presented him with. Though there'd been several opportunities to do so during the long waiting periods when the telescope was using its light gathering power to download a single photon per minute.

John had to console himself with the fact that at least he was in the place where he wanted to be. Ogilvy had mentioned the names of several experts in the field that John had heard of. He'd even talked of what had become almost an 'arms race' in terms of the development of more and more powerful telescopes. John listened as best he could to what Ogilvy was saying. The man was doing an excellent job of conveying his understanding of the process they'd come to observe. For John it was secondary. Being on site was far more interesting. Just being so close to the technically superior, though far from perfect, equipment on the elevated landscape where the land was sacred, was more than enough to compensate for listening intently to facts he already knew.

The Observing Technician made a gesture with his hand for them to view the monitors. Although responding to the signal, Ogilvy continued to talk. He'd started on a new tack. He was now talking about the star cluster studies he was involved with. John hadn't known Ogilvy was involved – still couldn't remember seeing his name. But was familiar with what Ogilvy was talking about. The observation of star clusters was a way of carrying out controlled studies not only the star clusters themselves, but given that all stars in a cluster were always the same age, of the same chemical composition, and the same distance from Earth, observational and astronomical history could be evaluated in the light of changes within individual clusters.

"Is there anyone in particular, currently working on observational error due to the shifting rotational axis of the Earth over time and the limitations of the reconfiguring of optical observations because of technical anomalies?" said Fielding out of nowhere.

John couldn't believe the man had actually asked the question. It meant he hadn't forgotten why they were here. It meant he was at least providing an opening for some further discussion on the thesis John had presented him with. He felt the tension in his neck, he didn't even realise was there, evaporating. He darted a glance at Angus, who in the preceding minutes had obviously drifted into a deep sleep. He looked as if he'd fallen from the ceiling, his body splayed out, his head back, staring at the roof, emitting a soft, almost purring sound.

For a few moments Ogilvy acted as if he hadn't even heard Fielding's question. He bent forward to peer at the computer screen.

"Almost," he said to the technician before straightening up and turning to Fielding. "Interesting you should raise the question, Brett. I had an email today advising me to check out a paper that's just been published in the Science of Astronomy journal." He turned back to the technician, "More tilt," he advised before turning toward Fielding and John. "Man called Franklyn, Dr Franklyn, I think…"

# 34 ADULTERATION

"Seems like the bastard has stitched you up, Man," Angus spat, as he threw the journal on the desk. "Fielding's suddenly gone incommunicado. He hasn't answered any of my emails. So either he's taken the usual break and joined the rest of the campus staff on the mass exodus or you're right."

"He hardly spoke on the way back from Kressa Peak," said John grabbing at the journal and rolling it into a tube. "Other than to attempt to clarify that the 'Franklyn' Ogilvy was talking about, was one and the same as my PhD Supervisor. I just…" He tailed off, stared unfocused at the computer screen in front of him.

"So he's decided to use your work as his own? He's crediting the work to himself," said Angus. "The guy is slime."

John placed the journal on the desk and put his head in his hands.

"Hey, Man."

He felt the pressure of Angus's hand on his shoulder.

"Don't get cut up."

He lifted his head – involuntarily shrugged Angus away.

"I feel…" He tried to pluck the right word from his mind to illustrate the feeling that erupted on hearing Franklyn's name, "Sick," he said. The word barely covered the sensation but it was all he could find. "I felt – feel sick."

"Man," said Angus.

"I just…" He paused. "When Ogilvy said his name. I mean, I had this great surge when Fielding asked him the question about research in the area of observational error and the limitations of the reconfiguring of optical observations because of technical anomalies." He laughed, picked up the journal again. "I thought it was the first step forward." He shook his head. "Then Ogilvy said Franklyn's name and my brain just seemed to shrivel to the size of a walnut. I couldn't even think straight. I couldn't remember what I – we, were doing there…"

"I guess it all makes sense now," said Angus. "Why he kept on pushing you to provide him with more and more evidence…"

"Had me doing his scut work…"

"Nah," Angus took the journal from John's hands. "It wasn't scut work, Man. You were the boy – the boy who not only came up with the ideas, but had the brains, the fucking genius – to turn an idea into a testable hypothesis. That's why he was speaking at the conference. Putting himself, big guy Franklyn, straight one hundred percent, in the forefront…"

"The reason I wasn't invited," said John.

"I thought the guy was cool," Angus was almost talking to himself. "So fucking cool he can rip off other people's ideas and calmly present them as his own. What do we do, Man?"

John said nothing. There was no way he could challenge Franklyn even if he wanted to. Many academics managed to achieve their Professorships, through the diligence of the research students assigned to them, simply because most PhD students took on research that formed part of their PhD Supervisors areas of interest.

The difference was Franklyn had pretended he had no interest in the particular areas John was working on. In fact he'd made him feel like a fool. The whole process, John thought, the continual demoralising, the ridicule – the pressure. The threat of disciplinary action, the missing files, the removal of the hard drive, it had all been premeditated. Greg knowing what was going down; yet Greg had never said a word. Greg, who could hardly keep his mouth shut because of the constant stream of verbal release, was able to omit something when it suited him.

"What do we do, Man?" Angus asked a second time.

"I don't think there's much we can do," said John. "Except hope someone takes more notice of what he's saying because of who he is. It's just that now…" John stood up before finishing and headed for the door.

"Now?" said Angus, following him. "What do you mean – now? You're scaring me, Man."

John stopped and turned.

"Angus," his voice was tight. "Now there's so much more he should be telling them – I've read the journal article. He's using my work but adulterating the predictions. He's no intention of expressing the truth. He's interested only in making a name for himself."

## 35 EVIDENCE

With the papers in his hands, the diagrams spread across the table; John hunted for the words he needed to explain what he was seeing.

Angus waited.

John tried to still his thoughts. It was so much easier to see what things meant, so much easier to understand the synchronicity than articulate it in the spoken word. It was the reason he'd done so well academically but failed in almost everything else. "D'you think Haziq will respond?" he asked, fully aware that he was in fact just stalling for time with the question. He'd really wanted to see Haziq under different circumstances. Circumstances where he could show Haziq that he felt for his loss. But Angus had made the communication and now they were waiting to see if Haziq would get back to them.

"Think so," Angus said. "I may have scared the b'jeebies outa him or sparked his intense intellectual curiosity." He frowned. "Either way, knowing Haziq, he'll want to know more if only to argue the possibilities…Or maybe we'll hear from him because he just wants to catch up with some people who were like family to him once."

John put the papers on the table, the sense of the irretrievable past a distinct emptiness inside him. "We were," he said. He turned away from Angus.

"Hey, Man," Angus touched his arm.

"I haven't been able to tell you," said John picking up the papers again. "In fact I haven't told anyone yet…"

"Jeez, what's going on?" Angus leaned forward in his chair. "You, you're not ill. I mean…"

"No…I…" John faltered.

"You're gay?"

In spite of himself, John laughed.

"It's no big deal," said Angus. "It doesn't make any…"

"I'm not gay," John paused. "I don't think so. There's never been any evidence to suggest… I just haven't really thought about…"

"So what haven't you told anyone that's so big, Man? You look as if your jaw's lost its hinge bones"

"I think I understand the meaning."

Angus sat back in his chair.

"The Jesus trip?"

John didn't have any idea where Angus was going. "Jesus trip?" he said. "What are you talking about?"

Angus took some time before answering.

"Well, you've been pretty stressed out, Man. It happens. It's not unusual. It happens."

"What happens?"

"The ideas – notions. One minute a guy is just an ordinary guy then stress…well it kinda tips the balance. Reality starts to slip away from him and his head is…well he thinks he's somebody like…"

"Like who?"

"Jesus, God. A guy suddenly thinks he's got special powers…"

John stared at the ceiling. Wondered if he should laugh, started to laugh anyway.

"Laughing is good, John." Angus was on his feet. "It relieves stress." He started to pace back and forth to the window.

"Angus," said John. "I'm not going crazy. Well maybe I am, but not in the way you think. I'm not having delusions…"

"You're not?"

"I don't think I'm Jesus – don't think I'm God…"

"Who then?"

"The same person I've always been only now – now I know what my roots are. I think I'm more aware of where I need to go."

Angus was silent.

"Angus," said John. "I'm not talking alternative delusions. I'm talking evidence about my past. The letter…"

"Letter?"

"From the solicitor, who handled my allowances, paid my fees and everything else I should have been doing for myself. What I told you. I always thought I was probably…" He paused. "Thought – well it doesn't matter what I thought. My mother – she abandoned me…"

"But your mother…"

John slid his hand in his backpack and withdrew the pouch, placing it on the table, before moving aside the papers and diagrams he had strewn across it.

"It seems, well the evidence, as I told you indicates she may be part of the Hopi Clan."

"Jeez, Man," said Angus, finally sitting down on the edge of the table. "You already told me all this."

"It's something else," said John.

"OK," said Angus. "Tell me, Man."

By the time he'd finished telling Angus the story almost all the natural light had gone from the room. He'd shown Angus the pouch, the leathered parchment, the tiny charms, the stone, the letter from Thomas Begvious. Now he was showing him the symbols displayed on the parchment.

He clicked on the lamp. "It's just so strange that all this happened within such a tight timeframe," he said. "That everything seems to be linking together – I mean I knew about the Dogon tribe, I'm familiar with a lot of esoteric stuff about the planets, the Universe, the great pyramids of Giza." He pointed to the shapes inscribed into the leather.

"They're all here – almost all the symbols. The signs relating to the work I've been doing, the thesis I've been developing. It's almost as if…as if all my efforts are being validated, something has been handed to me…"

"You gotta slow down, Man." Angus traced the shapes John was pointing at. "You'd need to talk to someone – maybe even Manda – Ma." He stood up and rubbed his back. "Just because the – well all this," he gestured toward the table, "it doesn't mean. It doesn't have to mean what you think…"

"It fits," said John. "The Blue Star Katchina Prophecy. When the Blue Star Katchina dances in the Plaza – don't you see it's what I've been working on…"

"You're losing me, Man. I thought you were talking observational error, reconfiguring of optical observations, rotational shifts, orbital irregularities, oscillations and fucking accelerating Universes." Angus slapped himself on the head. "You know, the normal stuff guys talk about, but this, it's…"

"Exactly the same," said John. "But the language is simpler. It doesn't need to define. It creates its meaning through the imagery. We're talking the same language only in different ways. I've spent years trying to clarify what's happening through mathematics, equations – document after document, when all I really needed to do was paint a picture." He pointed at the leathered parchment, his cloth. "A picture, Angus." He paused. "Like this one."

# 36 PATTERN MAKER

John opened his eyes, fixated on the ceiling, transfixed by the flickering light above him, and the faint distant buzz in the background. He couldn't remember when he'd fell asleep, or whether it was day or night.

He turned his head, slowly trying to adjust to the moment. His neck hurt. He was in the den, not his bedroom. Realised he was half folded on the couch. Could see Angus's feet propped on a table, the rest of Angus flat out on one of the chairs. He was making the same low purring sound as when they were at Kressa Peak.

John pushed himself up. Realised the computer was the source of the light on the ceiling – it was still on. There were papers strewn everywhere. It all began to filter back.

It had taken almost all night. But they'd done it. With Angus's help he'd been able to clarify his thoughts. Together they'd drawn everything out. They'd used the huge sheets of paper that Manda used for patterns – her pattern making. Now they'd created one of their own.

He wasn't sure if Angus was still harbouring thoughts about the sanity – or insanity – of what he was proposing but somehow he didn't care. They now had the pictorial representations to support the mathematical analysis and equations. He sat up.

Angus didn't even move as John reached over him to pluck a half full bottle of water, which teetered beside him on the edge of the chair. Unscrewing the cap John considered the madness of what he was proposing before tipping the bottle and taking a swig. He rolled the water twice around his mouth before swallowing.

He felt the old tightness in his throat. Despite his confidence and conviction of the night before he was still scared, Franklyn may have stolen his ideas; his thesis, the work it had taken him years to compile but Franklyn still only had the words, the numbers. In fact he only had half the picture. It wouldn't be enough.

# 37 ERROR

"Haziq," John said, unprepared for the sudden rush of feeling inside him as Haziq made his way through the gates at the airport.

"The man," said Angus.

Rejecting the images that presented themselves, John tried to think of ordinary things. Tried to remember if there were cultural differences, which meant he should display a low-key response when Haziq finally reached them? It had been so long – years. Yet Haziq looked exactly the same. The slight frame, the almost childlike features, but the brightness was gone.

Then Haziq smiled as he spotted Angus waving. So much had changed thought John. So much had changed since they'd last met.

"Good to see you," was all he said when Haziq was finally within hand shaking distance.

Haziq held out a hand.

John reached for it as Angus threw an arm around the shoulders of their friend. Within seconds the three of them were in an embrace. John found his own head pressed against Haziq's perfectly contoured skull.

"I'm so very sorry," he heard himself saying, "I didn't know, Haziq. Such wonderful people, your parents, I'm sorry."

The drive back to the ranch house passed in a mosaic of recalled memories. Haziq talking of his loss, the shock he was still dealing with. The pain that was there every morning when he opened his eyes to a new day, the work he was doing that was keeping him sane.

Angus managing to locate gems from the past that Haziq had shared with them as a boy.

It worked. Haziq took up the tales, told his own remembered versions of the stories. He laughed. Angus and John joined in. The conversation moved forward. Finally, Haziq asked how they thought he could help. John told him.

They were back at the ranch house, seated outside after the drive in, before Haziq took up the conversation.

"My father worked extensively in the area we have discussed, John," he said, before placing a document on the table. "He too, long considered that there were too many anomalies with regard to the historical framework. But you must understand, that despite his collaboration with western research scientists, he was careful to always bear in mind the political implications of his findings." He paused for a moment. "There are many theories associated with the Giza Plateau," he said, continuing. "All can substantiate their ideas in some way, because so little in the way of artefacts or conclusive evidence has so far been found."

John remained silent.

Haziq took a sip of the iced water Angus had provided them all with. "What you're saying, John, is not dissimilar to many other scientific researchers and commentators. In fact not dissimilar to what my father hypothesised in this paper. The energies emitted by, and surrounding the Great Pyramid, could be linked to the 'Uniting of the Two Lands' the event referred to in the ancient Shabaka Texts."

John nodded his agreement. Angus poured more water from the jug into their glasses.

"The scholarly opinion is that the reference is to a political and economic unification between both southern and northern Egypt," said John before nodding his thanks to Angus, "not the uniting of planets and stars orbiting in the cosmos through the power of, an as yet, unidentified, energy source."

"He's thinking capstone," said Angus.

"There's been a rotational shift in the Earth's axis dating back eleven point five thousand years," John said, his words spilling out faster than he intended. He sucked air before proceeding. "They use the spinning top to show how they believe the shift has occurred…"

"Believable," said Angus.

"But the flooding, the so called natural catastrophes, volcanic eruptions, earthquakes…" He could almost see the devastation.

"Global warming," Haziq said, slowing him down.

"Yes," said John. "The claim is Global warming…"

"And," said Haziq, "this is not what you believe. You think…"

"I think the Earth is moving progressively off course." He knew what he was saying sounded extreme, but that's because it was. "The architecture of the Great Pyramid, its design, its engineering all point to one thing…" He looked at Haziq and Angus, wishing either of them would say what he was thinking.

Both of them remained silent – expectant.

"I believed," he said, "it was a temple. Not in the ordinary sense, more of a sun temple – a temple of light. Consider…" He pressed his head against the knuckles of his hand. "I've considered how it might work. For someone traversing the night sky from beyond the Earth ten thousand years ago, consider the light it would have produced."

"I'm not sure…" Angus began

"I think I am," said John. "It's an anchor, a cosmic energy anchor. That's the reason for the precision with which the pyramids at Giza are aligned to the cardinal points. The change in the rotational shift of the Earth, the catastrophes, global warming – all of it. It's all due to the loss of the…"

"Missing capstone, Man…"

"Why the area was flooded?" questioned Haziq.

"Without it we've been moving off course," said John. He could feel the rush of blood flushing his face. "The 'Uniting of the Two Lands' was a reference to the Earth and the Sirius system. I'm convinced." He could feel the pulse of something inside him, was finding it increasingly difficult to remain seated. "Don't you see," he said. "Without the capstone, to sustain the balance – the energy, the magnetic forces of the Earth have been slowly depleting. Sirius, the huge burning mass of her…" He stopped. Exhausted.

Angus pushed the glass he'd filled with water toward him. "Chill, Man," he said. "I'll go top up this jug."

John took a drink before turning to Haziq.

"Sirius B may be a piece of the main star, formed when the capstone was lost," the words were shooting out. He wanted to say as much as possible before he started to question his own thinking. "Its off kilter orbit is acting as a plug. A volatile energy plug barely maintaining the equilibrium between the Earth and Sirius A …"

"They know it's likely to explode…" Haziq said.

"They believe …" John pressed his fingers into his temples. He needed to do something about the constant build up of tension. "They believe that Sirius B is the threat…"

"But it is not, you are saying, the threat is bigger than they are thinking?"

John nodded. "All the monitoring, all the programmes, everything they have in place to protect the Earth, they're working to prevent something that's already begun to happen."

Haziq sat back in his chair. They were surrounded by the sound of the breeze as it licked its way around the house in a precipitation of rain. Haziq spoke.

"You talked of the need for the reconfiguring of optical observations, John. I may be able to help you with that beyond the work you have already done. You know of the techniques I learned from my father?"

John shook his head. He couldn't think that far back now. His head was too full of the present.

"Not the same as the techniques you have been working with," said Haziq, "but with an advanced form of digital analysis which identifies minute – microscopic, alterations in images through light and reflection. Originally it was variations in temperature, which represented as light because of the energy source heat creates. It was useful in geological research and also in collecting geodetic data. It was the work my father did in this area that I was particularly proud. It was the basis of this work – his work that influenced the research into adaptive optics…" Haziq paused and smiled before continuing. "They now know that they could have saved billions by developing adaptive optics instead of pouring the money into space observations which will tell them very much the same thing."

Both Haziq and John looked up as Angus returned with a fresh supply of iced water. They nodded their thanks as he refilled their glasses.

"Maybe," said Haziq, "we could begin to look at what you have. I have my laptop. The programme is loaded."

"How about we eat first," said Angus. "We can't save the world if we starve to death."

They ate outside. A variety of foods Angus had retrieved from the freezer and microwaved or baked. Haziq put together a huge salad and John cut bread and prepared the plates and cutlery.

The night began to awaken in the valley below, the fine, muted, but unmistakeable scattering of illuminations in the distance as dwellings and workplaces switched on their lights. Haziq asked Angus if he was still using the medication for the pain. John was surprised. He hadn't realized Angus was suffering pain. He knew about the illness and the shock to Angus's system that had caused both the weight, and the hair loss, but Angus had never mentioned the pain.

Angus shrugged. "I stopped the pain killers about two months ago," he said.

"And the pain?" Haziq ducked his head as he spoke.

"You were in pain," said John, wondering why it hadn't occurred to him.

"Man," said Angus. "The withdrawal from the medication was even more painful." He dropped his gaze. "Nobody tells you about the anxiety and the raised blood pressure, the nausea." He paused. "Well maybe they do but I wasn't listening."

John thought about the first week or two when Angus had seemed to swing from one mood to another without warning. The mood swings had slowly retreated. Angus was almost his old self again.

They moved on to other topics before eventually discussing what had happened with Franklyn.

"He is not a good man," said Haziq. "But will his involvement progress your thesis – your predictions – in a way faster than you alone could have done?"

John was silent for a moment. No matter how many times he asked the same question, the answer was always the same.

"Yes," he said to Haziq, "and no."

Haziq smiled. Angus loaded another baked potato with soured cream from a tin.

"Yes," John reiterated, "because he is already a recognised scholar. He achieved his doctorate over twenty years ago. People are more likely to listen to him than me. He can probably command some respect because of his position. No – because he doesn't really seem capable of understanding the implications of the work I've been doing. He's unable to synthesise information. He places no value on the work of others unless he can use it to further his own goals. He is also vehemently opposed to anything outside of mainstream academic thinking and would ridicule anything related to prophecy, myth or religion…"

"Rejecting just about everything that shows a man has soul," said Angus.

"How much does he know?" asked Haziq.

"Know?" said John.

"Less than half of what he needs to, Man," said Angus before tearing another piece of pizza from the plate in the centre of the table. "Show him, John."

John stalled.

"Let Haziq see what we're working with."

It took several hours to go through the papers and diagrams. Haziq made little comment. He listened and nodded then asked for the opportunity to work from John's back-up files. He fired up his laptop as Angus had sunk back in a chair.

"This is not always a process which is an easy one," he said as he downloaded the files. "I will not save these to my computer I will only work with them."

It seemed to John that Haziq was conducting an internal dialogue. It didn't matter. He stood by and watched as Haziq layered each simulated image of the Sirius system, all six thousand and eight hundred of them. Each of which had already been formatted down from the original six million and eight hundred thousand images of optical configurations.

"The programme I am using," said Haziq, "will treat the light as if it were heat source. It will show us recordings of observed change in this column to the left." He indicated to an automatically controlled calculator. "Of course we will have to transform the calculations in order to relate them to your thesis."

To the naked eye the differences in the images were not, as John knew, discernable, but each encoded calculation altered at every hundredth image. Again it was slight. The encoded calculations on their own would not raise any eyebrows or start any alarm signals but the fact that they continued to increase may have, if anyone had taken the time to do what he'd done, and what Haziq was attempting to do now.

"There is, as you have claimed, a measurable change," said Haziq, the purring sound of Angus's snore vibrating in the background after almost three hours of diligent encoding had taken place.

"I have yet to determine if it could be classed as significant, but I will believe you are able to determine that with the calculations and the equations you have already done."

Haziq returned his attentions to the computer. "Now," he said. "Let me see." He scrolled down the page. "You have based each replicated image, which you have constructed from your reflected light based simulations, on a single light year of movement, yes?"

John experienced a sudden tightening in his gullet, a spasm of pain across his neck and shoulders. A sudden blackout of rational thought as a web of panic wrapped itself around him. He could barely move.

"And as we all know..." Haziq began.

"Haziq," said John, abruptly curtailing Haziq's words. "Please tell me there's an error in the programme you're using,"

Haziq glanced from the computer screen to John's face. "Error? There is no..."

"I can't believe..." John could hear the raised pitch of his own voice, could see the widening of Haziq's eyes.

"What's happening, Man?" Angus sat up in his chair.

"I thought we..." John grabbed a pen, ready to isolate numbers on one of his diagrams. Saw Haziq opening his hands in a questioning gesture. Saw Angus rubbing a hand across his bald, head. Was aware of them both watching in silence as he scrabbled through the documents, papers and diagrams before reaching for his calculator. Dread already leaching the breath from his lungs.

# 38 LIGHT YEARS

"This can't be happening." John couldn't believe what the figures were telling him. Sure he'd been using the right mathematical equations to calculate rotational shifts, orbital irregularities and oscillations on the basis of the mathematical model for light years – the Parsec. The Parsec, equivalent to 3.26 light years using the 365.25 days in the Julian year, the Julian year used in all Astronomy. Knew he'd based his calculations on the fact that light could travel nine point five trillion kilometres in one Julian year.

But he'd gotten something wrong. The figures weren't adding up. If anything, everything he had was an overestimation of time. He struggled with the equation, his mind refusing to operate. He knew all about the different calendars – the Julian and Gregorian. The Gregorian calendar which assumed the time between vernal equinoxes as three hundred and sixty five point two five, when in fact it was eleven minutes shorter. He hadn't used the Gregorian calendar.

His mind spun. Flashing back to the Hot House office and Greg's continual talk, remembering how difficult it had been to hold onto his thoughts. How the constant stress of Franklyn's demands and put-downs had affected his capacity to think. But it was still his mistake, his error – a stupid, unforgivable error. No wonder he'd been driven out of academia. He hadn't deserved to be there. He needed to look at his own computer programme. Maybe there'd been a glitch. Maybe he wasn't to blame. But he didn't need to.

The error he'd made was clear. Looking at the figures it was more than clear. He'd been calculating each Parsec, the standard astronomical unit of 3.26 light years, as if it was a single year. It was beyond belief, all his calculations now needing to be multiplied by that figure at least. That would give them just over two-years normal time but with the adjustment for the reconfiguring of optical configurations due to drift... He felt his head implode. He threw down his pen; turned to Angus and Haziq.

"I thought we had more time," he said. He slumped into a chair, covered his face with his hands.

"Man," said Angus. "What are you telling us?"

He raised his head. His chest constricted, his legs numb, and the pain in his temples almost unbearable.

"Tell us?" said Haziq.

He swallowed the lump that had lodged like a stone in his throat. "I've been working on the basis of six point eight light years," he said, aware that to attempt to hide his error would be pointless. "For some reason I thought I was using the Parsec, the standard astronomical unit equivalent to three point two six light years." He felt his eyes almost staring straight through his two friends. He wanted to blink but couldn't. "I thought we had at least six point eight years grace…"

"And?" Haziq's face loomed back into focus as he spoke.

"We'll be lucky," said John. "If we have six months…"

# 39 SWITCHED

John could feel the metal of the chair pressing against his bones as he, and both Haziq and Angus, sat straight-faced waiting for Ogilvy and Fielding to join them.

Angus said that Fielding had been reluctant to even consider discussing what he now believed to be the work of Dr Franklyn. The Dr Franklyn who was now working exclusively with the investigative team on the NASA Supernova project which included the investigation of the reconfiguring of optical observations, rotational shifts and orbital irregularities in the Sirius system.

"He won't listen," said John. Speaking for the first time since they'd left the house.

"He's agreed to meet, Man, that's…"

"Something," said Haziq, his voice calm. "You did work that is good, Angus."

Realising Haziq was waiting for further comment from him and realising he had nothing to give, John shrugged.

"He will listen when I tell him my father would have listened, John," Haziq said. "People have great respect for my father."

John noticed the way Haziq's shoulders became ramrod straight when he mentioned the father he adored. He only hoped that Haziq was right – that people would respect the memory. He didn't want Haziq hurt – didn't want Haziq to hurt any more than he already did.

Angus had already contacted his own parents who were currently overseeing the building of hospital facilities in Asia for which they'd raised the funds to establish the project. Both Paul and Manda Yeager had responded by saying they would help in any way they could.

Although John couldn't think of a single thing he could ask of them he was glad of their promised support. He'd even considered making contact with Thomas Begvious, his benefactor, the man who had found him and to whom he'd given so very little thought. He'd reread the letter from him over and over during the night, had surprised himself in discovering an unexpected sadness in his own heart for the man.

For the first time he'd recognised there'd been no need, no cause for Thomas Begvious to provide him with what he now knew to be a relatively safe and comfortable passage so far in life. But he couldn't deny there was a smouldering spark of anger, too. If Begvious hadn't fought for guardianship over the foundling, John now knew himself to be, maybe there would have been an adoptive family. Maybe he could have grown up with siblings – brothers. Sisters even. Lived a normal life where he wouldn't have tried to unravel the Universe in a bid to stop unravelling inside.

The click of the opening door brought him back to his current space in time. Fielding followed by Ogilvy entered the room.

"Sorry to have kept you," Fielding's tone was formal. He sat down and motioned to Dr Ogilvy to do the same. "We haven't much time," he said.

John reined in the desire to point out that the statement concurred with the exact reason they were there.

"You've all met Dr Ogilvy?" said Fielding.

John and Angus nodded.

"I'm not sure I …" Haziq began.

"Of course," said Fielding. "You didn't join us for the Kressa Peak meeting. Dr Ogilvy, Haziq," he gestured between the two men as he spoke. "Haziq has been working on the geological data team, he's an accomplished Computer Scientist."

"I am the son of Professor Hariz Oman."

Again John noticed the sudden change in posture when Haziq mentioned his father.

"Professor Oman," said Ogilvy. "Primary heat and light expiration, pre-cursive elements in optical definition?"

John saw Haziq smile. Fielding looked annoyed. John sat back further.

It took all of two hours to provide a brief on the findings to Fielding and Ogilvy. Haziq took the lead. John was amazed at how he managed to present the data and explain the thesis in such an assured way. Haziq was so slight, yet had the bearing of someone twice his size when he articulated the scientific data and the basis for believing that John's findings were not artefact. He stressed that it was imperative that they be given clearance to have NASA investigate, and set in motion plans to manage, if not completely forestall, the catastrophes that were now imminent.

Fielding and Ogilvy listened without interruption during Haziq's presentation of the facts, but an awkward silence followed. John noticed Angus closing his eyes, hoping Angus wouldn't drift off and start the soft snoring that would turn the meeting into a comedic farce.

The sound of the phone ringing precipitated the possibility.

Fielding snapped up the receiver. "I'll take it outside," he said. "Won't be long, feel free to further discuss the concepts you've been elucidating with Dr Ogilvy." He practically marched across the room before swinging out the door and letting it slam behind him.

For a few moments no-one spoke, John wasn't sure who to look at, whether he should speak, or remain as quiet as he had been since the beginning of the meeting. He was considering the depth of his own lack of understanding of how to operate in situations, when Ogilvy voiced his position.

"Interesting," Ogilvy said. "Compelling even – the evidence you're presenting." He straightened his back. "I'm not saying I can fully support you, but I'm interested," he added as he sat forward.

He's almost eager, thought John, becoming aware of the sudden spark of excitement revealing itself in Ogilvy's eyes.

"Much of what you have been discussing falls outside my realm of expertise," continued Ogilvy, waving a hand as if swatting an errant fly. "But I'm fascinated, and despite the narrow focus of my own work I can almost visualise the possibilities of what you're hypothesizing…"

"You can?" John wished he hadn't spoken. Even to his own ears his words, even the sound of his own voice, sounded like that of a child. Why did he have to act so surprised that the man could recognise some merit in his work?

"I can," said Ogilvy. "Most scientists begin by trying to disprove the existence of anything beyond the rational." He stood up and stretched his back.

John longed to do the same.

"Then," said Ogilvy as Fielding burst back into the room, "they find themselves convinced that everything beyond themselves is immeasurably volatile and refuses to be contained or captured in a framework of irrefutable static data."

Fielding made it part way into the room. Ogilvy smiled showing the fantastic teeth. John was aware of the reluctant stance Fielding had adopted. As if in some way he felt the group had been discussing him in his absence. Despite his size he looked almost frail when set against the bulk of Ogilvy: Ogilvy, who was still smiling in a way that could only realistically have been described as feral.

"I'd like to propose we eat," said Fielding, his eyes seemingly reluctant to make connection with anyone around him.

"Ah, food," said Ogilvy attempting another stretch.

"I can probably organise something here or…" said Fielding, distracted for a moment. He checked his watch before continuing. "Or maybe we could try the Oak House. The place that's just opened on the far side of town – I believe it's good. We can book a booth to give us some privacy."

John caught Angus's eye. He wasn't sure whether he wanted to eat with Fielding and Ogilvy. They'd talked most things through already.

Angus was giving nothing away. It was Haziq who gave a short nod of his head, which John couldn't determine as a signal of agreement or otherwise.

"That's settled then," said Fielding. "I'll go check they have a booth."

Once Fielding disappeared out the room for the second time, John got to his feet, as did Haziq, followed by Angus. Ogilvy reached for his jacket, which he'd slung across the back of a chair.

"The Oak House," he said. "The food is good? I've never eaten there."

"It's new," said Angus, "far side of town. I've not heard anything detrimental so far. Or good either."

They made their way out and across to the car park, Angus pulling Haziq into conversation with Ogilvy, each making generalised comments about the work at Kressa Peak. John couldn't think of anything to say. Haziq had covered everything they'd agreed to discuss at the meeting. He wanted to get the day over and move on.

Eventually Fielding emerged from the building in the distance; made his way over toward them. "I've booked a table – booth," he said, retrieving his keys from his pocket and clicking the fob to open his car. "I'll drive us." He motioned to Angus's truck. "You can leave that here. Just pack your stuff in the back."

John shook his head. "It's OK," he said. "We'll keep it with us." There was no way he was planning to leave all the documentation and his laptop in the back of a truck in a soon to be empty car park.

"Fine," said Fielding. "Whatever."

"I'll take the truck," said Angus. "We'll follow you out."

"Dr Ogilvy," said Fielding, indicating toward his own vehicle for Ogilvy to join him.

Ogilvy moved across the tarmac.

"I don't understand the sudden invitation to eat," said John, without thinking as he climbed into the truck. He waited as Angus revved the engine and began to follow Fielding's car through the gates on to the road. "I mean," he continued, "hasn't Haziq already explained everything,"

"Beats me, Man," said Angus. "Unless he just gets the munchies like the next guy, but he didn't look too happy in there when Haziq, was laying it all out. But like I told you, Man, he's a guy who likes to be in control."

"Or a man who likes to know the answers," offered Haziq. "He did not seem pleased that we were presenting possibilities that he could not yet argue with."

"And Ogilvy," said John. "What did you make of him?" He asked, continuing without waiting for an answer. "He seemed different somehow. As if, I don't know…"

Angus laughed. "As if he was getting some kind of a rise out of the situation, Man…"

"You think he was laughing at us?" John voiced his thoughts.

"I think he enjoyed that somehow Dr Fielding seemed so uncomfortable," said Haziq. Pausing, before adding, "I am not clear why that should be so."

By the time they made it to the Oak House, they were no nearer an understanding of the apparent shift with Fielding and Ogilvy.

Angus honed straight in on the food. "I'm glad we came," he said, loading his plate. "I'd forgotten I'd been told this place offered the full carvery facilities – I'm starved. Now I've seen the food I am seriously starved."

Haziq laughed. "Angus," he said. "You have always been a starved man. Remember as when we were boys how you ate our food?"

For a fleeting second John saw the boy Angus once was, scrabbling in the cupboard for food. The biscuits in the Sick Bay the day Angus had come to see him, wondered if Angus realised what he'd saved him from back then.

The booth, as Fielding had promised, was private. The privacy further enhanced by the fact that the Oak House was virtually empty. John wondered if it was the time of day or if maybe the food was not as good as it looked.

"Great," said Fielding once they were all seated. "Feel free to help yourself to some wine, or I could order some beer. There's water here too."

"Beer is good for me," said Angus.

"Water is fine," Haziq spoke softly.

Fielding motioned to the waiter who was leaning forlornly against the empty bar.

"Beer for me too," said Ogilvy, his feral smile flashing again.

John poured himself a glass of Wine. He wasn't sure he wanted it, but it gave him something to do with his hands. Fielding was driving and was unlikely to drink more than two small glasses. Unless, thought John, Fielding was less sensible and straight laced than he appeared. He still couldn't figure out why Fielding had invited them. As if reading his thoughts Fielding spoke.

"You're probably wondering why I suggested we eat out here," Fielding picked up his glass as he spoke and twirled it around in his hand. "Well," he said. "If I'm entirely honest I…" He took a mouthful of wine and then put down his glass. "The fact is I'd like to be able to engage with the ideas…"

"Not ideas," said Haziq, his tone firm, diction perfect. "What John has been working on are testable hypotheses. I myself, using a programme designed by Professor Hariz Oman, my father, can provide support for the hypotheses John is laying before you."

The atmosphere became tense. Fielding's face expressionless, Ogilvy flashed the same smile as before. Angus pushed back his seat, gave John a sideways look. Again John could not discern the meaning behind the look. Haziq poured himself more water. Despite being glad that Haziq was on his side, John wished he could speak for himself. He took a deep breath to prepare himself to do just that when Fielding spoke again.

"You know of course, Haziq, that someone else, Dr Franklyn from Bloomfield University is claiming credit for the work John is proposing is his?"

John experienced the familiar flare of nausea.

Haziq was unfazed. "It has been discussed Dr Fielding…"

"You realize my – I've…" Fielding floundered.

"It is my understanding," said Ogilvy, "that within the UK there is little to prevent people from assuming the credit for other people's works – other people's research." He turned to John. "Am I correct in my thinking?"

John wasn't sure. The papers he'd read from the Research Council on the subject of plagiarism had not been entirely or even vaguely clear.

"Dr Ogilvy," said Fielding. "I'm not clear about the position in UK universities but I'm quite clear about the position here in the states. Those found guilty of plagiarising content can lose federal funding." He turned abruptly and stared at John before continuing. "Falsification and fabrication of data is considered an act of scientific misconduct. I'm not sure what you're after here. It's more…"

"How come no one's laying any heavies on Franklyn, Man?" said Angus, curtailing Fielding's flow as he pushed his chair back and stood up.

John noticed that for the first time since he'd arrived Angus seemed to be packing the power he'd expressed when he was younger.

"You've put me in an untenable situation," Fielding again directed his words to John before standing up and reaching for his coat. He glared at Angus. "I don't appreciate your tone, Yeager. I thought I was helping out but I'm not prepared to have funding withdrawn or compromise my position…" He stormed out of the restaurant without finishing his speech.

"Ah," said Ogilvy. "And I thought he'd be paying the bill."

Angus insisted on using his card to cover the cost of the failed dinner. Ogilvy argued.

"No, Man," Angus waved him away. "I was the guy who…"

"My fault," John said. He'd kept his own mouth closed so that he wouldn't say the wrong thing to impact on the positions held by Angus and Haziq at the university. But, he realised now, keeping his own mouth shut had probably implicated his friends adversely anyway.

Angus's unexpected outburst hadn't been taken well by Fielding. Even Haziq's considered account of the findings had, in retrospect, seemed like the confrontation Fielding appeared to interpret it as.

After Angus had settled the bill they headed outside to the truck.

"I should have spoken for myself." John considered his two friends and the reserved countenance of the wolfish Dr Ogilvy. "I was holding back because…" He paused. Why was he holding back? It was a fact that Haziq presented the findings in a way that he himself seemed incapable of doing. Was that a good enough reason to let other people maybe pick up the flack from people like Fielding? "The truth is," he said. "Is given I've found it so hard to get anyone to listen…"

"You mean Franklyn?" said Angus as he clicked the truck open.

"Yes." John pulled and held open the door of the truck while the others climbed in.

"Where shall we drop you?" queried Angus, with a quick turn of his head toward Ogilvy as they drove back out onto the road. "Back at the campus, good?"

"It would be," Ogilvy said. "Only I haven't a car. Dr Fielding picked me up. I'll need to book into a motel and get back to Kressa Peak tomorrow."

"You could…" Angus seemed to be considering something as he switched gears before accelerating. "You could stay over with us at the house – that's if you want?"

Now Ogilvy seemed to be considering.

John felt uneasy – unsure. He still wasn't sure of Ogilvy, or how excluding Fielding from any discussions may affect Angus and Haziq.

"It may be a good idea," said Ogilvy. "We can talk."

It seemed that none of them wanted to discuss Fielding's sudden departure. They drove in silence, most of the way back to the house until Ogilvy decided to brief them on his own background, his current unexpected stint at the Observatory.

"The man you would have expected to meet would have been Professor Van Heuson," he told them. "Interestingly he was called by NASA to investigate the work of your friend Dr Franklyn. That is how I knew of it when Dr Fielding opened up the subject while you were on the night shift with us at the observatory," he said. Then explained that now as he knew what John had been working on he realised his textbook talk at Kressa Peak must have been very tedious.

"Silence tells me when I talk with students that they are either one of two things; deeply impressed and scared to speak in case I ask them a question, or they are so bored they are planning some exciting event." He patted John's shoulder. "With you I thought you were impressed, yet scared. I find myself after today's revelations questioning my powers of observation." He laughed, before adding, "Not very good for an Astronomer, eh?"

John saw the joke but didn't laugh. He'd already seen something else.

Angus had too. "Shit," Angus said, swerving the truck to a stop.

John saw Haziq's eyebrows rise, as Ogilvy leaned forward. The house, he'd hoped it wasn't, but it was. Angus's house, as bright as a beacon on the rise ahead of them.

"Tell me I didn't leave the gas on," said Angus as he pushed open the door and leapt out of the vehicle.

Ogilvy was quick. Out of the truck in seconds, grabbing Angus's arm and slowing his progress before Angus had a chance to head toward the leaping flames.

"Your house?" Ogilvy's question bit the air as he hooked a second arm round Angus, rendering him immobile.

Angus tried to shake free, but it was a feeble attempt. John felt himself rooted to the spot – all his things. The weeks of work, the diagrams, he grasped his rucksack, thought of the gifts from his mother, suffered a wild flash of breathless panic as he searched and retrieved the pouch, before he allowed himself the luxury of inhaling. Haziq already had his mobile phone in his hand, speaking to an operator. John started to cough. His mouth scorched with the taste of smoke.

# 40 ILLUMINATE

The fire didn't make any sense. The suggestion was that it had been the work of amateurs. In some ways it seemed so. The wind had pulled the flames outwards onto the decking area, catching the porch roof. The traditional apex holding the flames as they tore upwards into the night, saving the main house from serious damage. The effect of the smoke wasn't so good. It had permeated everything, and the debris of the porch had to be cleared.

It hadn't taken long to discover that along with the two PCs, his back up drive was missing. The documentation that had been in the den was gone. The police believed it had been used to start the fire. Though why, thought John, would thieves want to bring attention to the scene of their own crime? There seemed no reasonable explanation.

Between them, they'd identified a list of missing things. Again, the simple lifestyle of Paul, and Manda Yeager, meant there were no supposed valuables.

John was aware of the great help Ogilvy had been. The fact that he didn't generally sleep at night when at the Observatory, meant he'd been pretty sharp well into the early hours when Angus, Haziq and he himself had flagged. He'd been amazed to discover that Paul Yeager, the 'Wild Man of Rock', one of his own music heroes, was father to Angus. He'd spent part of the night, in between the arrival of police and fire services, trying to level the stress they were all under by talking about music.

John even finding some space in his addled thinking to share the fact with Ogilvy, that the guitar he'd torn through the house in search of, as soon as the fire crew had given the OK, had been gifted to him by Paul Yeager.

Unbelievably the instrument was safe and undamaged, had lain untouched under a quilt that John had thrown over it.

"The Wild Man played this?" Ogilvy asked with something akin to awe, his hands opening and fingers splaying as he spoke. "Could I...?"

John saw the longing. Lifted the guitar, held it forward watched as Ogilvy gently took it from him.

"You play?" Angus said, as Ogilvy sat down.

Ogilvy made a slight move of his head. "Is it OK?" he said. The question directed at John.

John nodded, watched as Ogilvy's fingers moved with dexterity over the fret-board picking out the notes of Trojan Mind. The Snow Leopards' seventies number-one hit, that had every novice guitarist in the country desperate to replicate.

They'd all laughed. Amazed. The fire and the fear unexpectedly displaced, temporarily forgotten.

Now as morning had arrived Ogilvy had hitched a lift into town from Angus who was dropping Haziq of at the university before arranging for a salvage team to come in and do the bulk of the cleaning. He was also looking for a local craftsperson to rebuild the traditional porch. John had stayed back to start the clearing up outside. He was sorry he had now.

Pushing the broom across the flagstones he realised the ache in his head was distracting him from having any coherent thoughts. It was hard to discern whether it was the lack of sleep, the effects of smoke inhalation or the fact that once again his work had disappeared. The police and the fire team had crawled all over the place. The insurance team had already been in to estimate the damage and ascertain liability. The place had been trashed.

It was ridiculous but he felt somehow exposed, on edge – could almost feel as if he was being watched. Reminding himself the police had said it was likely a random event; he tried to shake off the feeling of threat. The police seemed pretty convinced it was no more than a group of teenagers out for some fun – a crackpot dare of some sort.

He hadn't considered motives. The fire and the smoke had been shocking enough. He'd just been glad that the damage was limited and so very little had been taken. Managing to convince himself that even if the PC's and his own back up drive had gone along with the documentation and diagrams, he still had all he needed on his laptop and a full set of copies of everything – almost everything, related to his research findings. His precious guitar was safe, and the insurance people would finance the work to make good all the other damage. The leather pouch and its contents were still with him. It was hard to tell if it was the after effects of the shock of the fire, the loss of his things or the wanton damage, but whatever it was there was an uneasiness stalking upwards from the pit of his stomach.

He rested the broom against the low brick wall that framed the empty pool. He wanted to lie down and rest but felt reluctant to go inside the house. What if someone was watching – someone waiting for a chance to get him alone? For the first time since he'd read the letter from Thomas Begvious the question occurred to him. What had the woman, believed to be his mother, been running from?

His hand slid inside his jacket to the pouch. Was there something in the tiny gifts, the artefacts she bequeathed to him, or the symbols and words inscribed on the leathered parchment that she needed, or wanted protected? Maybe the thieves were looking for the pouch. He sat down on the wall, aware of the vulnerability of his back.

Already he'd synthesised the information his mother had given him. Everything had fitted with his work – his theories. Or had he made it fit? The man, Thomas Begvious, his letter too, it had almost been an invitation to join him in something. *'I returned to the libraries of my past'* he'd written in the letter, *'those vast places where knowledge and records are stored. They illuminate me. I hope you find they illuminate you too.'*

What had the man been talking about? It was if there was some agreed link between them – some secret hidden understanding. Maybe the man, Thomas Begvious, really was his father and the pouch meant nothing. All the artefacts, the symbols, even the tiny silver cross, had they been carefully gathered together and presented to him as a test – but a test of what?

There'd been a lot of things happening: the missing papers, Bloomfield University. What had been going on with Franklyn? Where did Greg fit in?

He felt as if he was too relaxed, yet somehow constricted. He still had the stuff on his Laptop. It didn't matter if stuff was vanishing again. Maybe there was something bad in what he was doing. The work…maybe it was wrong in some way. Now the police were involved.

Maybe this was all part of some wider plan. Another experiment like the one Berke carried out. Only this was more sophisticated. They were saying he was lying about his work. Fielding had talked about falsification of data – even tried to get Haziq to understand that Dr Franklyn was the person behind the research.

Feeling a trickle of cold sweat run down his back, despite the heat, he shivered. Felt something wedge in his brain then twist and shift. He raised a hand to his head. It seemed unlikely, but it was possible that they were all involved – maybe even Angus and Haziq. The letter, the pouch, the parchment were all some sort of a joke – a set-up. A carefully designed puzzle to send him on a wild goose chase where he'd cast all rigorous scientific methodology and thinking to the four winds, grasping at the nebulous clouds of myth and prophecy to support him on his journey in search of the truth. To make the pieces fit to create a picture he believed only he had the power to see.

Angus had alluded to the fact that there could be something going on. John now realised he was in the dark again. Were they all laughing? But Franklyn, if it was all madness, why had Franklyn taken the credit for the research? His head was starting to pound. There was too much space around him: the valley; the mountains; in the distance; the endless sky. Where was he – what was going on?

Everything was moving. He guessed it was happening. The predictions – the prophecy, everything was unfolding. The numbers started to run through his head followed by the images, as if the kaleidoscope of his mind was moving on fast forward. Everything around him was circling. Gripped by an extreme dizziness he tried to steady himself. Realised there was nothing beneath his feet. He'd failed. The world was finally spinning off its axis. He was falling into the blackness of space. He tried to catch hold of the edge of the world. Too late – it exploded.

# 41 PEACEFUL

"Hey, Man…"

He could hear Angus's voice somewhere far off in the distance. Tried to open his eyes. He was still in the blackness. There was something on his face. He tried to raise a hand to find out what it was. Realising it was probably the blindfold Berke had made him wear he wanted to remove it. He tried but his arm wouldn't move. He was too tired; just wanted to slip backwards into the darkness again.

"If you don't talk to me, Man, I'm gonna have to call an ambulance."

Angus's voice again. John didn't remember Angus being in the class. Thought Angus had been a friend.

"Here…"

He could feel his body being moved as the person spoke. He tried again to speak. Maybe he was dead. He remembered where he'd been before he fell off the Earth. A ranch house in Arizona – why was he there? He'd been scared. He'd been right to be scared. Someone hidden in the hills had taken aim and shot. That's what the explosion was. The gun going off as they shot him.

"Dehydration, probably heatstroke," the voice was saying. "How long was he out here? He may need a line."

What sort of a line John wanted to ask? He was asking but the question was in his head, his lips weren't moving. He let himself drift again.

He couldn't determine whether he was dreaming or still asleep, the light searing through his eyelids, shifting and changing colour with sudden unexpected shadows. There was something in his arm. He was on his back almost flat out. He commanded his eyes to open. Reluctantly they did so.

He saw the ceiling above him and the light from the window to his left. Felt the coolness of a breeze. A curtain was lifting and falling, casting light and shadow as it moved, revealing the day outside, against the dimness of the room he was located in. There was a soft purring sound to his right.

He turned. Angus was resting in a chair. John felt clammy, his head an almost impossible weight. The door swung open. Angus lurched forward knocking a glass of water off the side of his chair, stared for a second, before grabbing a towel from the small hook on the cabinet beside the bed.

"John, Man…" he said dropping the towel as he spoke. "You're awake."

John tried to respond. He almost expected Angus to start searching for food as he had all those years ago.

"You're doing fine, there, baby." The nurse patted him on the arm. "Behave yourself and you'll be outa this place before sweet Marie here has time to make you fall in love with her." She laughed. "Here," she said, throwing a wad of paper towels at Angus. "The water." She pointed toward the floor, where Angus's plastic glass still lay in the pool it had spilled out.

"Sure," said Angus dropping the wad and standing on it to soak up the spill. "How you feelin, Man?"

John was aware of Angus's face in front of his own.

"Scared the beejeebies…" Angus began.

"Floor," said the nurse.

John watched as Angus, taking in the stern look from the nurse, tailed off and bent to retrieve the damp wad from the floor. He threw it in the bin before turning back to the bed. "John, I…" he said.

"Sorry," John felt the croak in his voice rather than heard it. "My head, what happened?"

"Exhaustion, sweetie pie," the nurse swiped a cloth across his face as she spoke. "Too many parties, too much fun."

Her face emerged close to his as the cloth was removed. She unclipped a drip machine from the side of the bed.

"You need a nice girl like me to keep you home at nights." She pulled the clipboard chart from the side of the bed checked it, then attached a monitor to his thumb before gently taking hold of his wrist to record his pulse.

John moved his other arm across his chest.

"Keep still," the nurse scolded, "or Marie…"

John sat up. The pouch. What had happened to the leather pouch?

"You OK?" Angus was beside the bed, his eyes wide.

"My things," John said, trying to lick his lips to moisten them to make it easier to speak, but his tongue was dry. He reached for the empty glass Angus had lifted from the floor.

Angus hurriedly filled it with water from a jug and held it forward, while Marie, the nurse, tut – tutted.

John swallowed a mouthful, then another. "I need to get out of here," he said as he tried to swing his legs from the bed, but couldn't do so. "Who's got my clothes, my Laptop, the things my mother gave me?"

Seeing the look in Angus's eyes he felt his throat start to close. He could barely breathe. There were too many coincidences. Why were they holding him in here? The nurse with the singy-songy voice, what part was she playing in all this? If it was a plan between them to keep him quiet they'd made a mistake. Is this what they'd done to his mother? Set her up, drugged her. Is that why she'd had to run away – why she'd never come back for him?

He tried again to wrench his legs out of the bed, but his breathing was tight, his chest almost bursting with the effort. Maybe they'd given him something. He felt the chill of deception. He'd never expected Angus to be part of a plan to hijack the truth.

Angus was looking at him now. John couldn't read the look. The nurse was jabbering on about hyperventilation. Angus was trying to press him back on the bed. There was a buzzer going off somewhere. The sound was cracking through his skull, the vibration across his skin like a thousand electric currents. Master Berke. He was in on this, John was sure. Why hadn't he realised?

Why hadn't he realised that Angus... He couldn't remember what he was thinking. There was a man coming towards him. Who was he? The features in the man's face were dissolving and reconfiguring. He had something in his hand – a syringe. The bastards were holding him down. They were going to kill him. The man with the syringe started to smile. John realised who it was. He wasn't going to let him get him.

He summoned his strength. Thrashed from Angus and the nurse, tried to free his arms. Couldn't. Wasn't strong enough. Forced himself backwards, rolling, twisting, lashing out with his feet. Then everything became peaceful as if he was falling through space, the light of the Universe disappearing.

# 42 OVERWHELMED

"I thought I'd only been out a day," he spoke as Manda moved around him. "When I opened my eyes I thought you were…" He stopped, conscious of the well of feeling ready to rise up and overflow whenever he thought or began to speak the word.

Manda sat down beside the bed. "How are you, John?" she said.

"I thought you were my mother." He saw the fleeting veil of understanding move across her features.

"That's not so strange, John."

He wanted to tell her he knew that, and would be eternally grateful for her kindness when he was a child, and even now. But that wasn't what he'd meant. It was the colouring. The dark hair pulled into a braid – her eyes. He'd never realised how much Manda looked like a Native American Indian.

"Did Angus tell you?"

"He told us how ill you were." She reached forward, took his hand in hers. "Told us how hard you'd been working." She stroked his hand, rested it back against the cover, before sitting back in the chair. "Told us how difficult things had been for you."

"Have I gone crazy, Manda?" He felt the beseechingness of the question, closed his mouth quickly to prevent more words from spilling out.

"No more crazy than the rest of us, John." She pushed a stray strand of hair from her face. "You should have talked to someone sooner." She stood up and treaded toward the open window.

He noticed her feet were bare. She turned. Appraising him with the look he remembered from childhood. He felt the unmistakeable sensation inside the bridge of his nose. He wouldn't cry. He was a man now. Yet the scared boy still lingered. He turned his head away and focused on the hand woven blanket, which hung from the wall. "My stuff…"

"It's all in the safe, John."

"The leather pouch?"

"Everything," Manda reassured. She came back to the bed and sat back down again. "Sarah and Dan have emailed us that all your stuff back home…" She smiled, "It's all safely stored in the facility where you left it, and all your other things here are in the safe. Now what I want to know is if you'd like to try and get yourself up and we'll sit outside in the shade for a bit. You need to think about getting back on your feet, and off the medication as soon as possible."

The walk from the bedroom to the kitchen was hard. Outside on the porch he took in the air. He felt as if the space around him had no substance, the distance in front of, and above him, endless. He kept his hand on the doorframe for security.

"Come sit, Man," Angus said as he pulled out a seat.

"The fire," said John. "Did I imagine the fire?"

Manda encouraged him forward. "There was a fire," she said. "Not too much damage – just a lot of smoke."

John recalled the saying that there was never any smoke without fire. So there must have been a fire. It wasn't all in his mind.

"Good work, eh?" Angus waved his hand taking in the outside of the house that John remembered as forming a torch in the night. "Took less than a day for them to repair," he cupped John's elbow as he spoke.

Guiding him, John realised, to a seat. "So I didn't imagine everything?" he asked as he sat down.

"Nah," Angus said. "You're...well you were just exhausted, Man."

"When?" John heard himself ask. He still didn't know how long he'd been in this half world. When he tried to work it out he had to close his eyes because of the pain in his head.

"Three weeks," Angus said. "We found you collapsed up here. Three..."

John watched as Angus glanced at Manda for confirmation. She nodded.

"Three weeks ago, Man. Scared the beejee..."

"Was I in a hospital?" John cut in. He could still see the man bearing down on him with the syringe. At first he'd thought it was Berke. He was sure that Berke was going to blindfold him again. The way he'd blindfolded him in school. Then Berke's face had changed. It was Franklyn. He was impersonating Berke for some reason. But why was Franklyn in the hospital? The memory made the top of his chest start to vibrate.

"Why was he trying to kill me?" John heard the hoarse rasp as he spoke. "Why was Franklyn...?"

"It was just a doctor, Man."

John glanced sideways. How did Angus know?

"You thought it was someone else, Man – someone who's been screwing with your head for a long time."

By the time he was back inside some of the fear had abated. He'd eaten the first food he remembered eating since they'd all been at the Oak House with Fielding and Ogilvy. He recalled that for some reason the meeting had been incredibly important yet he'd hardly spoken. Now it seemed so long ago. Everything had seemed so vital – crucial. It was as if he, some skinny guy, who could barely speak in front of people, knew how to save the Earth. His head was full of exploding stars, celestial catastrophes, the Great Pyramids of Giza, acoustic waves. He couldn't remember where it had all come from. He remembered the diagrams illustrating the big picture – The Sirius System something about expanding or accelerating Universes and planets dancing in the sky.

He'd been so sure of something. Manda said he should have talked to someone sooner. He remembered he had. There'd been a woman named Julia. A painting. A watercolour hung on the wall. Did Julia paint, too? There was something he needed, something that made him feel safe but he couldn't remember what it was. He climbed back into bed wishing he could stop forgetting things. The tiredness overwhelmed him. He had to rest.

# 43 MEANING

It was as he remembered it. If he walked up the ridge he could turn and view the sweep of the mountain leaning across the sky to join the sea. He'd almost forgotten a place could flaunt so many shades of green; dips and folds; hills that rose and peaked to mountains - the sanctuary of his distant childhood.

He was glad they'd brought him back here. The welsh farmhouse. He could walk for hours.

"Just keep putting one foot in front of the other, John, and you'll get there," Manda said.

He hadn't fully understood. He knew now. It was about getting well again. His head – his thoughts, were less fragmented. The memories were returning, the fatigue no longer holding – crushing. He was painting again, had even begun practicing the guitar in earnest. As near to mastering 'Simple Twist of Fate' as he'd ever be.

Manda had insisted he come back with her, nursing him back to health with her quietness and simple activities. Listening without interruption when he'd told her about the letter from Thomas Begvious – the links to his past. She'd fashioned him a silver chain so he could attach and wear the gifts from his mother.

She'd handled the tiny artefacts with something akin to reverence. Later she'd drawn up his astrological chart from the dates and times on the leathered parchment, and explained the meaning of the planetary positions.

She'd taken him to the Healing Well. "I read all about this place when we first came to live in these parts, John," she said. "I'll never know whether it's the belief and faith people place in Holy Shrines that initiates the healing process – the energy to create a miracle or whether there are places…"

"That capture the pure, and complete energy of creation…" he said.

"We'll just sit a while, if you like," she said. "You don't have to go in the water if you don't want to. I read that St Beuno helped a lot of people, before he healed Winefride. Would you like to go in?"

He said, "No." Too many people were there, entire families plunging into the pool, which collected the healing waters. He sat alone in the small side chapel. Lit a candle and knelt down to pray. He hadn't been able to think of anything to say, aware of the people outside, the hope and the prayer, the children laughing. He'd closed his eyes and asked only for guidance in all that he did.

He was aware of that guidance being somehow with him now as he followed the track he'd started on. A gentle enough slope to make him feel he was making progress. It was time to speak with Manda. She needed to be with Paul, her husband – Angus's father. Manda and Paul Yeager had hardly spent anytime apart since they'd met. He was grateful for Manda's care, but couldn't quite dismiss a sense of guilt for being responsible for creating a hiatus in the close relationship of the two people in his life, to whom he owed so much.

The sun was still high in the sky when the path opened up forming a grassy bank, around the foot of the rock, which angled upwards providing a natural viewing point.

Experiencing the old remembered flicker of anticipation he manoeuvred himself onto the ledge to view the scene unchanged since he'd first climbed here over fifteen years go. He sat down, closing his eyes for a moment, inhaling the clean air. Felt it cool and comforting in his nostrils, a promise of redemption. He wasn't crazy. He just needed to find his way back. The weeks he'd spent recovering from exhaustion both physical and mental he'd been operating as if in some netherworld – some timeless space. He'd not watched TV, listened to the radio, spoken on the phone to anyone, or even browsed the Internet. It was almost as if the world had stopped turning.

It hadn't. Angus had brought the news, along with the documentation he'd collated with the help of Carlos Ogilvy from source. Despite Manda's attempts to draw the conversation along different avenues, he'd confirmed, what John, in some part of his mind, already knew. Franklyn had made a name for himself on the back of the research work he'd stolen.

Franklyn had now managed to secure a position on the team at NASA, and Fielding had been seconded from the University to assist on the now international 'Giza Star Track Operation', to work with him. It had hit the news across the world whilst John had been clawing his way back to some sort of sanity. The detailed research he'd been working on for the greater part of his life, which had been adulterated in its essence by Franklyn, had now been given credence by scientists and astronomers around the globe.

"It's Franklyn's baby, now," Angus stormed. "He's making a name for himself, and Fielding is basking in reflected glory."

"The 'break-in' and the fire…" John could hear the flatness in his own voice.

"You knew, Man?"

"Some part of me did…"

"Can he do this?" Manda asked. "There must be rules. I mean you trusted these people, John." She turned to Angus. "And Fielding, isn't he, wasn't he connected to…"

"He was – is, a control freak, Ma. I should never have pulled him in," he said, before darting a look toward John.

"I'm sorry, Man." He paused, shook his head. "It was just…well…I knew he could get leverage if we needed it. I didn't think he'd be party to…"

"Angus," John said. "It doesn't matter…"

"How can it not matter, Man?"

John saw how Angus squared his jaw. How bright his eyes were. "Because," he said, "it means I'm not crazy…"

"Who ever said?" Manda began.

"Even I thought I was," conscious of his raised voice, he took a deep breath. "I've thought I was going crazy for a long time. This means I wasn't. I'm not. It doesn't matter if Franklyn…"

"Has ripped off…"

"No, Angus, Manda, don't you see I feel as if all the hours, the days, months and years of my life, the obsession, the focus, it hasn't…it isn't," he took another breath, "it means my life has had meaning."

"Has meaning, John. Your life has meaning," Manda said.

He saw Manda's distress, how close she was to tears. Reached out and grabbed her hand. The first time he'd ever initiated contact. "Manda," he said, trembling inside. "Angus," he looked from one to the other. "It's not over," he felt a swirl of panic as he voiced his thoughts. Knew his system was being flooded with adrenalin, his heart beating faster, his muscles tightening, his breathing more rapid; the thin film of cold perspiration moistening his skin, all symptoms of the sympathetic division of the body's autonomic nervous system fight-or-flight response.

Julia had explained it all in fine detail: the importance of cognitive appraisal of a situation. There were always choices a person could make. He chose. Making a decision in the space between heartbeats, feeling the sudden unexpected calm as the noradrenalin response kicked in. He felt more in control than he'd felt in a long time. Ready for battle – glad that Manda had eased him off the medication. "It's not over," he told them both a second time. "It's barely begun."

He clicked the stop button on his thoughts, scanned the horizon. From where he sat all appeared serene, the curtain of sky melding into the darker blue of the sea, the rocky outcrops of the land leading the eye to the far distance view of possibility. He pulled himself up. It was time to go back.

# 44 APEX

"It is moving forward at great speed," said Haziq. "They are working on the theory of magnetic oppositional reversal which you presented in your thesis."

"And?" John said, his own sense of excitement, almost a reflection of the heightened animation Haziq was generating.

"They are very much intrigued," Haziq continued. "In fact, I too am very much intrigued." He narrowed his eyes. "Why, I am asking myself, has this never been measured before?"

John thought of the hours that turned into years spent reading the esoteric texts, the accounts of others who'd deciphered hieroglyphic accounts, the theories of those individuals outside of mainstream academia who were shunned by the scientific and academic communities. All of it had inspired him to explore the mathematical possibilities of unity and balance within and between the Earth and the planets and stars revered by mankind. "Time," he said. "Maybe they didn't have the time." He almost laughed at the ridiculousness of the statement. There'd been aeons of time. The earnestness of Haziq's stare stopped him.

"They have much less time now," Haziq confirmed. His expression serious, some of the spark in his eyes dimmed.

"Even the work on Neutrinos has almost taken a back seat, Man," said Angus opening the manila folder on his lap. "Lo-tech communication here, guys." He handed both Haziq and John a sheet of paper. "They seem to be following the line of thinking you set forth in one of your earlier papers. Take a look at the diagram."

"The depth and shadow hypothesis?" said John, staring at the copy of the diagram, almost a replica of the one he'd produced at age fifteen. Franklyn was pretty much home and free now to appropriate, and take credit for everything he'd ever humiliated him for producing. It irked. But, it didn't hurt the way it had in the beginning. At least Franklyn and Fielding had the position and background to be taken seriously. If it weren't for Franklyn's blatant theft of his work, John knew he'd still be sweating it out in the Hot House.

"The one," said Angus.

"The geological survey, it has shown there is evidence for the greater depth of the pyramid," said Haziq. "Although it is still not easy to determine not only the actual depth, but if the greater depth readings are…"

"It was always assumed to be a rock formation upon which the Great Pyramid was built," said John, tracing the line of shadow across the page Angus had given him.

"John," Haziq said. "The scientists are considering seriously that the precessional shift that will have occurred will, as you identified, have created an apparent distance between what the believed exact locations of…"

"Of the apex of the pyramid and Sirius A?" John spoke, unable to control his excitement, aware of the trigger of something intangible opening up his mind as he posed the question. He could sense the eyes of both Haziq and Angus upon him.

"Man," said Angus.

"It appears they are focusing on the capstone theory," said Haziq, his hand moving across the page almost as if he was casting a spell, "as a predicted focus for the theory of magnetic oppositional reversal, which you presented in your thesis, John."

"They're looking for something pretty big out there, Man," said Angus, creating a shape in the air as he spoke.

Haziq held up both hands to draw the attention of his friends. "Work has already begun on the design and possible reconstruction of a new capstone should it not be possible to locate the original. I have been made aware of this."

John considered the size of the hypothesised missing capstone. It was massive. Even if it could be located, how would they lift and move it back to its rightful place? Even with modern technology, reinstating the missing capstone would be as much of an engineering miracle as the building of the pyramid itself. To reconstruct would be equally challenging. Given the limited time frame, the ticking clock, both options would demand extensive resource and expertise.

That such a course of action was being considered showed that his thesis, his research, his work, now masquerading as Franklyn's, even though adulterated was being validated across a range of disciplines. Yet the news reports had stopped. There was nothing new being reported through any source. Even the Internet was failing to throw up any information relating to the 'Giza Star Track Operation'. If Angus and Haziq were not affiliated to, and engaged with, the University, and if Ogilvy hadn't come on board as a friend they'd know nothing of the progress being made.

"I can't understand…" the words slipped out before he could properly formulate his thoughts. Angus and Haziq looked at him and waited. He felt limited enough being a bystander, but the sudden blackout in communication from all media was hard to fathom.

"There's not much you don't understand, Man," said Angus. "Seems like half the scientific world is falling over itself to grab a piece of the pie you baked with a recipe all of your own design…"

"But why has it all disappeared off the radar? I don't understand why…"

"You are questioning why it is suddenly 'top secret'?" Haziq said.

"Chaos, Man," said Angus.

"Panic!" said Haziq. "Angus is correct, John. There are vast implications if people panic. Not least of which will be the financial implications across the western world…"

"Financial implications?" John knew his question and sense of outrage were futile. The Earth was shifting on its axis but maintaining the stabilisation of worldwide markets would still be top priority for governments far and wide. Maybe it was best that people were kept unaware of potential threats. The longer they didn't know, the less fear and despair to be experienced.

"John," said Haziq. "There are still many ways we can be involved. It is possible I can make further contacts. My father has…" The halt in Haziq's sentence was momentary, the shadow across his eyes brief.

John felt a snag of pain for Haziq's loss.

"My father," Haziq began again, "had many friends. There are some who will not be too afraid to help us."

"Ogilvy's on board too," said Angus. "The man is a fiendish rock fan, the musical as well as the cosmic kind. He's got every album the Old Man made. How wild is that?"

"The focus isn't right," said John. "Franklyn is using only the material elements of the work I presented."

"Man," Angus opened up his hands, his shoulders lifting in question.

"Some of the texts," said John, "illustrate the possibility that during the time of dynastic Egypt there was some form of spiritual cataclysm that resulted in mankind's degeneracy to a lower level. Mankind coming to believe that the material world was the only reality, and the spiritual world no more than a reflection of that reality…" He stopped, suddenly aware of the look on Angus's face. He slanted a glance at Haziq, whose expression remained the same as always. Neither of his friends spoke. "I'm not losing it," he said.

"Maybe," said Haziq, his face breaking into the semblance of a smile, "you are finding it. That something we are all looking for."

# 45 NO DEFENCE

"You can't just trek off, Man."

John noticed an unfamiliar edge to Angus's voice. Stole a look at his friend, but continued to fill his rucksack.

"Haziq – Haziq and me, we've been setting everything up…"

"I'd just like to find her, Angus. Speak to her. Ask her. Why?" John felt the hunger of desire even as he spoke.

"But, Man." Angus threw the orange he was holding from hand to hand.

"When I didn't know…" said John, "it was hard." He frantically pressed the contents of his bag to make more space. "So guess what?" He dragged a tee shirt from the bag and hurled it toward the door. "I fantasized, Angus. I made up stories. It didn't fill the emptiness but it filled the space in my mind where the rejection was – even if only for a short time."

"I hate to say this, Man." Angus rubbed the back of his head before starting to massage the back of his neck with one hand. "I mean…but how do we know this guy Begvious, Thomas Begvious, was telling the truth?"

"She must have been running from something or someone, Angus. Why else would she be on an embankment with a child – a baby? Why would she abandon a child – why? There must be a reason."

"John, Man,"

John waited, watched as Angus looked again at the letter from Thomas Begvious.

"Even if the guy is telling the truth," Angus said. "How about he added two and two together and came up with five. What if…?" He averted his eyes for a second before looking John straight in his. "What if she'd…?"

John watched his friend falter on the words he'd asked himself.

"What if she wasn't my mother? Is that what you're asking me, Angus?" John dropped the bag. "What if the pouch, the gifts, were things she'd stolen to sell and not for me at all? What if she'd just dumped me there so I'd fucking die in the night because I wasn't even worthy of a life then. Because…"

"She was some poor terrified young girl with a half breed child.

She…" Angus didn't finish.

"I've already thought that too," John removed the letter from Angus's hands as he spoke. "It doesn't explain things." He stopped and folded the letter before returning it to the pouch.

"We need to decide what we're gonna do, Man."

John touched the tiny artefacts, now safely hung around his neck on the chain Manda had crafted for him. "I think I want to keep searching," he said. "There's just so much that fell into place after I found out. The Hopi connection – the idea that to be Hopi involves a state of total reverence and respect for all things, the mythology, so much of it resonates…"

"John, Man," Angus said. "You were ill. Everything you read started to have meaning…"

"Because I was searching for some – some meaning, some reason for being…"

"She…" Angus began.

"She left me Angus," John said before Angus could finish. "Know something? Despite all my fantasies about whom my parents were. Why I was sent away. Why my life had to be lived behind the closed doors of a boarding school. Through all of it I never really envisaged a mother…" He stopped, his arms hanging straight to his sides, his hands opening and closing as if clutching at something. He could feel the tension in his jaw as if his mouth was reluctant to move.

Angus stepped forward, "Man," he said reaching out.

John found himself moving backwards. Watching as Angus withdrew the hand he was offering in comfort. "I never envisaged a mother, Angus," he said. "Somehow I never really thought of someone real. Someone who held me…" He let the words wrap around him. "But now I know. I must have meant something. Why would she fashion me the gifts? I need to know why, Angus. I need to know why someone…my mother, abandoned me." He felt his body slump, the trickle of tears a trace on his skin. The pain in his chest as if the world he wanted to save was resting upon him. He sat down.

They both sat in the almost silence, the air conditioning a constant vibration of sound in the background. John wiped the damp from his cheeks. Imagined the ticking of a clock where his heart was. Thought of how small he was in the Universe, aware of the slightness of his pain amidst the growing terror of the catastrophe of impending world events. Wondered why with so little time he had been handed a key to his past, while the possible future was shrinking with each moment. The door of oblivion waiting to slam if the national and international space and defence agencies, along with the scientific community, were unable to recognise the flaws in Franklyn's distorted, and adulterated version of the research he'd falsely put his name to, and, because of those inabilities, were unable to respond in time to the true threat identified.

"We need to decide what we're going to do, Man."

John looked up. So deep in his own strangling thoughts he'd almost forgotten Angus was there.

"Ogilvy can get us on a team. We'll be registered as postgraduate students on an Internship. It'll give us a way in. They're locating teams at fifteen sites worldwide."

John attempted to release the tension in his head by rubbing his temples. "Decide?" the single word was almost too much.

"Man," Angus's voice was strained. "You set this ball in motion and Planetary Defence…"

"Has three phases," John pulled himself up from where he was sitting as he spoke. "Angus," he said. "I need something for the pain."

# 46 NO CONSENSUS

The painkillers started to kick in.

"We need to drink more water," said Angus. "Ma always says that dehydration causes headaches. It's a sugar thing too. We need to eat more," he said, "or more often. It's about sugar drop how it affects…"

"I can't believe I was so naïve," John spoke.

"About?"

John shook his head. "About planetary defence, it…I, the three phases…"

"Phase one," said Angus, "is all about recognition of the threat or hazard of cosmic impact, and Phase Two is about surveillance of specific threats by several programs around the world. That's where we come in as part of Ogilvy's team. We'll be monitoring what's happening…"

"Angus." John said. "You realise that Phase Three is…"

"About impact mitigation, Man."

"And no matter how long it's been part of the agenda there's no universal consensus on how impact threat should be handled."

"But, Man, they're already working on the find of, or reconstruction of the capstone. All of the land sea and air services are being prepared for mobilisation…"

"Angus," John said. He wanted to say it might all be too little too late, but fought back against the sense of negativity clawing its way to the surface. Instead he considered his own incredulity. Recognising just how vulnerable the world was to cosmic threat was becoming more and more mind blowing.

"Angus, it's crazy," he said. "Can't you see how crazy it all is – that there's been nothing in place – a three stage planetary defence with no preparations to deflect or intercept a threat to this planet?"

"They're working on it, Man. Are we in on the Chile excursion with Ogilvy or not?"

"Yes," said John. "But first I want to find…at least try and find…my mother."

"Working on it, Man," Said Angus. "Working on it…"

# 47 RATTLED

John felt the grip of fear but refused to respond to its embrace. He'd not considered that the trip to Chile would demand this excursion in what appeared to be no more than a tin can of an aircraft. Angus had sensed his building anxiety as they boarded.

"Regular means of transport," he'd said. "Safe as your standard jet flight, Man."

He noticed how Angus didn't look quite as confident now as they appeared to be cutting above some serious storm clouds. The light aircraft almost rattling in its efforts to keep on course, as the bank of grey ahead suddenly enveloped the plane.

"Gonna get a little rough here, Man," Angus's voice sang out at the same time as the sudden vanishing of the light.

John felt his stomach plummet and the grip of Angus's hand on his arm. The terror of flying he thought he'd almost overcome resurged tenfold. He froze, but willed his heart to start beating again. He closed his eyes.

It seemed like hours, but was probably within minutes that the plane appeared to stabilise, the light of the sun bursting through the small space; scalding the flesh of his eyelids.

"Through, Man."

John released the breath he was holding. The pilot was silent, focused only on the controls.

"Freak weather front. It's cleared now. Take a look out of the window, Man," Angus said.

John tried to comply, tried to relax his muscles, but his neck had seized in a solid unmoving column.

"I can't," he edged the words out.

"No sweat, Man. If it's any consolation my guts took a parachute jump back there too."

"What's landing in one of these like?" John didn't really want to know the answer, but talking seemed preferable to remaining in terrified silence.

"Pretty good," said Angus. "Getting out alive and onto the tarmac is even better!" He laughed. "Kiddin, Man. This guy up front flies this thing all the time."

# 48 FRIENDS

The attempt at landing was everything he'd tried not to think about, but had. They circled, dipped, almost landed, but didn't because of a vehicle on what he assumed passed as a runway. If he'd have managed to eat anything before they'd set off, he was pretty sure it would no longer be residing in his stomach.

He felt the way he had all those years ago after joining Angus in sampling the marijuana that one of Paul Yeager's roadies had forgotten to safely conceal. An overwhelming nausea accompanied by the feeling that his head was blowing up big enough to pop. Tex was the guy's name. He'd gone ballistic when he'd realised the missing joint had been smoked by the two kids the 'boss', Paul Yeager, the Wildman, had brought along for part of the tour. He'd begged them never to do it again and pleaded with Angus not to tell the Old Man.

They never had done it again – at least John hadn't – and Paul Yeager never knew. Tex had become a firm friend, whose American drawl had outdone even Paul Yeager's and lived on in Angus long after Tex had moved on. Angus had loved the guy.

"Preparing to land."

It was the first time he'd heard the pilot speak. There'd been no quips or jokes, no running commentary on the features that defined the landscape below. Angus, who John could see out of the corner of his eye, looked relaxed, though his gaze was fixed on something in the near distance. John tried to do the same as the pilot took them down. By the time they'd climbed out and spotted Ogilvy, at the far edge of the makeshift airstrip, climbing from his own truck, accompanied by Haziq, the pilot was already taxiing off again.

Ogilvy was heading toward them, his determined strides deleting the distance between them in moments. He grabbed Angus's hand to shake first, before turning and gripping John's shoulder as he greeted him with a firm handshake also.

"Glad you could make it. I've sorted all the paperwork. Looks like you had some freak weather coming in. This place usually boasts the clearest skies…"

"Is it not to be expected?" Haziq had reached them; his question offered as he gently pummelled first John's arm, then Angus's, in a gesture of friendship.

Ogilvy suddenly looked grim – the smile gone. "A significant amount of work has already been done, but it's not an easy task," he said as he motioned them toward the truck. "There has never been an international synthesized response mechanism or strategy, for reasons that are obvious."

"But the weather changes are already showing on the radar?" Despite knowing that the answer would be yes, John asked the question.

"Freak storms and unexpected eruptions – yes," Ogilvy pulled open the back of the truck as he spoke.

Angus and John took the cue and threw in their rucksacks.

Ogilvy slammed the door shut. He continued, "The key problem has always been that most of the radar and space surveillance systems set up by International Security have been set up in order to identify and deflect nuclear threat…"

"The warning systems," said Haziq, as he pulled open the passenger door, "are using the technology developed to differentiate between nuclear attacks and asteroid impact."

John acknowledged Haziq's comment with a movement of his head. His own research had thrown up the fact that every year about thirty asteroids entered the Earth's atmosphere before exploding. Miraculously many of the explosions occurred over uninhabited landmass or ocean. But the western world had to be alert to the impacts, which could release as much energy as the Hiroshima A-bomb simulating a missile strike and precipitating nuclear conflict. It had been argued by key people, that the US should take responsibility for alerting the world to asteroid or near-Earth objects that threatened life through impact, or instigation of a nuclear response from less developed countries, who may unwittingly perceive the collision of an asteroid as a nuclear attack.

They climbed in the truck. Ogilvy took the wheel with Haziq beside him. John and Angus settled in the back.

"Afraid the ride here may well be as bumpy as you found the flight," Ogilvy fired the engine causing a rising mist of sand as he spoke. "I've organised for our team to stay on one of the lower reaches," he continued. "There's more air there and we'll be more isolated and have less contact with some of the other teams that have been flown in…"

"I think it would be correct," said Haziq curtailing Ogilvy's flow of explanation, "to tell John and Angus who else is here." Haziq turned in his seat to face John and Angus in the back.

"It wasn't planned," said Ogilvy.

"This team some kinda top secret or something, Man?" It was the first time Angus had spoken since they'd landed.

"Fielding and Franklyn were flown in last night as part of the NASA advisory team," Ogilvy caught John's eye in the rear view mirror as he spoke. "They were not listed previously for this mission."

"Bad pennies, Man," Angus almost snorted. "They always turn up."

John felt his face flush under Ogilvy's rear view mirror scrutiny. He was only just beginning to lose the flight-induced nausea. Already it was tearing back.

"So, what's the plan?" Angus questioned as if the whole atmosphere in the truck hadn't changed.

"We'll go up of course," answered Ogilvy. "It's what we've planned. I've just tried to rearrange the timing. We'll need to get you both medical clearance first because of the..."

"Altitude," said John, glad his voice hadn't dried up.

"Yes," Haziq agreed. "Oxygen tanks will be necessary. They will provide you with a run through of what you need to know. It is procedure."

"How long is he here for?" John asked.

"Franklyn?" Ogilvy needlessly sought clarification.

"Yes," said John. "Franklyn," Just saying the name layered anxiety on top of the nausea. "I don't want to come into contact with him. Not yet."

"It is understood," said Haziq. "He is a man here on false pretences."

"Fielding," Angus spat out the name. "Man, I bet the Guy doesn't even realise he's going to be taken for a ride."

John considered his options. He wasn't sure why he was here or what could be achieved. He certainly didn't want to find himself in the company of Franklyn or Fielding either, but the thought of a return journey on the light airplane, before he'd even recovered from the one he'd just experienced, wasn't something he was keen to do. He touched the gifts from his mother, which hung around his neck. At least he had the sense of some protection. He'd stick with it. Keep on trying to work things out.

"I have my mobile for contact," Ogilvy said, moving the conversation on. "I've asked for clearance in the control room down here tonight as the others will be either on the summit in the observatory, or in conference with the other teams. We'll be able to monitor the situation as it is at present."

"The international multi agency strategy," asked Angus, "is it coming together?"

"As well as can be expected under the circumstances of decades of secrecy." Ogilvy paused to change gear in order to take the truck up a slope. "But," he continued, "despite the threats there are experts from all related disciplines."

"Physicists, astronomers, geologists, cosmologists..." said Haziq.

"The Military too," added Ogilvy.

"It is almost, as if this is something that goes beyond politics and cultural differences. So many are prepared to work together..." Haziq tailed off.

John guessed he was remembering that the inability to disentangle the cultural and political from the scientific and the greater good had cost the lives of his parents.

"Yet there is still the fear of sharing too much expertise and knowledge," Ogilvy's voice rattled and shook as he spoke. "Surveillance grid," he said by way of explanation. He slowed, pulled on the brake as a small rectangular concrete building came into view. Turned toward Angus and John in the back seats, "Our hotel, my friends," he said, a smile tugging at the corners of his mouth.

# 49 FACE IT

"This is one weird place to be, Man." Angus was staring out the now open, previously closed, metal shuttered window in the bunkroom Ogilvy had advised was to be their accommodation.

Haziq had gone to make coffee and rustle up some food.

"It's almost like being in a..." Angus continued, "like being on an isolated uninhabited planet." He turned to John. "I feel bad for dragging you out here, Man. But you're the guy who set all of this in motion; you should be part of the action. I didn't know the bad guy would be here too."

John shrugged off his jacket. "Sometimes," he said undoing the catches on his rucksack, "sometimes the things, the people," he added sliding the laptop from the bag, "we want to avoid, or escape from, have a nasty habit of refusing to disappear." He retrieved his notebook from the side pocket then sat down on the bed and laughed. "I still can't believe I keep on getting on these planes. I said I'd never..."

"You always had to be distracted, Man."

"And now it's almost as if I keep on having to face the things I've tried so hard to avoid. I thought we were going to die on the way in on that..."

"Tin can?" said Angus.

"Tin can," John agreed.

# 50 SHIFTING

Haziq had set up the computer with a direct wireless network link to the mainframe in the control room before he and Ogilvy had set off. He'd flicked the switch and the screen had flared.

Within minutes they were watching the recreation of the images recorded by telescope from the previous days. John, despite his knowledge, and the years of research that had led him to hypothesise and predict the changes that would start to occur apparently randomly and unexpectedly before accelerating as a result of celestial chaos, was mesmerised by the evidence rapidly emerging.

He couldn't take his eyes of the incredible reconstruction. He knew that the birth of the solar system was the result of a volatile capsule of time over four billion years ago. Collapse, condensation and collision in the part of the galaxy known as our own had led to the formation of a glowing red sphere igniting its nuclear furnace and becoming the Sun. He knew how the debris of those collisions and explosions – the dust, pebbles, boulders, the so called 'dirty balls' called comets, had taken billions of years to be swept up by the revolving planets. Yet now the debris – the dust, was forming again.

To the untrained eye it may have seemed no more than a mild and unthreatening meteorite storm – the type of spectacle that often had people sitting in their gardens and yards, or hanging out of windows to watch on a clear night. This was more than that. It was, if they didn't move quickly – maybe even if they did, the signal of the beginning of the end.

Three hours later, John was again working on his own laptop. Angus who'd lain down and dozed for an hour or more was now awake and up hovering over his shoulder. John tried to ignore him.

"You're supposed to sleep, Man."

John turned, taking in the tension in Angus's voice, recognising the pallor of tiredness on his face.

"Angus," his voice was harsh. He could almost hear the frustration seeping out of him. "I can't sleep. Don't you understand? It's taken billions of years for the world – this Earth – to reach the state of semi-stability we've known in our lifetimes."

"But, Man," Angus said, before turning abruptly.

John looked at Angus's back. "I've got to do this," he said, though even to himself his words sounded weak. His mouth was dry. He kept on reaching for the bottle of water beside him. "I didn't expect to see the dust swirls, the debris already forming." He glanced back at his laptop. "I've got to keep working on this."

"You don't think it's gonna be controlled. Is that what you're saying? Tell me, John. Is that what you're saying?"

John felt an unmistakable shudder run through him. Maybe Angus was as aware as he was that time could be slipping away.

"What I'm saying..." He tried to think of a way to say what he was thinking without inspiring even more dread than seemed to be already present in Angus's eyes. "I'm saying that I need to keep working on the calculations. The hundred and one factors I've been trying to synthesise. Franklyn has taken what he wants from my research and..."

"Bastard," Angus punched the wall as he issued the expletive, obviously regretting it as he shook his arm to relieve the pain.

John put his laptop on the bunk and stood up. "Don't..." he said, reaching for Angus's arm.

Angus pulled himself away; sat on the one metal chair by the wall he'd just struck.

"I'd like to have done that to that Franklyn slime, Man."

"Me too," said John.

They both laughed.

"But my main concern right now is that he's using disparate elements of my work. I know I've said it before, but it may not be enough."

"Cherry picking – Is that what you're saying?"

"In a sense – he's using the big stuff the..."

"Man," said Angus. "It's all big stuff..."

"No it's more than that, Angus. He's focusing on the major factors which will provide him with status in the international science community and..."

"The military, the political, the bastard's got a whole bunch of people from several countries eating out of his hand. He's got a fucking entourage bigger than Madonna!"

"I know," John said, then sat back down.

Angus started to laugh. "And the guy can't even sing." He flexed and unflexed his fingers; balled his fist before rubbing his hand. "If quantum physicists are right, John, and matter is no more than energy without any real solidity, why the hell does it hurt so much when you try and put your fist through it?"

John couldn't help himself from smiling. But he wasn't going to be pulled in to a debate on quantum physics, despite the unwarranted desire to do so, when there were so many other important things to consider. It was still something he was desperately working on in his mind.

He already knew of the research being conducted, where energy was converted into matter. It was no fantastical theory. Particle accelerators were known to convert energy into subatomic particles. The difficulties were in collecting the particles that were created. There were conservation laws, and the unfortunate ability of anti-matter combining with matter and turning itself back into energy. Like everything else it was complex. But the fact remained that Angus was still in pain and rubbing his hand.

"D'you need to go up to the Infirmary? It may be…"

"Nah, Man. I was just pondering the reality of pain. Just an attempt to think about something more ordinary than exploding Universes! What is it you're looking at besides the calculations?" He stood up. "But wait. Let me find us something to eat first."

The sandwiches were as tasteless as all the other food they'd eaten. It had all come pre-packed in cling film in chill boxes. John guessed it was all pre-frozen then defrosted before being delivered. It may as well have been cardboard, but Angus was right they still had to eat, and judging by Angus's empty plate John reckoned that even cardboard tasted good to Angus. He swallowed the lump of defrosted dough in his mouth and offered his own remaining two sandwiches to Angus, who smiled broadly before taking them and proceeding to wolf them down.

They swallowed the last of their coffee.

"Brief me," said Angus. "Tell me where we're up to. I'm losing track of where all this is going. I thought, well I guessed, that once we were here we would chum up with some of the good guys and infiltrate. Ogilvy thought so too."

"They're both still up there?"

"Seems like," said Angus. "Haziq is making connections with as many…" He paused, thoughtful for a moment. "No, I think he's sussing out who he can make connections with. Franklyn and Fielding turning up with the entourage is…"

"Limiting things," John said. It was true. He felt stifled. The journey, the flight in the tin can of an aircraft, and being caught in the freak storm all so he could be part of Ogilvy's team and find some way to communicate the elements of the massive puzzle that his research had identified, now seemed to be no more than a wasted exercise.

But had it? He'd been able to link up with the data gathered from the control room. He'd been able to read the observations, the light gathering from some of the best telescopes operating in the driest of skies in the clearest of nights anywhere in the world. He'd viewed the seemingly innocuous changes and knew that they were anything but.

"It's only limiting things in that I don't know where to go from here."
He paused. "It's hard trying to keep a tether on my thoughts. Every time I
make a new calculation, or see something that confirms what I've been
thinking, a whole new set of ideas comes hurtling in."

"That's why you're not sleeping, Man."

"I keep on writing things down," John said. "Things that might
connect, but even I'm losing track. I've tried to keep everything recorded
by writing it down getting it on the laptop backed up on the pen drive…"

"The back-up hard drive being, we assume, stolen by our esteemed Dr
Fucking Franklyn – academic extraordinaire? Weasel of the first kind."

"We've been through this before, Angus."

"The weasel?"

"No, trying to synthesise everything. You asked me to brief you on
where I'm up to. I need to, because if anything happens to me…"

"John, Man." Angus moved forward. "Don't go there, Man," he said.
"This is why you're supposed to sleep. Ma will kill me if you flip again on
my watch. She only flew back to be with the Old Man on the condition
that…"

"You looked after me?" John felt something stealing his breath.

Angus frowned, rubbing his jaw, which had suddenly slackened as if
the muscle beneath his skin had dissolved.

"She just worries, Man. She's doing everything she can to trace the
lady – your ma…"

"My mother…?"

"She's got all sorts of searches going on. She's looking at the
background to what was happening during the period of your birth. Not
everything associated with the Hopi people is recorded. They have their
secrets. Things they don't want to share with outsiders."

"She'll contact us if…"

"No sweat, Man. Ma, she'll contact us. So what's this brief I need to
know?"

Two hours later, after going through as much as his brain would allow
him to, John felt as if his head was a splintered mass. He'd been struggling
to simplify the pictures of his thoughts and transform them into words. It
wasn't easy. It had never been easy. The key factors remained the same –
Sirius A, Sirius B – the shift that hadn't been calculated for. His own
unbelievable error of calculation, the use of so many different calendars, the
evidence for an expanding Universe, Sirius B the reason it was understood
by the ancients – the reference to night, the dark. The capstone as anchor
to maintain the stability of the Earth now that it was clear that Sirius B was
shifting, and would be unable to act as the volatile cosmic energy plug to
hold the massive Sirius A and the Earth from collision. The positive and

negative energies, the need to understand the architecture of sound – the wave forms of quantum physics, acoustic resonance – the tendency of an acoustic system to absorb more energy when forced or driven at a frequency that matches one of its own natural frequencies of vibration, redshift and blueshift, the shifting frequencies – the known Doppler effect.

How could he explain that somehow he had a feeling beyond his own thinking – that the vibrational waves in matter were linked to something higher in the octaves of existence – the levels of being. How did he explain the existence of something even bigger than the Universe? Angus looked as exhausted as he himself felt.

"I don't know, Man," said Angus. "It's mind-blowing. We know some things for sure and that's the shift. We've already seen the evidence of the shift, so all your calculations and theories seem to be accurate. But it still all seems impossible." He leaned forward. "I mean…everything is still turning. We're still here. Ma and the Old Man are hauling rock to help build a new hospital. I can still turn on the radio, can even eat a sandwich that looks and tastes like cardboard and enjoy it. It just…" He stood up, moved over to the window. "Everything up there looks exactly the same as it always has. Only it's less pretty up here – though cleaner somehow. I don't think I can comprehend, grasp, or maybe accept what you're saying, Man."

"I don't think I can either, Angus. But it's all in my head gathering momentum."

"D'you think we should split, Man? Try and find another way – find someone else to listen? I mean…"

The throbbing pulse of the mobile phone cancelled out the conversation. John, distracted, watched as it danced with the momentum of its own sound across the metal bedside unit before reaching for it. He clicked on the display and read the message.

"They want us up at the Infirmary for the check up," he said. "I'd have thought Ogilvy or Haziq would have given us the call first." He clicked off the phone. "Does this mean Franklyn's gone?" He felt a weight lift off him as he asked the question.

"Guess he must've, Man. Means we'll have to walk. Ogilvy's got the truck."

They grabbed their things. John put his laptop and notes in his rucksack. Angus disappeared to the side room that housed the kitchen and bathroom off the narrow hallway then returned. They set off.

# 51 PARAMEDIC

They trekked in silence. Following the track upwards, stopping as the grey squat building came into view.

"Guess this is the place," said Angus. "Glad it wasn't so far. It's kinda surreal out here, Man. All these vast expanses – we should be touring, staying in some hotel in the foothills – eating fantastic food."

"Endless landscape," said John, "strange, barren. As if the life has been sucked from the Earth, makes me feel as if I've been trapped inside for months."

"The bunk room, Man?" said Angus, "pretty claustrophobic in there, I'm sure glad they buzzed us up here."

John adjusted the weight of his rucksack, aware of an empty feeling in his chest. "Me too," he said. "When I'm inside working on things, it's as if I can't let go. I just want to keep on. Yet once I'm outside I just want to keep moving. It's like I never want to go back in again." He gestured around him. "This place, like you said, the terrain, it's like a landscape from an uninhabited planet – an empty dry desert of mountains." He tracked the horizon with his hand. "Running North to South in three great ranges," he added, dropping his hand back to his side. "I read that the soil out here is almost indistinguishable from the soil – or sand, on Mars. It can't sustain life."

"Something else, Man," said Angus. "I know what you mean about wanting to keep moving. The wilderness – powerful as any drug; you keep on wanting just a little bit more, 'cos the thought of going back squeezes something dry at the base of your spine."

"If you hadn't got sick?"

"I'd a kept on movin, Man. The charity gigs I did across the Jordanian desert – the other places too. It was hard to come back. I didn't want to be closed in again." He pointed toward the sky. "I can see why they located this place out here. It's like being part way to the heavens."

"Yes," said John, "enabling a steady, cloudless view of the night – the nearest thing on Earth to the dark stillness of space."

"Maybe not quite as still as it should be, Man. And if all your hypotheses are right it's not still at all." Angus stopped, surveyed the building. "Do we knock or is there some kinda signalling device?"

John considered the blank façade. There were no buzzers or bells, nothing that could be interpreted as an intercom. "Maybe we're on the wrong…"

Before he could finish, part of the face of the structure opened, revealing a young pony-tailed man, garbed in a paramedic's suit.

"Ha!" said Angus. "Neat or what?"

The man came toward them. "Yeager?" he asked, his eyes squinting slightly against the brightness of the rapidly falling sun, "Begvious?" He thrust out a hand. "I am…" he began. "You will need…"

John saw the struggle in the young man's frown, guessed it to be the struggle to find the right words. "You need to see our security passes?" he said, reaching into his pocket as he asked the question, nodding to Angus as he did so.

"Sure, Man." Angus retrieved his own pass from the back pocket of his jeans before presenting it with a flourish. "We had a buzz to come up."

"Yes," the frown deepened as the passes were scanned. "Follow, this way with me please."

John and Angus did as they were bid. Entering a narrow foyer inside the building, before being taken through to what appeared to be a small operating theatre.

John saw Angus's face pale.

The Paramedic grinned. "No fears," he said. "It is a sump…no, a small…"

"Procedure?" said John, in an attempt to help.

The paramedic nodded. "My name is Edelmo. I like for you to sit please." He pointed toward a metal-framed table with a thin mattress rolled out across its surface.

John moved forward at the same time as Angus did.

"One only is better, please."

John noticed how Edelmo's use of English had suddenly improved and realised that, despite the faltering start, he probably needed to speak at least the basics of all the languages of the nationalities that came here. The earlier frown was probably more to do with the struggle of accessing the right lexicon to communicate in an appropriate language, than a struggle with the language itself.

Angus seemed to suddenly hold back so John sat on the bed.

"I am needing to check your blood." Edelmo took John's hand, reaching for a small blue peg as he spoke.

"Blood test," Angus's voice sounded at a slightly higher pitch than usual.

"Yes," Edelmo pressed something on a machine as he answered.

"Needles?" said Angus.

Edelmo smiled. "No, no," he said. "Is no needles just this." He clipped the peg onto John's finger. "Thees is the check for the blood. See the light ees there." He pointed. "It illuminate the blood…is calculate the oxygen levels to see if it safe for you to go up. I check also the pressure of blood. It is for safety. If all OK I prepare the tanks for you."

# 52 FEAR

"I'm not sure this was one of our better ideas, Man," said Angus, staring hard at the length of track in front of them. "Maybe we shudda waited."

"It's steep." John stopped, moved sideways across the track trying to see beyond the curve in the mountainside.

"Didn't seem that steep from where we were," Angus looked concerned, his comment almost a question to himself.

"Maybe it's the wrong track," John said as he re-hitched his backpack, weighed down even heavier now with the addition of the oxygen tank strapped to his side. "It seems amazing that this is necessary." He gestured toward the tank.

Angus shrugged his shoulders. "Beats me, Man. Guess it must be, otherwise we wouldn't have been buzzed up. Glad to get the pretty clean bill of health from Edelmo, though."

"We'll just keep on a bit further," said John, checking his mobile for the twentieth time. "Maybe there's a problem with signals up here – a time gap between sending and receiving. Ogilvy or Haziq should have called us by now."

"Edelmo said the pick up was on its way down, Man." Angus glanced at his watch before continuing, "That was almost an hour ago."

John considered the position. "Let's just try beyond that ridge," he said. "If there's nothing in view we'll head back down to the Infirmary."

They trudged on, the bend less easy to navigate than John had thought. The shape of the curve almost as hard to discern as the incline of the path was to climb. He picked up on the slowness of Angus's tread; the slight pallor of his friend, even before Angus stopped.

His own chest had begun to feel tight. He looked up ahead, aware that despite a further hours walk they seemed no nearer to the summit. The light was beginning to change, the sky already moving toward a deeper darker blue. He checked his cell again. Nothing.

"I'm going to try and see if I can pick up a signal," he glanced at Angus's white face as he spoke. "Just sit on the rocks at the side. I'll move around a bit; see if I can pick anything up."

Angus complied. "What did Edelmo say about the tank?" he asked, trying unsuccessfully to disentangle the straps of his pack from the oxygen tank.

John crossed the dusty track. "We use them on the lower numbers if we start to feel tired," he said. "Is it tiredness, just tiredness, or are you feeling breathless?"

"Kinda dizzy, bit nauseous, Man. I'll be OK. I'll just rest a bit. Just gimme a hand getting this."

Picking up on the slur of Angus's words as he tried to move the tank across his backpack, struggled to manoeuvre the breathing tube, John felt a rush of worry.

Aware that Angus's robust appearance, and even the checks at the Infirmary may not be taking into account the fact that he'd not long recovered from a seriously debilitating illness he moved forward. Shrugged the bag from his own back before helping Angus put on the mask and turn on the oxygen. Nothing happened.

He retrieved the tank from Angus. It felt lighter than the one he'd been carrying. He examined the controls and the nozzle, tried it to his mouth. He couldn't be sure because he'd never used a tank before but it seemed as if there was very little oxygen inside it, maybe none at all. He reached for his own tank and carried out the same procedure he'd just carried out on Angus's.

The slight hiss told him at least the one he was carrying wasn't faulty. He slipped the mask on Angus's mouth.

"Just keep it on till the nausea subsides," he said, fixing the empty tank in the side strap of his own bag before hoisting it onto his shoulder. "I'll track a bit further up – try and get a signal."

Angus grabbed his arm. Attempted to shake his head, took the mask away from his mouth. "No need, we'll share this…" He closed his eyes.

Feeling the chill already starting to seep into his back John shivered as he fitted the mask back on Angus's face. He wasn't sure if it was safe to leave him here. Neither of them was prepared. They hadn't even looked at a map. Edelmo had pointed in the general direction of the track they were now on before jumping on his moped and setting off back down toward the small town.

He rigged the backpack so that it was supporting Angus, keeping him fairly upright. He'd learned somewhere that breathing was more difficult when lying down. He took off his Jacket and placed it over Angus's shoulders before grabbing his bag.

"Ten minutes, no more," he said. "Then I'll turn back and we'll head back down."

He set off. Walked on. Couldn't deny he was beginning to feel progressively drained, wasn't sure of the distance he'd covered, but was sure it wasn't far enough to be making him feel the way he was feeling. He kept telling himself it was the sudden unexpected fear gripping his chest and making it more difficult to breathe as he continued toward the summit.

He glanced at his watch. He'd been walking no more than ten minutes. Realising he'd told Angus he'd be no more than ten minutes he'd already come too far. The ten-minute return trek would mean Angus would have been alone for at least twenty minutes by the time he trekked back. He faltered, stood unmoving, making a decision.

The light from the sun had almost disappeared. He should have remembered that night came on suddenly in places like this. There were no streetlights and the hulk of the barren mountainside was enough to cast a giant shadow across the track to exacerbate the rapidly deepening dusk. He focused ahead; sure he could see a light in the distance. If he just kept still maybe he could expand his lungs a little, stop his head from spinning, regain some strength in his legs.

He stumbled to the inner part of the track, mindful of the fact that even if the landscape appeared to stretch in a wide expanse of undulating hills, sudden, unexpected, sheer drops could go unseen at this height.

The wooziness was making him want to retch. He tried to focus on the light ahead, tried to discern if it was static. Maybe part of the building structures he was heading to. Maybe he was closer than he thought.

He wasn't sure if it was the dizziness or some kind of optical illusion but the light seemed to be moving. Moving toward him growing larger and wider, a spherical illumination moving fast, he staggered backwards. The light – it was blinding him. He tried to raise his hands, felt the sudden swoosh of air. Heard the sound of the engine as he threw himself sideways out of its way, was aware of rolling forward on the ground. Whoever it was mustn't have seen him. He tried to breathe, praying that Angus was still propped against the rocks out of harms way, as he tried to pull himself up. Sure that the danger had passed when it came toward him a second time.

The light and sound united. He felt himself turning, reaching out, yet spinning. The night awash with the crackling of adrenaline boosted fear. The spray of dust, the image of Angus propped against the side of the path a flashbulb recollection, the smell of his own sweat filling his nostrils, the anger that erupted from someplace deep as he grabbed for the tank. It was fast – too fast, everything moving at once in a twisted synchrony.

# 53 RELENTLESS

He could taste the salt of his own blood. Feel the pain of the gravel burns on the side of his face and his arms. The bike had gone back in the direction it had come from. It had to. He rolled over on his back and opened his eyes, the sky above him an explosion of billions of stars, a Van Gogh masterpiece – an expanding Universe. It took his breath away. A galaxy of secrets, relentless mystery – one he knew he still had to solve.

He needed to move. Get back down to Angus before either, or both of them, were added to the statistics of people who died on the mountains. Hyperthermia or lack of oxygen was usually the cause. Not a set up with empty oxygen tanks and an unexpected lone biker intent on driving someone off the ridge of the road.

It seemed beyond comprehension. Someone was seriously trying to kill him, maybe Angus too. He hefted himself up. The rucksack was gone. Only God knew why he'd had the flash of insight that made him hurl the empty oxygen tank. The bike had skittered and spun, the rider, his or her face hidden inside the helmet, struggling to keep control, the gravel spraying in an ark, the bike heading toward the edge before suddenly turning and disappearing the way it had come.

He started to edge his way down the mountain, continuing to pray that Angus would still be alive.

# 54 CONFRONTATION

"Why would a person do this?" Haziq said, his eyes unnaturally bright despite his tiredness.

"For a bag full of sandwiches, Man."

"That tasted like cardboard," added John. Remembering how when the rider had torn the bag from his shoulder it had been too quick to consider what was going on. The tank had slipped to the ground and rolled and somehow he'd grasped it as he fell and used it.

"I have not heard that there are bandits here." Haziq was shaking his head nonplussed.

"Haziq," Angus seemed much recovered, only the faint quaver in his voice belying his apparent confidence and assertions that he was fine. "Haziq," Angus said again. "Why would a bandit...?" He appeared to consider what he was trying to say. "No," he said. "How would a bandit have my mobile number? We were buzzed to go up to the Infirmary. That's how we set off on the..."

"Foolhardy expedition?" Haziq said.

"We assumed Franklyn had gone," said John. "We made a lot of assumptions."

"We were stir crazy here," added Angus.

"You think someone wanted to kill you?" Haziq's forehead furrowed as if he couldn't believe the question he was asking.

John turned away, an unexpected sense of shame forcing him to break eye contact.

"I know I've been ill," he spoke to the empty space in front of him before turning back. He stood in silence. Acutely aware of the time he'd spent at the hospital, the recuperation in Wales with Manda taking care of him. It was only now occurring to him that nobody had witnessed what had happened on the track. The bruising and the gravel burns could have been the result of a simple fall. The missing bag could just be a missing bag. His skin started to prickle. He could feel the faint mist of perspiration forming on his forehead. Haziq's eyes were unblinking. Angus was quiet. John could feel his heart beating. It felt weak, the beat no more than a tremor. He turned away again. Ogilvy had already gone to investigate who had made the call to the mobile phone.

"You are saying – said," said Haziq, "it was Ogilvy's number on the display?"

John wondered if Haziq was directing the question at Angus.

"Maybe it is possible we could check …" Haziq continued.

"You think I'm lying?" John could feel his hand forming into fists. His breakdown could – no – would, make everything he said or perceived questionable. Wasn't he the guy who thought the doctor in the hospital back in Arizona was Franklyn trying to kill him? He could sense the eyes of his friends through the skin of his back.

"You think it didn't happen?" He said the words to the blank wall in front of him.

"John…"

Haziq's voice sounded far away even though John could feel the strength of his friends grip on his arm.

"I didn't…"

John turned around before Haziq could finish, saw Haziq recoil. Saw the expression of surprise in Angus's eyes.

"I'm not crazy," he ground out the words, resisting the urge to smash his fist into the wall the way Angus had done. "I'm not crazy," he said again. "But I'm fucking angry."

"Man." He heard Angus say as he pushed his way past Haziq and out of the room.

He stood outside the slab of the accommodation block. His heart didn't seem weak now. It was practically breaking through the bones of his chest. If someone hadn't have tried to kill him last night he'd have marched out into the wilderness. A power walk – anything that would help free the tension that was locking his muscles into rigid spasm.

The landscape spread out before him offered no clues to the mystery biker. Any tread from the wheels, or evidence of the attack would be blown away. There was no way any imprints could be taken on such dry, gravelly and dusty ground. He wondered could it have been Edelmo?

Even if both he and Angus had seen Edelmo taking off in the opposite direction it didn't mean Edelmo couldn't have skirted some other path that took him upwards so he could make the return journey downwards. All he'd have had to do was lay in wait before having a perfect view of the two of them making their approach toward the ridge. Then John alone after Angus had taken ill. It seemed a strange coincidence that Edelmo had given Angus a clean bill of health – blood pressure, blood oxygen, when it was clear that Angus was not as fit as claimed.

He realised they'd both taken Edelmo's words and health clearance as fact. Neither of them checked the readings. Edelmo then provided them with faulty tanks – or at least one faulty oxygen tank. He'd known who they were. He'd had a call too. Had his call come from Ogilvy's cell too? He walked back inside.

There was no further talk till Ogilvy returned from his investigation. "There is no Edelmo," he announced as he sat down

"No wiry guy with a ponytail?" Angus offered the description that could fit a thousand or more young locals.

"He doesn't exist," said Ogilvy. He looked at John. "There are no records of anyone by that name and the Infirmary was not staffed yesterday evening."

"Hey…" Angus stood up from his bunk.

Ogilvy motioned for him to sit back down. "The facts you've given me. I'm not questioning the facts," Ogilvy said as he nodded toward Haziq. "The facts you've given to us." He looked at his phone. "The only way a call could have come from this cell is if someone had access to the lockers at the Observatory. I did not, I assure you, call you." He turned to John. "The rucksack, the bag torn from your shoulder by the biker, it was Angus's bag?"

"With my mobile, tucked in the side pocket," Angus sounded weary.

"So," Haziq said. "It is not possible to check any…"

"Of the details of the call," John finished for him.

"John," Haziq said. "It doesn't mean that we, or I, at any time did not think you were telling the truth."

John aware that Haziq looked nervous, his words sounding clipped, said nothing, wondered if there was any point.

Haziq held out a hand toward him. "I am sorry if I made you think that, John. If I made you think I did not believe you. You are my friend." He turned toward Angus. "You are both my friends. I know you would not lie – either of you."

John felt sick to his stomach. Haziq seemed cowed since the outburst, incident – confrontation, whatever it was that had dislocated their friendship earlier. He reached out and touched Haziq's wrist. "I know," he said. "I'm sorry too."

# 55 PLANNED

With no direct evidence to provide to police or security personnel there seemed little point in wasting time by making statements. Ogilvy had been wise enough to investigate matters regarding Edelmo and the Infirmary without drawing too much attention to what had happened.

The background to the whole scenario was unclear. The biker may well have been Edelmo; there may well have been an intention only to steal from two unsuspecting Postgraduate Interns.

Or the intention may well have been, as John and Angus suspected, a planned attempt to steal John's laptop with all its up to date data and information. What was clear, Ogilvy had said, was that there were obviously issues of safety. As their Supervisor, even if only in name for the purposes of gaining access to the Giza Star Track Operation team, he had to take responsibility for removing them from danger. He was organising a flight out. They were going back home.

# 56 BACKTRACK

"Something stinks, Man," Angus retched out the words before throwing a hand over his mouth and backtracking out the open door onto the patio.

"Stinks?" John dropped the bag he was holding. The mask of fear, which had almost instantaneously formed on Angus's face, a signal, which quickly revealed unthinkable possibilities.

John reached for his mobile. "Do we need to call the police?" he said, terror rendering his fingers almost immobile.

Angus was backing away from the house, wavering from side to side; moving slowly sideways till his legs touched the stone of the low wall that curved around the flagstones. He sat down.

"I don't know, Man. There's been nobody..." He seemed to be searching his thoughts.

John was just about to speak when Angus did.

"I think maybe..." Angus began; then stopped.

"What?" John heard himself shout, as Angus's mouth opened, just as his eyes became blank.

"Ma..." the roar erupted from somewhere deep in Angus's belly as he leapt to his feet and ran toward the house.

John saw the possible picture forming in his own mind too. The swell of emotion propelled him forward.

He lunged at Angus from behind. Tackling him to the ground; rolling him away from the door, pressing his forearm against Angus's chest, using his own full body weight to stop Angus from moving, "Angus," he heard the desperation in his own voice. "You can't go in there." He could feel Angus's heart thumping, could hear his rattling breathing. Feel the tension of his friend's muscles as Angus tried to fight him off. "It may be an animal," he said, all the time wondering if the crashing, thumping arterial crescendo against his ribs was maybe his own heart; not Angus's at all. "Something may have got in while we were in Chile," he said. It was the preferred scenario.

Angus was motionless, a glassy look, like a deflected mirror, dulling the expression in his eyes. "I'm going to phone 901," John said as he brought the phone up against Angus's shoulder, careful not to give any leeway for movement to his friend. "I'm staying here till they arrive."

The three squad cars arrived in minutes. John didn't move from where he was, lying atop Angus. He didn't want Angus making a run into the house. His faulty thinking became unpleasantly clear as the doors of the three police vehicles sprang open and a team of armed police took up position around the extended patio courtyard.

# 57 ABSENCE

John loosed the gag he had around his mouth. Angus did the same. Every window in the ranch house was open. The entire contents of the freezer had been binned, but the smell still lingered. Even in the outside courtyard there was too little breeze to clear the air.

"Man, I don't think I've ever been so scared." Angus clicked open a can and passed it to John before opening one for himself.

They both sat down.

"I switched the fucking freezer off, Man." Angus laughed out loud. "Why did I switch the fucking freezer off?"

John shook his head. He'd have liked to laugh but he couldn't. Not yet. "I can't believe how terrified I was," he said. He put the can to his mouth but didn't drink. "I reckoned it was my fault, was taking the blame. I've already drawn too many people into this, Angus. Maybe I should…"

"Should take up wrestling, Man. You're stronger than you think."

John looked at his arms, wondered where the strength had come from. Took a swig from the can in his hand, savoured the sharpness of the cool ginger beer on his tongue. Thankful for the functioning drinks fridge in the den. He removed the can from his lips. "I still can't believe what happened in the desert," he said, "then this today. I started to think…"

"Me too, Man." Angus downed his beer. "Once the armed squad didn't kill us, once they'd fell about laughing and taken off our handcuffs, all I wanted to do was speak to Ma and the Old Man. Thank God they're OK. Ma'll kill me if we don't have the stink cleared by the time she gets back, but other than that, Man, she loves me – loves you too, John boy."

Angus chinked his can against John's. "Juanita musta fled in terror when she opened the freezer." Angus grimaced. "I'm not surprised she didn't stay. Ma asked her to come over when she knew, when we texted we were heading back – let her know my phone had gone missing in case she was worried I'd not answered calls. I'll have to give her a call – apologise. I never knew a freezer could contain that sorta potential. Man. It was horrendous. What's it been four five days?"

John didn't have to calculate. "Six," he said. He took another taste of the canned ginger. Then placed the can down, wondered how they'd ended up back here cleaning the place. It was beyond a joke. It was ridiculous.

"We're going round in circles, Angus?" he said. "Why? We don't seem to be making any progress. I know they're supposed to be working on the capstone but…"

"Hey, chill," Angus, said. "Things are movin, even if it seems we're not. Folks in higher places are progressing things. Lucky they already had so many plans in place, Man. I didn't even know they'd planned to relocate the stone for the millennium. D'you think they can construct what's needed? From what I heard of the millennium plans it was more about a visual. They came in for some flack on that gig though, Man."

John considered. Maybe Angus was right. Things weren't entirely static, even if it seemed as if they were at a standstill. "It seems an impossible exercise," he said. "The belief is that the original capstone was made of gold." He paused, captured by the picture in his minds eye. The apex of the great pyramid a pinnacle of brilliance, reflecting the rising or falling light of the Sun. "Although," he continued, "there's no proof. You know the history?"

Angus smiled a resigned smile. "You're gonna tell me anyway, Man."

"Fact is," said John. "It seems hard to believe, but there are no records of anyone ever seeing a capstone on the Great Pyramid. We're talking as far back as the time of Christ, over two thousand years."

"Long stretch, Man," Angus acknowledged, before taking another drink from his can.

"Those who visited the site reported its lack – its absence," said John, continuing the story. "Some argue that it was maybe never finished. Which, when you consider the magnificent feat of engineering the pyramid represents, the idea of it never being completed is…" He reached for his drink. "I don't know. Why would something so fantastic, so incredible be unfinished?"

Angus shrugged in response.

"You know it's all about…" John said, moving the can around in his hands, "symbolism. The Egyptians called the capstone the pyramidian or sometimes they called the capstone the Benben…"

Angus held up a hand. "I'm gonna surprise you here, John boy."

John watched as Angus folded a hand around his jaw.

"Benben," he said, before putting down his drink. "It's a bird. It's tied in with the symbolism of a bird. Just give me a moment, Man. The picture's forming." He closed his eyes. "Yes, the symbol of the Bennu bird. Symbol of rebirth and mortality, like the Phoenix rising from the ashes, nothing ever dies it's just reborn, or can be." He opened his eyes. "How'd I do, Man? I'm not Manda's son for nothing."

"It means something," John said. "There's some link. The Phoenix as an immortal bird, that after death is reborn from the ashes of the flames that consumed it. But why the twigs – why does it need to ignite? How does it ignite itself?" He glanced at Angus. "Why is its cry like a beautiful song? Did Manda – your ma, talk about the sound of the song of the Phoenix?"

Angus shook his head. "Not that I remember. She sorta likened some of the myth to the Hopi belief. She gained enough respect to be included – invited to be part of one of their ceremonies. But she's so tender, Man. She was pretty cut up about the Eagles ritual…"

"Eagles ritual – The band? You mean something to do with the band – their music?"

Angus laughed.

"Wish I did, Man. No. The Hopi have a ritual, which involves the freeing of an eagles spirit through its sacrifice. The sacrifice is part of a religious ceremony to enable the eagle to carry messages between the spiritual and physical worlds." Angus gestured with his arm as if he was cutting through space. "She sobbed her heart out when she came home. But she recognises the rights people have to follow their own culture, even researched the meaning so that she could provide evidence to support new regulations which enable indigenous people to carry out their ceremonies without breaking any laws. You know, Ma."

"Maybe we need to finish the cleaning," said John. Conscious of all the Yeager's had done for him. Even now Angus was sticking out his neck, threatening his position at the university, getting himself tied up with people robbing and setting fire to the Yeager house, being stalked by so called bandits on lonely tracks. "It's not good that I've managed to get you caught up in all of this with me," he said.

"Hey," said Angus. "No sweat. You're my honorary brother."

"The breakdown, everything that's happened," said John. "Sometimes I feel more of a…well less of an honorary son or brother," he paused, "sometimes I feel more like a burden…"

"Man," said Angus. "Remember the song – He Ain't Heavy, He's…"

"My brother?" said John.

"The one," said Angus. "Hollies 1969, worldwide hit. Written by Bobby Scott and Bobby Russell." He laughed. "How come a young dude like me knows so many songs from the past?"

# 58 BADLANDS

"I know we agreed," said Angus. "But no-one wanted to talk to us, Man." He turned in his seat and faced John. "Ma, she…" He hesitated. "She's got some way in with these people…"

"Just another wasted journey," said John. "I shouldn't have dragged you out here."

"The guy, Begvious," Angus said. "How come you didn't try and find…"

"I thought if I didn't know I couldn't be any angrier than I already was."

"We tried, Man," said Angus. "Shot in the dark but we tried."

John closed his eyes, the longing for a miracle still holding him hostage to hope. They'd travelled out to speak with the small group of people who refused to be forced into a way of life outside their beliefs and culture. There was a woman. Maybe Manda shouldn't have told them. A woman whom she'd traced. A woman she'd found who had special responsibility for caring for pregnant girls and woman within the Hopi Clan during the period from nineteen-sixty-nine onwards.

There was some possibility, Manda had explained in the email she'd sent him, that of all the people involved with the natural childbirth methods of the Hopi during the time of John's birth, Joanna had a special role. If anyone outside of mainstream medical care could remember a Hopi girl, either pregnant, or one who had recently given birth, disappearing, it would be Joanna. Manda had gone on to explain how she was working through an intermediary to try and arrange a meeting with Joanna outside of the Hopi reservation.

John hadn't wanted to wait. He knew he was wrong now. He'd barely read the email before he was pulling out maps and planning the journey. Despite Angus's initial refusal to go along with the plan, the pressure John applied meant he'd eventually capitulated.

"Man," he said. "If it makes you happy we'll go." He'd started printing off maps straight from the Internet.

John remembered waving the ones he'd already set aside to go in the bag.

"No good, Man," Angus, said. "These people like to stay clear of the beaten track. Ma'll kill me. But we'll find the place."

They'd found it. It had taken them from before dawn till after six in the evening to complete the trip. The radio reports on the journey warning of unexpected weather change. He'd wanted to tell Angus to turn back, but the desire to speak with someone who might know of his mother had stolen the words. Part of him knew what he was doing wasn't right. Manda would be hurt – maybe angry. But he couldn't, didn't want to, deny the longing.

They parked miles from the site, which Angus had only been able to locate with the help of Manda's paperwork associated with the work she'd engaged in. Checking the radio before they'd left the truck. The weather news wasn't good, but the sky turning from the pink of dawn to the clear blue of morning above them gave no hint of change.

John knew the weather was no longer something that had any power to keep its promise, but the sense of urgency to find the woman who'd given birth to him was stronger than his sense of survival. Given the accelerated timeframe of the possibility of cosmological catastrophe he couldn't afford to wait. The chance to make connection, he'd reasoned, may never be possible again. It had been another wild, ill-considered plan. Like everything else he did, doomed to failure.

They'd travelled out to this place, The Painted Desert to its people, for nothing. Both of them had been treated with suspicion. No one answering their questions, and, if the woman Joanna, had been available to speak with, both she, and the people he and Angus had spoken to, hadn't wanted to admit it. The news of the swiftly moving volatile weather front had drawn a sharp indelible line under any further opportunities he and Angus may have sought to find a way to engage with a people who had tired of the questions of strangers. He realised he'd probably made things much worse with his anxious behaviour.

He'd been trying desperately to take in his surroundings, the faces of the people moving around him, searching for some likeness, hoping for some recognition some way to know if he belonged. He hadn't found it. But he'd seen a look in the eye of a woman they'd attempted to speak to. Her eyes had been so dark. Yet almost warm and welcoming till Angus had mentioned the year nineteen eighty-eight, asked if she remembered anything about a missing girl. She'd averted her eyes too quickly. Then in a flash she'd returned their gaze with eyes no longer warm, the pupils of which had shrunk to the size of pinpricks.

"No," she'd said before turning away again. She'd retreated from them, shouting over her shoulder that she needed to prepare for the incoming storm.

Angus, keen to get moving, and scanning the horizon in a flurry of maps and concern identified a route that would take them around a ridge away from the dust that was starting to swirl up. They'd walked the distance. Now they were back. Glad to be in the safety of the truck.

They'd hardly spoken on the journey to the parking spot, had been more involved with keeping to the route Angus had chosen.

John, disappointment entwined with the pressure of guilt at exposing them both to further danger was silent as Angus fired up the engine, waiting for the slow steady hum that would inform that it was safe to shift gears and move.

Angus clicked on the radio. The static of transmission settled. The news report advised that nothing had changed. The five hundred mile wide storm with winds of over eighty miles per hour was surging across the landmass with New York and other large cities stationed along the predicted path.

"They're not telling anyone," John said, closing the uneasy distance that had settled between them.

"I'm hoping she'll move," said Angus, fixated on the challenge of attempting to start the engine.

Belatedly, John realised that just because they were safely inside the truck didn't mean they were going anywhere. Angus had expressed his concern that the engine could get clogged with sand before they'd even set off. John had ignored him just like Angus was ignoring him now.

A whirring sound came from the front of the truck. Angus slammed his hand against the steering wheel. "Why aren't they telling anyone?" he said, trying again to start the engine. "You're asking me why they're not telling anyone. The truth, Man, you wanna know why they're not telling anyone the truth?" He tested the accelerator. A high-pitched whine emanated from somewhere behind the dashboard. "This baby's playing for time," he turned as he spoke.

Seeing the beginning fabric of fear in Angus's eyes John quickly surveyed the indigo and purple streaked clouds heavy with rain advancing across what had began the morning as a clear blue sky.

"Is it not going to move?" The question was a pointless one. Even if the entire vehicle wasn't flooded with sand and other debris the approaching storm would surely get them before they'd be able to cut back up to the higher reaches and some sort of protection.

Angus turned off the engine. The radio continued to spill out its incessant reminder of the suddenness of change. Several million people were being ordered to leave their homes as part of a massive evacuation. Over two thousand shelters were already being erected.

"I should have known," said John. "But I can't believe the speed it's happening..."

"Faster than anticipated, Man."

John noticed the sudden calmness in Angus's voice, watched as Angus began collecting things from the glove compartment.

"We're going back up?" Angus said as he reached behind the seat and grabbed his rucksack.

John grabbed his own from the footwell, kept there to protect the precious laptop.

Angus climbed from the truck and waited. His gaze fixed on the gathering cloud sweeping across the horizon.

"I'll get what we need from the back," John said.

Angus said nothing just continued to stare. His hands clutching the rucksack, his throat moving almost imperceptibly in an attempt, John imagined, in swallowing the same kind of terror he could feel in his own.

Heaving the truck door against the weight and strength of the wind John felt the hope inside him begin to ebb. The news report had advised that people were already out on the streets, battling floods or preparing to defend against them. Emergency services were being stretched to the limit. There were rescue teams already gearing up for what could be a full alert. Over four hundred trucks had been loaded with supplies and in excess of a hundred thousand troops of the National Guard were on standby. Still the world didn't know. John couldn't deny the creeping sense of self-hatred he was experiencing for dragging Angus here. Out into a place with no immediate shelter, on a mission driven by needs that were his alone.

Easing his body through the narrow space that the gale was allowing between the inner security of the truck and the squall of the building storm outside, he mentally ran through the options for safety in the here and now. They could stay here, barraged by the metal of the vehicle, in the hope that the threat of the hurricane would veer past them. If it didn't, and they were trapped inside, the whole tonnage of metal could be wrested and moved in the hard rain that was preparing to burst from the darkening clouds.

He looked up the rocky path. Angus had said there were caves up there. Places where some of the peoples who couldn't cope with the changes had fled. He could see Angus still staring at the Horizon. Although maybe not. He couldn't see his eyes maybe they were closed. Maybe Angus was praying too.

Unlocking the rear door, John battled against the gusts to pull the container of food and water through the available opening before stretching for the jackets. He felt the sudden smattering of rain anoint his skin as the thunder rolled, followed almost instantaneously by a burst of lightning that lit the blackness the sky had become. "Angus," he heard himself shout. "We've got to move."

They stumbled up the track, a strange absence of sound around them. The sky had stilled and the rain that had momentarily touched John's face had stopped. He wondered if they'd have been safer in the truck. Angus still wasn't speaking. His back was slumped and despite the need to move quickly his pace was slow.

John tried to think clearly. He knew so little about the wilderness. The threats, the topography of this place, Angus would normally have been the one to know what to do, but he'd gone somewhere in his head. Or maybe he was conserving his strength in case he lost the ability to breathe as he had in Chile. At least the tempest that had threatened was stalling in abeyance as they made the climb. It was giving them the gift of time.

The feeling in his ankle was fleeting. Yet the ground rose up to meet him at speed, the weight of the rucksack on his back propelling him forward without mercy. The cry that escaped his lips as he rolled on the ground surprised him. Then he saw it. Half hidden by some abundant desert scrub of plant life he had no experience to identify. The opening was narrow, but wide enough for a man to squeeze through. It was positioned up from the path by a boulder shaped step. "Angus," he shouted, the pain in his ankle forgotten. "I've found a cave."

The flash of lightning blazed the sky. From where he stood in the frame of the opening in the rock, the plain below lit up, the lavender, red, orange and pink brushstrokes of some unseen artist flattering the long expanse of badland hills and buttes.

For seconds the world was bathed in light then eclipsed by the jet of night. The clouds cracked open. The deluge began.

# 59 TERROR

John forced himself to move. Hands wary against the damp rock as he felt his way along the walls of the cave, struggling to block out the skittering sounds; the fear of the oppressive darkness cramping his throat.

He needed a way out of the cave – a path to a higher level, an opening of escape. It was clear it led upwards. The ground beneath his feet was curving. He could feel the incline. How far it went, or if it went anywhere at all he didn't – couldn't know. He needed to find out. As, despite the relative safety of being protected within this chasm on the elevated path, the torrent of rain was forming a river between the ridge of the rocks outside. He could hear it even if, in the periods of inky black darkness, he was unable to see it.

If only there was some daylight. The voice in his head nagged like a faulty mantra bringing no comfort or peace. He continued his slow progress. If there were daylight he would be able to see if this fetid smelling tunnel led anywhere. The path outside the cave was no longer safe. The water flowing down was carrying all sorts of rock and rubble. They'd barely pulled away the overgrowth of foliage and climbed in before the track was running in flood. The rise to the mouth of the cave no more than eighteen inches, he'd hoped it would be enough. But the dampness he felt in the softness of the mulch under his feet indicated the place took in rain and maybe even flooded completely.

He thought of Angus stumbling inside the cave, positioning himself against the wall. Not speaking. Wordless. His hands clasped in front of his face, his teeth pressing into his knuckles.

John bent down. Despite his resolve he was trembling. The terror of the dark had never left him, but, he kept reminding himself, he wasn't blindfolded now. There was no Master Berke in control. No bunch of quietly sniggering pre-pubescent schoolboys watching him. He was alone in this space. It was his choice.

He'd asked Angus to turn on the emergency lantern at periodic intervals. Hopeful that the distance he'd travelled would be easier to gauge if he could see the flicker of light behind him. There was no light now. He inhaled. The dank smell of rotting plant life assailing his nostrils. He placed his hand on the ground. Feeling the sudden urge to retch as his diaphragm and oesophageal muscles contracted as realisation dawned. It was wet. The entire cave must flood at some point.

He was moving back now, afraid for Angus, afraid for himself too, hoping that the emergency lantern hadn't run out of charge. It was supposed to be good for eight hours. He moved faster, unable to hear if the storm was continuing to rage because of the sound of his own racing blood supply. He began to call out to Angus. His voice echoing off the rock walls, the panic inside him twisting and turning. There was no answer. He opened his mouth to call again. The sudden flash of lightning sending him reeling.

The mouth of the cave illuminated. Angus was lying face down on the floor of the cave.

# 60 VULNERABLE

"Anguuuuus…" the sound that ripped from his throat, reverberated along the tunnel, wrapping, moulding and bouncing against the rock on its defined course before returning and exploding in an echo through his skull. He scrambled forward, legs barely able to hold his weight.

Without the light he couldn't mark his progress. Only the change in air quality gave evidence that he was nearing the hollowed out space in the rock where Angus lay.

He tripped and fell, his hands touching the remnants and wastes of nature. He shuddered, awareness of the threat surrounding them, firing his brain with the volt of an electric line. They could die here, trapped in this hidden crevice, this secret crypt. All his doing – his fault, he'd involved too many people. Put people he cared for at risk. Failed to take responsibility for the truths his research had uncovered and gifted to him. The world was in danger of being destroyed. The beautiful Earth, the spinning globe of mountains, raging rivers, forests and lush pastures, vulnerable and helpless against the might of the Universe, if Angus was still alive he had to get them out.

Fighting off the shame that threatened, he edged forward on his hands and knees listening for the sound of Angus's breathing.

Touching the softness of flesh he let out a long narrow hiss of sound. Angus was still warm. He moved quickly in the darkness. Checking the pulse in the wrist of the hand that he'd grasped, thanking God he could feel the weak but steady throb. Pulling his friends body into the recovery position, the simple skill he'd learned – thought he'd never use.

He could feel Angus's breath against his own cheek. Angus was still alive. They both were. Fumbling for the lantern he found it, pressing the on switch as he dragged it toward him. The light glimmered then brightened. He felt helpless, Angus's head; maybe even his life, in his hands. He knew so much about outer space yet so little about the workings of the inner man.

He remembered Julia in the counselling room, the soft sway of her hair as she moved her head, her half closed eyes. Something she'd said. It escaped him now. He thought of her mouth. Wondered what it would be like to kiss her. Would he be too scared? He'd always been too scared of everything, had always known so little about the world.

He pulled a towel from the rucksack, rolled it and rested Angus's head upon it. Tried to think, there had to be something he could do. There was no point trying to call for assistance. All the emergency services would be fully occupied. He checked Angus's pulse again, placing his face against Angus's mouth. Registering the awareness that Angus seemed to be in some sort of unconscious state.

Why had Angus become suddenly withdrawn then keeled over? Again he felt the crush of guilt. He should have insisted that Angus saw a doctor when they'd returned after the collapse on the mountain track. Instead they'd come out here.

If Angus was in some sort of a coma there had to be a reason. He chased the thought around in his mind, swinging open doors from the past searching for memories, some way of understanding, trying to find an answer to the question screaming in his mind. "How can I help him?" he said out loud, the words, a prayer, flying into the vacuum of the half lit prehistoric space.

Sugar! It came to him. People went into comas through lack of sugar. Angus was always eating. Always had been someone who couldn't go long without food. Reaching for the holdall that held the food container John hoped he was right.

It wasn't immediate, but Angus's eyes eventually flickered open and closed again several times. John continued to rub the chocolate bar across his friend's lips, letting it melt into Angus's mouth in gradual stages. Terrified he may be doing the wrong thing, but aware of the paucity of alternatives. Time seemed to be stretching and narrowing out. His back ached. His shoulder and arm where he held Angus's weight were numb. He wondered if he was wasting his time. Then felt the unmistakeable pull as Angus tried to move.

"Man," Angus said as he opened his eyes.

John felt the sudden lift of hope.

"We still alive?" Angus said, his eyes struggling to focus in the dim light.

John lowered his arm, felt the sharp jag of pain from nerves deprived, then suddenly supplied with blood. "Just about," he said as the tears started to run down Angus's cheek. "Angus," he said, "You're crying... Don't... I...it's OK. It's OK..."

"Nah," Angus sobbed, as he pulled himself upright and wiped the tears away. "My eyes are just leaking, Man. That's all."

# 61 CONNECT

"I'm going to have to learn to drive."

"Drive?" Angus turned.

"I should have learned to drive years ago," John straightened his seatbelt as he spoke.

"Sure," said Angus. "Like me to teach you before or after we save the world?"

"Before would be better," said John. "There's just so much I've never done."

He knew it was ridiculous but he didn't care. Who in their right mind wanted to learn to drive when almost half the roads had been washed away in the storm that had now thankfully abated?

"You did a good job on the engine, Man." Angus motioned forward with his head. "Never thought I'd see this baby again, or these mountains or skies."

"Cleaned out the filters," said John. "Tried to remember everything I'd ever learned when I opted for car mechanics instead of football or Rugby. I took a lot of options to save myself the shame of falling on my face or scoring a goal in the wrong net or getting crushed to a pulp by…"

"Hefty guys who wanted to take the ball away, Man?"

"I'd have just handed it over, then."

Angus chuckled. "We all find ways of escaping what we're scared of, Man."

The radio crackled, followed by a whine of static. "Contact," said Angus as he swerved around a bank of mud left behind by the diminishing flood.

John's fingers were on the dial before he could even think. He tried to find the semblance of a station. In the flood-washed desert with the sun emerging above the mountains to the east it appeared as if the Earth was at peace with the horizon, the dome of the sky still intact. But was it?

When they finally reached the highway the sky was a clear cerulean blue. There were no clouds buffeting its surface, and the heat from the sun was already drying things out so fast a steam cloud was rising like mist from the ground.

The news reports surprised them both. There'd been flooding and storm damage. People had been evacuated. But the storm had turned, dissipating over the Atlantic Ocean.

"It's a miracle – so little damage. How a storm can just turn like that." John said.

"Sure seems like one after the surge that came in, Man. I kinda lost it when that howl started. The truck movin even before the water lifted its wheels."

"Lucky." John touched the dashboard on the passenger side as if for luck. "She moved about a hundred metres with the force of the flood. But the side sway left her lodged against the rocks." He touched the dashboard again. "Never dreamed I could get her going again, just opened everything, shifted the sand, let the sun to do her work."

"I couldn't have done it, Man." Angus laughed. "I'd have been stuck out there forever."

"Lucky you can drive or we both would have been," John said. "How you feeling?"

"Glad to be on my way home. Last night…I thought…thought maybe it was over. I was totally freaked. It's been…well it's been as if what you've been saying, Man, as if it was happening somewhere else. Like some kinda…"

"Alternative universe?"

"Kinda," said Angus. "Though I'm not too sure what that kinda place is either…I was thinking about Ma and the Old Man. They know only the bones of all this stuff. They're just carrying on – sorta oblivious. I haven't told them, and last night when that storm, well I realised – well, I guessed that if the…if it was the end…maybe I'd left it too late to say goodbye."

John thought about Angus starting to come round in the cave – the tears. He touched Angus's shoulder.

"You called them today – on the mobile?"

"Yeah," said Angus. "And guess what? All I had the courage to say was hello."

# 62 REFLECTING

The roads back up to the ranch house showed signs of severe weather damage, but all the buildings they passed were still standing.

"I've seen worse," said Angus as they drove further up the mountain. Both of them surveying torn down gates, and trees that had fallen being chain-sawed to logs for internal wood burners.

"Might sound crazy, Man," said Angus, as he pulled into a passing place to let another truck squeeze by, "but could there be some sorta stabilization process taking place? Maybe it's not as bad as you think."

Stifling and rejecting the desire to lie about the probabilities associated with the mathematical equations and the astronomical and cosmological evidence of change and instability John searched his mind for a truth. He found one.

"Despite everything I know," he said, wondering how much he, or anyone, else really knew at all, "everything I've learned, the evidence I've seen with my own eyes…"

"The freak storm last night, Man,"

"The freak storm last night, too," said John, reflecting Angus's words back to him. He hesitated. How could he say he knew that last nights storm had only been part of the series of waves predicted and there was much worse to come. He struggled with the thoughts. He'd probably never been more certain about anything. The truth as he knew it was clear. Without massive international intervention, and even with it, the indications were that the Earth might not survive.

"Angus," he said again, aware of the sound of his own voice. It sounded different. As if it belonged to someone else. It was hard to define. Yet something had changed. He moved the words he was planning to use around in his mind. How would he order them? "The truth is," he said, running his tongue across his bottom lip before continuing. "Even knowing all the things I know, believing, what I believe. I know something else too." For a moment he listened to the silence, aware of the turn in his own thinking, the reality of being, the memory of overcoming his fear in the darkness of the cave. "I know," he said, "that despite what we expect and think we know, God's plans are his own."

"Sheeesh, Man." Angus let out a long whistle before starting to laugh.

"You really are the Old Man and Ma's honorary son."

They pulled up part way along the drive. Parking some distance from the house. The outdoor furniture had been blown about in the storm. Some of it now lay damaged or broken across the path. The newly erected porch, only recently restored following the fire, had taken a second battering though still intact.

They climbed out of the truck, moving the pieces of torn trellis and the broken bench seats to one side as they made their way to the door.

John's eyes fastened on the apex of the porch. It was still in place, although some of the length of roof that ran along the house had partially collapsed. He tried to work out the secret of its strength. It had acted like a funnel for the energy of the fire. Saving the house from much greater damage after the robbery and what appeared to have been a deliberate act of arson. Now it had survived the gales of the night before. He went forward, considering.

Thankfully the electricity was still on. Either power had been restored or it had never been lost. Leaving Angus to check the messages on the answer-phone John unloaded the truck. He knew there was no escaping the fact that he had to persuade Angus to see a doctor. There would have to be blood tests. There was no way they could continue until they'd had some assurances. He hauled the rucksacks and bags over his shoulders and grabbed the holdall with the food container and the chocolate that had probably saved both their lives. John shook the thought away. He'd speak with Angus now. It couldn't wait.

# 63 STAR TRACK

Glad to see the hospital disappearing into the distance John sat back. The place held too many bad memories – the memories of the breakdown that had slowed his mind and ability to function while the Giza Star Track Operation had been implemented.

The forty-eight hour stay for Angus had thankfully confirmed a hypoglycaemic condition, which had to be managed but wasn't life threatening. As long as Angus followed the plan he'd been given he'd be OK. Given the amount of regular snacking involved it suited Angus fine. Though he'd been testy about the types of snacks he'd been told to avoid – the sugary and carbohydrate foods he'd always craved. The diagnosis also explained the mood swings, which had been in part, wrongly attributed to the withdrawal from the painkillers.

The forty-eight hours had also confirmed for John that despite the miracle that had been the lull in the storm, the effects of the shifts taking place had produced what to many commentators seemed random environmental or ecological events. John knew they were anything but random.

Already several underwater volcanoes had erupted. The bubbling sea had been captured on camera, with a video of the spectacle running on the Internet. Heavy snows had fallen across many parts of Britain in what was described a freak weather front. The pictures to accompany the unexpected and unpredicted fall showed children joyfully playing in the streets building snowmen and dragging out sledges. It all seemed so innocuous. Just as the pictures he'd seen of the children of Bikini Atoll when nuclear fallout fell like snowflakes from the sky – the result of Operation crossroads. The children had played, excited and unaware of the threats then, too. This was different, but the innocence was the same.

Floods in America and other parts of the world had mercifully spared the majority of the population and the hatches that had been battened down were being opened. Not a word of what was going on to create the sudden weather changes had been offered by government spokespersons. It was clear the Giza Star Track Operation was operating undercover.

"I'm glad you didn't tell Ma."

Angus's voice flipped John back to the present. "You asked me not to," he said. The reality was he'd struggled with the promise he'd made. Manda and Paul Yeager had a right to know if Angus was ill. But he knew Angus was right. It would only scare Manda; have her catching a plane over to look after her son. Given what the doctors had said, Angus was fine, as long as he took on board the advice he'd been given.

"She wants to get back anyway, Man. I think she was freaked by the reports of the storms here, but worried 'bowt the floods where they are – you know…the kids an families they're working with out there."

"The reports say rescue operations have been initiated across many of the areas close to where they are," said John. "Mostly it's been manageable. In fact it's almost as if the freak weather has charted a path around and beyond habited areas."

"Any theories?" Angus put his foot down on the gas as he asked the question.

John had been working on every possible explanation while Angus had been getting the medical overhaul. "The only thing I can think of," he said while rubbing the muscles above his knees, "makes no real scientific sense or maybe it does, but I don't understand…"

"I'm all ears, Man," Angus managed to interrupt just as he fell into the outside lane and slowed his speed.

"OK," said John. "This is no more than a thought, it's not a theory or thesis, and has no basis in anything…"

"Man," Angus gave him a look then turned back to focus on the road. "Everything you've come up with so far has been the deal so cut yourself some slack and just say what the hell it is you're thinking."

"It's almost as if…" John paused, aware of how completely off the wall what he was going to say would sound. "As if…" he still couldn't say it.

Angus released a long sigh. "I'm going crazy here, Man," he said. "Just spit it out – tell me."

"It's as if the storm," said John, "the energy – is looking for something." He sat back, the temporary silence in the truck a balm. After poring over the reports, and following the satellite maps depicting the course of the weather front that had wreaked havoc across the globe, for almost all of the forty-eight hours Angus had been confined in the hospital, he was exhausted. He could blame the lack of sleep and food or the excess of coffee sapping his adrenal glands, but it was the constant struggle to try and decipher the signs.

It was mentally draining trying to make sense of everything that was going on. The thoughts spinning in his head, the science; myth; religion – it was all converging. He'd read somewhere that the reason it was virtually impossible to explain the building of the Great Pyramid was because it wasn't built on the earth plane. He'd almost had the conversation with

Sarah. The argument was that it had been built on some other dimension and had only descended into matter because of some fall from grace due to mankind's attachment to the material. It tied in with what he'd talked to Haziq and Angus about. The spiritual cataclysm believed to have occurred in the time of dynastic Egypt, which led to the degeneration of mankind.

"What I can't fathom, Man," said Angus, breaking the silence. "Is why it was full on and then stop. What's goin on there? You said it's not stabilising so why?"

John pulled his mind back. Reaching to capture whatever it was Angus was talking about.

"The storm," said Angus. "Why…I mean like you said, how can something so powerful just dissipate?"

John still didn't know. The diminishing magnetic forces of the Earth were measured and reported but were yet to be explained. Like the storms there was a force and energy that had dissipated and could even be about to disappear.

"Equilibrium," he said. It was the only word he could find that could begin to describe what he believed to be taking place. "Forces are acting against each other. But inherent in everything is the desire for balance. It's why, at least I think it's why, and the experts – all the specialists from diverse scientific disciplines – have failed to investigate the changes. They've always read the evidence as random when equilibrium has reigned. It's why governments can renege on promises to reduce carbon footprints by suggesting that global warming has no real scientific basis." He shook his head. "Remember all the jokes about global warming when we had six or more weeks of snow in Britain a few years ago? The raised eyebrows and humorous comments when even the summer temperatures struggled to get into the low seventies?"

"I was out of it, Man."

"Yes," said John, remembering. "But it's fascinating me. I'm seeing this massive global shift that has this energy, or opposing forces of energy. Or maybe it's even tied up with the repulsive energies of the Universe. I don't know but there's this straining toward balance…"

"Equilibrium," said Angus. "Isn't that what you think the capstone will do – act as some kinda harmonising force?"

"The capstone," said John. "Why haven't we heard from Haziq and Ogilvy?"

Angus was silent.

John waited. The truck gained space on the vehicles on the road ahead. "Angus," he said. "I'm still not sure about the capstone," he felt as if he was talking to himself. Angus didn't respond. "I know Franklyn has managed to make it top priority but it was only ever part of the system of things outlined in my thesis. Yet from what little we've found out it's…"

"John," Angus said. "D'you think we should make contact with Haziq and Ogilvy?"

John glanced at his friend. Hesitating before he made a decision.

"I've never liked pushing things," he said. "I've always…" he paused, remembering how he always waited for someone else to make the moves. But that was then, "At some point," he said, "I guess we'll have to."

Despite the time of year the ranch house seemed strangely cold as they pushed open the porch door, the thermostat on the wall blinking a mild, almost wintry, twenty-one degrees for the desert location. John shivered, not so much from the chill as the sense that things were changing almost imperceptibly while he was doing little more than marking time.

"Air conditioning needs adjusting, Man. That's all." Angus moved toward the control panel located in the alcove to the side of the porch door.

"I didn't put it on," said John, heading toward the kitchen before Angus could respond.

"You got food?" said Angus as he turned and followed across the hallway. "Please say you've got food."

John pulled open the fridge. It hadn't occurred to him to shop. Didn't Angus realise he'd spent the past forty-eight hours camping in the visitors room at the hospital with only occasional forays across the car park to the truck and back.

"Wow," said Angus, as the fridge revealed its bounty of fresh salads, cheeses, a full roast chicken and a variety of other edibles. "Maybe you should marry me, Man."

John blinked. The food he hadn't bought but had unexpectedly manifested in front of his eyes was still there. It wasn't the hallucination he'd thought it might be.

"Stay cool, Man," Angus said. "You're safe with me." He laughed. "Juanita, she's the one. I'll have to put up the Banns or something." He turned to John. "Maybe she put the air conditioning on too," he said as he started to investigate the contents of the trays.

John experienced a sudden unexpected but welcome feeling of hunger as his mouth began to water.

They'd barely finished eating when the phone rang. It switched almost immediately to answer-phone, the repeated bleeps indicating several waiting calls. Whoever it was ringing the house put down the phone before either Angus or John could reach it. John reflexively reached for his mobile. Angus snatched at the receiver and held it in mid air.

"Who's ringing us on landlines?" He replaced the receiver almost as if it had stung him. He pressed the display.

"Thirteen messages," said John.

"Unlucky number, Man," said Angus as he pressed the message button and Paul Yeager's voice broke through the line.

By the time they'd listened to all the messages, which included six from Haziq, six from Paul Yeager, and one from Sarah, it was clear to John that while so much seemed apparently unchanged there was something going on with the radio signals. The last time Angus had connected with his parents was the day after the storm. The lack of emails also indicated some problem with the Internet. There'd been no contacts received from the Yeagers, Haziq or Sarah. Though the frantic messages they'd left on the landline indicated they'd certainly tried to communicate.

Angus immediately began calling everyone to let them know both he and John were OK. Leaving messages where he couldn't get an answer. Paul Yeager was the only one to pick up. John guessed he'd been sitting aside the phone in the hope of hearing from them since the last contact.

After Angus put down the phone and explained that both parents were already making preparations for travelling overland before catching a plane back to Arizona he'd become visibly agitated, pacing the room, stopping every now and then to stare out the window at the deepening blue of the sky as it slipped toward night.

"Tell me again what's goin on out there, Man," he said, rubbing his hand across the glass, as if by clearing the view he could see what was going on in the Universe with his naked eye. "Tell me what Haziq was talking about in that message which made no sense, Man," he said turning abruptly from the window. "He's saying it's no secret that we have to meet to discuss planetary matters because it's all part of general congress. Man, what is that supposed to mean?"

John sat up straighter from the table where he'd spread out a map and several diagrams. He made an effort to stretch the muscles of his neck and back.

"I think he was trying to tell us something, Angus. I'm trying to break down the content of some of what he said…"

"You mean like some sorta riddle, Man?" Angus started to laugh as soon as he said it. "Why can't he just say what he has to say – what the fuck he means?"

Experiencing recoil at Angus's added expletive John put down the pen he was holding. It wasn't as if he wasn't used to Angus swearing but the intonation was aggressive, directed at Haziq. "Maybe it's something he isn't supposed to know but it's something, we're supposed to know," he said. "He left six messages. In each one he said something that didn't make much sense. It wasn't Haziq talking."

"The way Haziq talks?" asked Angus.

"No," John agreed. "He was conveying something. I'm not sure what.

I'm going to play the messages again – try and analyse what he's telling us."

"Maybe I should clean the house." Angus looked around him, a wild expression on his face. "Get things ready for Ma and Pa."

Angus was still stalking the house without any real purpose when John discovered what appeared to be the meaning in the cryptic messages left on the answer-phone.

"Angus," he shouted. Angus appeared in seconds. "Seems like we've got less than twenty four hours, we…" he could feel the rush of his own voice as he saw the colour drain from Angus's face before he'd even finished speaking. "No," he said. "Not what you think, Angus." He paused. After two hours of moving around slips of paper, with the out of synch words Haziq had left in his messages written on them, he wasn't thinking about the effect of his words on the already hyped Angus. "I mean," he said. "I think Haziq is telling us there's a meeting…"

"Meeting?"

He saw Angus's colour return as he spoke. "The International Planetary Congress meeting," said John. "There's been nothing reported but Haziq's message indicates, well it might indicate, that leaders from around the world are getting together." He felt his insides flip. Forced himself to continue, "He mentioned the incredible views coming from Kressa Peak. I'm reckoning that's where the meeting is going to be held. Kressa Peak. It can mean only one thing. We're going to find out what the international perspective is."

"What's going on?" said Angus.

"Maybe," said John, reckoning that if Haziq was telling them, what he appeared to be telling them, Haziq was doing so for one reason, and for one reason only. Haziq expected them to go. "The meeting, Kressa Peak," he said. "I'm going to have to find a way to get in."

Angus shook his head. "The place'll be teeming with security, Man. How do we get through?"

"Gatecrash," John tried to swallow the heart that seemed to have leapt into his mouth as he said the word. "We're going to have to gatecrash." He tried to lick his lips. Marvelling at how quickly his tongue had turned to something with the distinct feel of sandpaper.

# 64 KRESSA PEAK

Angus was right. The place teemed with security. But given the fact that it was top secret, and only those who were attending knew what was going on, it was hard to spot who, amongst the plain clothed police, guards and military, was likely to suddenly tackle any gatecrashers or interlopers to the ground. To the innocent unknowing observer the people who'd been arriving at the bunker at the eastern reaches of Kressa Peak were just the usual site personnel – astronomers and technical staff, along with the visiting groups of academics and students from diverse locations.

John could feel the hairs on the back of his neck starting to vibrate as Angus released the handbrake and powered the truck forward. After showing the passes, they'd used on their last visit to the observatory complex, to the almost sleepy guard they'd been allowed through to the main site. Angus allowing a slow whistle to escape through his teeth as he backed the truck into a designated parking spot before cruising backwards and jerking the wheel to spin them round and across the slope that would take them down the dirt track used as a running strip by observatory personnel.

"Let's hope it's all eyes on the entry way, Man," he said as he flicked off the beam. "This is the runner's path. Let's hope all those poor guys who need to watch what they eat and sprint to stop the pounds piling on are otherwise engaged tonight." He slowed to almost a crawl. "There's enough of a ridge somewhere down here where, if we keep the truck close enough to the swell of rock, we'll be able to negotiate our way across. There's a torch in the glove compartment. You'll need to use it, Man."

John felt for the torch. His hands were shaking. Some of the ridges were only barely wide enough to take two runners side by side if his memory of his last visit here was right.

"No sweat," said Angus as if reading his thoughts. "In the daylight I know this place like the back of my hand."

John glanced out the window to his left. Angus was missing something. The day had slipped away. Despite the clarity of the night skies up here if there were a massive drop he wouldn't see it.

"Open the window," said Angus. "Just aim the torch downward to the left. The drop is on your side. I just need a little guidance, Man."

"I can't understand why we didn't just park the truck and go on foot," John said as Angus scraped the truck around a barely passable hairpin bend.

"Too long," said Angus. "We've already covered some distance. It's three miles as the bird flies, but six if you follow the main path. Besides we couldn't have stayed in the parking space up top. It belongs to someone else – pulling in just makes us guys look bona fide."

They continued forward, John ridiculously gripping the side of his seat with one hand as if he could prevent the sudden fall into nothingness, all the time aiming the torch into the darkness. The beam suddenly hitting space, "Keep right," he shouted to Angus as the track ahead looked set to disappear. "Just stop!"

Angus flicked on the headlights momentarily. "Sheesh, I think this truck is bigger than it was," he said, braking, even as he spoke.

They sat in silence for several moments, John wishing that Angus had tried to dissuade him from launching such a ridiculous mission. Instead Angus had leapt into action, pulling out clothes to wear and checking the Kressa Peak ordnance survey maps. Drawing up the plan of approach and execution of what he was excitedly calling Operation Kressagate. The hyperactive state he was in suddenly channelled.

"It's possible," said Angus. After what John assumed to be internal strategic deliberation.

"Possible we can scrape through, but you're gonna have to climb out and scope the track ahead."

John shone the torch downwards through the open window. "I would," he heard his own almost disembodied voice saying, "but from where I'm sitting there isn't any track to walk on." He coughed trying to clear the airways that had suddenly threatened to close. "The track – the road, Angus, is just about holding the wheels."

"And the drop," said Angus.

"Like a black hole," said John.

"Just close your eyes, Man," said Angus as the engine once again stirred.

It seemed like an age had passed in suspended animation before Angus changed gears, slowed, braked, and turned off the engine. John slid out of the truck. His legs felt boneless. He'd been unable to speak once Angus had moved the truck forward. He'd done as Angus bid him. Closing his eyes, trying to cut out the sound of the spin of the wheels as they occasionally lost purchase on the ground beneath them. In contrast Angus seemed to be almost buzzing.

"Knew it could be done, Man. Now look over there."

John followed the direction in which Angus was pointing; could see the long low building in the distance flanked by several smaller buildings. "That's the bunker?" he asked, surprised at its size. He'd expected something more the size of the control room. "It's almost the size of a football…"

"Houses the full gym, bunk room accommodation, swimming pool – even a football pitch, Man," said Angus. "Well baseball but you get the picture. The techs can still use it for five-a-side. They've done conferences associated with the university here before…just not top secret ones…" He paused. "Unless they were so secret I didn't know…"

"And the building running alongside?" said John.

"Exactly where you and I are going," said Angus. "If it's the caterers who know me and my fondness for food they're not going to be surprised to see me."

"They know you?"

"I've always made good friends with people who have food. I'm just hoping they haven't brought in a contract team. That's why we came across the back track. It cuts out miles and there's a little snicket, Man. We just slip through and we're in…"

"In?"

"In the catering section – the kitchens, I'll point you in the right direction and you'll be able to grab some uniforms. Then all we have to do is push some trolleys through, follow the designated plan and we're in and can find out what…"

"The world isn't being told," John said wondering, as he followed Angus, just how they were going to pull this off.

Slipping through what could only be termed desert brush he could just about see why the approach they'd taken was a wise one. The back track they were on was deserted. Angus, all confidence, gave the second briefing on the agreed plan as they made their way down. Just like the old days, thought John. Once Angus was given, or had taken control, he assumed everyone would be enjoying whatever was going on just as much as he was. John didn't have the heart to tell him, that after all his own big talk, his own confidence of seeing the plan through was touching zero.

Angus led the way across the gravelled area toward the concrete structure that was used by the caterers.

John hovering behind in the background foyer, as instructed, as Angus pushed through the doors and strolled through into the kitchens.

John held his breath. He didn't need to. Within seconds he saw Angus high-fiving with a Latino looking guy before exchanging some sort of joke. Across the kitchen he could see the loaded trolleys. He'd expected more people to be working but there were only half a dozen, at most, that he could see. They all had the same dark blue chef's tunics with the Kressa

Peak logo on the back, jaunty little sailor type hats, and what appeared to be black pants or black denims. He understood now why Angus had rooted out the tailored pants.

He was watching Angus helping himself to something off one of the trolleys while gesticulating to another guy, when he heard the sound of voices from behind him. For a second his blood held in suspension. Franklyn's voice was unmistakeable. He'd heard it so many times in real life, heard it running round his head when he'd relived their discussions, and Franklyn's continued humiliating putdowns, all in an effort to work out what he should have said, or done, to stop the guy wanting to crush him.

"There could be considerable opportunities for advancement..." Franklyn was saying. Then silence.

Maybe Franklyn was alone and talking to someone on a mobile phone, thought John. But why was he outside the catering block and at the back entrance? John needed to find out. He edged his way along the wall, moving closer to the exit with every step.

"There's no way that the appropriate data could have been analysed within such a tight timeframe. We..."

Again silence. John couldn't hear anything other than the clatter of trolleys emanating from the kitchen. "These people are politicians..." Franklyn's voice was audible again. John strained his ears. "The scientists amongst them are hamstrung in their ability to..."

Swinging round as the rattle of wheels behind him announced Angus's appearance John raised his hand, quickly placing a finger to his lips indicating the need for silence. He moved his head in a gesture suggesting retreat. Angus looked perplexed but obeyed. In the split second lull John heard Franklyn laugh, before he heard the sound of footsteps moving away across the gravelled path. He sagged against the wall.

"OK," he mouthed as Angus moved forward with a trolley that just happened to have a stack of laundry including two blue tunics and a pair of jaunty caps on its lower shelf.

He allowed himself to be led along toward one of the smaller blocks Angus had pointed out earlier.

"Wash house," Angus said. "Laundry room, whatever you want to call it. We'll throw these classy Armani suits on soon as I've dropped the washing off."

"Armani?" said John.

"Man." Angus shook his head and veered toward a small block where several other small trolley baskets were lined up outside. He stopped. "Dress up time," he said, as he reached for the clothes and tossed some to John.

They slipped on the outfits in moments. Taking up stationary positions with their backs huddled against the side of the block and their eyes focused on the doors to the main building till they heard the sound of a vehicle approaching.

"Could be," said Angus as what appeared to be a group of civilians emerged from the main doors.

They watched as the vehicle came to a stop. A group of men moved forward.

"Donovan," said John, as the tall athletically built man climbed out of the car.

"President, no less, Man." Angus said, his voice low. "Dark Chieftain, that's what the name Donovan means. Perfect. Irish, mysterious roots there, som…"

"What if someone shoots us," said John. "We walk in there and security has everything under control, know we're not part of any team…"

"There's people – celebrity stalkers," said Angus. "They make a living out of doing this sorta thing, Man."

"Living?" John whispered.

"We slip through that side door pushing the trolley now," said Angus by way of response. "All eyes and hands will be on the arrival of President Donovan. Trust me, Man."

John ducked his head. They pushed through the door. All he needed was to be spotted by Franklyn and the game was over. The jaunty sailor hat mercifully stayed in place, his surroundings little more than cloudy fuzz as his vision narrowed with the terror of being spotted.

"No-one is paying any attention," Angus said the words loud enough for anyone to hear. But no heads turned in their direction. "Just keep movin, Man."

John did. Within seconds Angus had negotiated around several groups of serious looking men and women of diverse nationalities seated around a central raised platform, and through two double doors into a small side room that appeared little bigger than a large closet, which was obviously, by the lockers running from floor to ceiling, some kind of changing room.

"Check that door," Angus said. "It's another way out if we need to split before the end of the party."

Legs and hands trembling with the fear of being caught, John did as he was bid. Quickly undoing the internal bolts and twisting the key that was thankfully still in the lock. He tried the handle. It turned, and the door opened inward toward him. The cool air from outside touched his face and he immediately had to damp down the desire to escape the building and the plan already in progress.

"Let's lose the costumes," Angus said, pulling off the tunic and stuffing the hat in its pocket.

No one turned as they re-entered the main area. As Angus had promised, the attention in the room was focused on the fact that the arrival of President Donovan had been confirmed. Taking in the faces of several key statesmen and women seated around the periphery of the raised stage platform, John attempted, as Angus had advised, to establish a cognitive map of the place. He was terrified. Angus beside him appeared unfazed.

Taking in the layout of the setting John tried to see if Franklyn was with the main group on the platform, or seated around the periphery as part of the audience, or whatever else the group, of what he assumed could only be international scientists and experts, could be called.

Despite the visual search he couldn't locate him. Gathering that it was possible Franklyn's face could be shielded from view by one of pillars he tried to relax. It was impossible, but at least he was breathing and no-one could see the perspiration trickling between his shoulder blades or measure his heart rate, which, he was sure, was definitely off the scale. He needn't have concerned himself because all eyes were now on the platform as President Donovan entered and moved immediately centre stage to begin speaking.

"Thank you for joining us here today." President Donovan placed his notes on the lectern in front of him. "Or maybe I should say this evening…" He laughed. Then added, "Under cover of the night." His voice was clear and strong. No edge to indicate the expediency of the gathering.

"Firstly," Donovan stated as he adjusted the mike that was attached to his lapel.

Or maybe he was turning up the volume, John couldn't be sure.

"Let me state my position," Donovan continued, allowing a few moments of silence to carry the import of his words. "I am not a scientist. My background is in law and politics. A background that has demanded that I understand that evidence to support a case must be robust. The law makes decisions on evidence. It acts and makes judgements where the facts of a case point clearly in a direction from which there can be no reasonable doubt that the evidence is telling us, with reasonable certainty, the truth of how things happened or came to be." He paused, took a sip of water from the glass that had been strategically placed at his side by an Aide.

"If you're asking yourselves why I'm talking about law, when we're here to discuss the sudden and volatile changes in the Earth's climate and the possible threat of cosmological catastrophe, that's because my learned friends in the scientific community, recognise the importance of robust evidence to support the judgement of a case also." He smiled.

On cue there was a smattering of soft muffled laughter from the audience.

"Where's he going, Man?"

John swung round abruptly. Sure Angus's voice was loud enough to alert others. Saw no other heads turned in their direction. He shrugged. He couldn't be sure where Donovan was going. He just wished he'd hurry up and get there so they could decide on the next stage of the plan, carry it out, and disappear.

"Consequently," Donovan continued, "I am advised that as the scientific community work on the basis of empiricism – which means that all theoretical stances must be supported by evidence. We can only work with what we know and have evidence for. Currently the position stands thus: Dr Octavia Franklyn who is with us here today…"

"Octavia?" Angus's jaw dropped. He swung an amazed look at John. "Doc Ock?"

John ignored him. It didn't matter what Franklyn had been named, as long as he didn't have to go near him. He glanced back at the platform. The President was indicating toward a seating position, which was obviously filled by Franklyn. John couldn't see him because of the pillar, but at least now he knew where Franklyn was.

"Dr Franklyn," Donovan said, "has been sharing his expertise, and the results of his evidence based research, with the international community as part of his now working role within the Giza Star Track Operation team."

John wondered if Franklyn was actually preening as Donavan spoke.

"Dr Franklyn, who will be delivering a presentation to detail the current state of play…" Donovan gestured toward the space John now knew was occupied by Franklyn, "…has demonstrated that we are currently facing the possibility of threat from the explosion of the white dwarf we know as Sirius B.

"Previous estimates of the white dwarf's distance, and indeed the Sirius System itself, have been shown by Dr Franklyn's research to be incorrect, the error being as a result of the limitations of the reconfiguring of optical observations because of technical anomalies. Once Dr Franklyn identified this he has been able to identify that a threat we assumed to be far in the future…a threat, which we thought we would need to address for the safety of our great grandchildren may be with us now." Donovan reached for his glass and took another small sip. "That threat," he said as he placed the glass back down, "is, we believe, under control. The massive undertaking to reconstruct the capstone of the Great Pyramid is approaching completion.

"We are advised by Dr Franklyn that, as The Great Pyramid lies at the centre of the landmass of the world, its key purpose may well be to maintain the correct orbital axis of the planet through channelling the gravitational pull of the Earth, the energy of which creates the appropriate repulsive energy to ensure that planets, both within our own galaxy, the solar system, and Universe beyond, cannot approach the Earth."

John stared. If he'd held any lingering doubts about Franklyn being behind the fire; the theft of his documentation and back up hard drive at the Yeager's house, the doubts were quashed. Franklyn had very conveniently utilised as much of the data, and the developing hypotheses from the outline John had provided, as were possible. He waited for someone amongst the audience of cosmologists, astrophysicists and astronomers to challenge what had just been stated as fact by the President of the United States, waited for someone to challenge the whole concept of gravity as a known and definable force. Not a single hand was raised.

Franklyn had managed to convince the entire science community that he knew the answers. Nobody laughed, or even smirked as far as John could see. Yet the language, the framework, varied little from John's own thesis. The differences were there though. Close to almost everything John had endeavoured to articulate. Yet there were clear gaps in the analysis. But Franklyn was obviously presenting the evidence of his supposed work to the science and political community as if it was beyond challenge.

He cast away the thoughts; listened as the President continued talking. Donovan was making reference to the collaboration of partners worldwide, the planned presentations on capstone realignment, inter – global emergency strategies, the continuing need to ensure that the media kept a blanket on the happenings in order to manage public panic and protect the economy. He was pouring praise on the technical capability of both national and international security systems. He addressed the need for the facilitation of formal discussions with the international community of scientists, national security experts, and diplomats, to explore the implementation of strategies for an international emergency response notification system to ensure that the accidental initiation of nuclear war could be prevented. He was talking, thought John, as if they had all the time in the world. He glanced at Angus before starting to move forward.

With his brain racing in overdrive he hadn't heard what point Donovan had finished his speech with, but the entire audience were on their feet and clapping. The noise, and the general low-key pandemonium, as people started to move about, made it easier to approach the platform from which President Donovan was making a slow exit as he shook hands with people on the periphery. The President, John realised, would need to be ahead of Franklyn's field of view, before it would be safe to slip forward and inveigle himself into the throng.

He was still considering his position when he saw Donovan introducing someone to a man who could only have been Franklyn. Even in the briefest of profiles Franklyn was easy to recognise. The body language he was using to announce his own perceived importance was much in evidence, as was the slimy smile when John caught a glimpse of Franklyn's face. He tried to figure how the man could have pulled it off. Considered how the painstaking years of research had been appropriated – stolen. The key evidence mangled, and yet Franklyn was now rubbing shoulders with presidents and the scientific elite, who for some reason were unable or unwilling to challenge the claims he was making. The man was a total fraud, but obviously a genius at influencing others. John felt the sudden rush of anger propel him forward as Donovan moved down the steps.

With a sense of his heart about to fail all normal functioning he pushed through the groups of people milling around. Donovan was looking amazingly relaxed for a man taking the international lead on strategies to prevent cosmological catastrophe. But then, courtesy of Franklyn's rejigging of the research findings, or maybe just his complete inability to translate the meaning of another person's analysis, Donovan had been fed what Sarah would have termed a pile of crock and wasn't really aware that catastrophe could be where they could be headed, was he?

Feeling the dull persistent beat in his temple as his fury toward Franklyn elevated further he tried to let go of the thoughts and focus on actions he'd promised to take.

The President was moving forward. About to approach the seating area to view the planned presentation as John sat down in a vacant seat then swiftly stood up again to enable Donovan to choose his preferred position. Donovan gave him the benefit of a brief smile, apparently interpreting John's actions as John hoped he would – as a sign of respect. Then he sat in the seat John had just vacated, his Aides moving to strategic points around the floor space to monitor the wider area. John took his chance and sat down in the empty seat beside him.

Aware that there may already be guns trained on him he tried to moisten his mouth. The internal terror doing battle with his desire and desperation to speak and let the truth be known had rendered his lips close to useless. They wouldn't move. They had to. He tried to steady his focus on a single pinpoint within his visual field. Julia's face swam into his mind. Again he wondered what it would be like to kiss her. He felt the tension in the back of his neck dissolve as he stepped momentarily into the possibility, before remembering where he was.

He turned to Donovan. "The evidence," he heard himself saying. "The hard evidence for impending catastrophe is beyond reasonable doubt." He noticed the muscles in Donovan's face flex. "I've spent almost my entire life absorbed in researching the science and mysteries of outer space…" He waited for a response or the sudden rush of security but none came. "President Donovan," he said. "The Earth is a beautiful place. I've spent so much time staring at the stars I almost missed the flowers growing at my feet. Now I've seen them."

He could see Donovan struggling to make sense of what he was saying, almost as much as he himself was trying to make sense of why he was saying it. It was hardly the intended speech or the confirmation of evidence he'd planned.

The stretching silence of what he could only assume was disbelief reached maximum tension before Donovan broke it.

"And now you've seen them?" Donovan said as his eyes flickered back and forward as if monitoring something beyond his immediate field of view.

"Yes," said John.

"So?" Donovan asked.

"So," said John feeling his own insecurity challenging his right to speak. "I…" he swallowed the sense of smallness. "I can't walk away from the possibility of it all disappearing."

Despite his attempts John felt he was floundering. The planned speech, the words he had so carefully chosen to make his pitch, had morphed into the mad ramblings of a failed poet.

He saw Donovan alter position, noted the almost indiscernible tilt of Donovan's head, the split second signal in his eyes.

"I'm not crazy," he rushed out the words. Immediately realising they were a confirmation of what he was trying to deny. It didn't matter. He could see Angus, little more than a speck in his own peripheral vision moving toward the escape route of the side closet changing room. He started to unfold himself from his seating position. "Please revisit the evidence," he said battling to keep his movements slow and fluid so that anyone watching could see his hands were free of any weapons. "The threat we're facing is not the explosion of the white dwarf, Mr President…" he was full on his feet now so if there was a gun trained on him he'd be an easy target but he kept on talking, "it's the spinning out of control and the fall from the heavens of the main system star Sirius A. We need to identify and harness the energies. There's something far more profound…" the flow of his words was prematurely stalled as he felt, rather than saw, the movement of someone approaching from the side as the sudden crash in the distance had everyone on their feet. He turned as planned, in the same direction as everyone else before moving swiftly sideways as the audience crowded together, just as the previously low key almost invisible security team materialised from strategic points around the floor.

# 65 INTO DARKNESS

He was out the side door, pulling on the tunic Angus thrust at him, and heading back across the gravel path by the time the security inside had located the site and source of the sound that had erupted. The trolley of laundry Angus had appropriated from the catering block just happened to have a stack of glassware stacked upon it. Which, given the loosening of the trolley wheel, meant it was simply a matter of carefully calculated time and gentle but forceful pressure from Angus's foot before it collapsed and smashed to the floor.

"We're going off road," said Angus as they dived back in the truck, "downwards toward civilisation." He turned the key in the ignition. "I can handle the back wheels trailing over the edge but maybe not the front…" He gunned the engine without beam. Taking off before John had time to protest. "Don't worry, Man," he said.

John fumbled for the torch, which he couldn't find. The road ahead a sprawl of darkness, but at least it seemed flat, judging by the contours visible in the strange luminescence provided by an unpolluted star filled sky. The first bump sent the truck spinning. A whirl of sand and grit surrounding them as Angus pulled the truck toward the turn and out again. By the fourth bump John could see the lights of distant cars on the highway and the possibility of making it back.

# 66 GRAVITY

"Can't believe we just did, what we did." It was the most in terms of talk John could muster after running off at the mouth to Angus, on the way back up to the house, about what was being conveyed as indisputable fact.

"It's off the wall, Man." Angus said. "What you've been telling me. Why didn't you tell me before? I thought we all knew these things."

"What things?" John felt distant, vaguely coming to terms with the fact they were both still intact after the crazy escapade, which, like everything else he initiated, had netted them nothing.

"The things you were telling me on the way back, up here. When you were talking faster, and more furious, than I've ever heard you speak, Man. I thought we knew these things. Kinda took it for granted. Gravity – remember those pictures when we were kids…"

"Pictures?" John asked his mind still a constant swirl of images of the happenings of the night.

"Everyone falling off the Earth, Man." Angus laughed. "Used to crease me up, Man. But know something?"

John shook his head, barely following what Angus was talking about.

"It terrified me. Terrified me, Man." Angus stopped pacing. "Is that what's gonna happen – we all fall off the planet?"

"It's…" John snagged the gist of Angus's articulated fears, posed as questions. Couldn't stop the picture forming in his mind, the stationary globe of the Earth, all the Lowryesque figures spinning into space. "It's not that simple," he said. "It's more…"

"I just can't figure how all those people…" Angus cut in before John could find the words to explain.

"Were falling off the Earth?" John questioned.

"All those people in the bunker up there – I mean." Angus gestured to the middle distance.

John felt the pull of exhaustion, wondered if Angus needed something to bring him back down from the hyper state he was in.

He watched as Angus resumed his pacing. Tried to figure out what to do as Angus moved back and forward from the window, glancing expectantly at the night sky like he had before they'd left, as if it were possible to see what was happening in the cosmos with the power of the naked eye.

"Angus," he said. "Maybe we need to try and get some rest. You did a fantastic job tonight. I'm still in some sort of delayed shock."

"Magnetics, Man." Angus swung back from the window waving his arms as if the room was full of energy he was trying to fight off. Forestalling any plan for sleep that John was intending to suggest. "How come they never explained these things in our Physics lessons?" He turned back to the window, as if vigilance would keep them safe. "What you were telling me on the way back down…"

John racked his brain.

"You were telling me that we…" He waved his arms again. "Telling me that we don't even understand the principle of magnetics. The Earth's magnetic field is diminishing – has been diminishing for…"

"Angus," John said. "There's lots of things we…"

"But gravity, Man…"

"You know all this, Angus. Gravity is one of the four fundamental forces of the Universe. Considered a none-contact force - what holds the planets in orbit, as well as the very Universe itself…"

"So what? Donovan was saying…"

"There were partial truths. Franklyn has managed to use what I've written but…"

"He's doctored it, Man?"

"He can," said John, the urge to sleep suddenly slipping away. "Gravity is still one of the biggest mysteries of Physics. We treat it as a known, when in fact it's an unknown. The mystery of what gravity actually is happens to be one of the main stumbling blocks to providing a universal theory that can accurately describe the functions of every interaction in the Universe." He indicated with his hand. "The people up there, all the scientific community, they know these things as well as we do."

"I don't…didn't, Man."

"They know these things, but given that gravity is still an unfathomable they're not prepared to argue…"

"With the President…?"

"With the President, or anyone else, or any place where they may look foolish amongst their peers for not knowing something everyone else may know. The person who's willing to speak out is usually excluded, isolated…"

"The bridge too far, guy – remember that film?"

"Yes." John resisted the desire to punch his fist into a nearby wall. "The dangers of Group Mind," he said in response to Angus. "Ignoring the truth is nothing new."

# 67 CUT OFF

The dawn had almost arrived. Angus had finally slept. John was aware that he had too, but fitfully; for less than three hours. Still brain fuzzed from exhaustion he was now investigating the latest news reports of the strange weather fronts across the world. Most of the reports were playing things down, as Donovan had advised they should. There were still many things that were hard to grasp.

With the need for air, and the hope of gaining some clarity of thought he took himself outside. The still dark sky revealed no secrets. The impending threat gave no indication of its existence. Instead he was conscious of a sense of peace being carried on the wind. He closed his eyes. Savoured the coolness of the breeze against his skin and wondered for the millionth time if he could be wrong.

By the time he returned inside Angus had woken, had already resumed his pacing upstairs. Evidenced by the soft footfalls John could hear above him.

John returned to the desk and the papers and diagrams he'd abandoned. He was beginning to feel that was all he ever did. Paperwork. Moving things around, trying so see if they fit, playing with a cosmic jigsaw. He was still trying to work out the pattern of the storm, his calculations suggesting a building strength of force coming in waves.

He still couldn't be sure if the storms that had just stilled could be classed as a single wave, or whether the movement of the storms across the landmass of the world were separate waves. He felt the heat building in his temples. He should know. He'd had long enough to work things out.

He was considering what to do next when a voice signalled Angus's return.

"This is how we'll play it, Man."

John stared at his laptop his mind fixated somewhere else.

"I said this is how I think we should play it."

John raised his head. "Play it?"

"With Ma and the Old Man," said Angus. He frowned. "You look out of it, Man. What's going on in your head? You don't usually blank me out."

John felt his eyes narrow as he took in Angus's beleaguered expression.

It was becoming increasingly difficult to switch his thinking.

"I'm sorry," he said before returning his focus to the laptop on the desk in front of him, then at the papers and diagrams strewn in disarray. "It's just," he attempted to track the thoughts that were zigzagging around his head, pulling him from one possibility to another.

"Just what, Man?"

John pointed toward the table, pulling first one sheet then another to lay them side, by side.

"It's this." He took a breath. "The fact that the masts have been taken down by the storms." He drew co-ordinates across some of his diagrams. "The reason we've had no contact from Haziq and Ogilvy except for the answer-phone message asking why we aren't responding to the email contacts." He shook his head as if to readjust some internal error in his brain – some glitch that was stalling the hard drive of his logic. "It's almost as if the storm is cutting out the radio waves across different continents."

"Why would the storm…I mean, Man, how would the storm…" Angus left his sentence unfinished and continued to pace. "I know you said it…" He stopped. "I know you said that the storm seemed to know where…"

"I said it seemed to know where it was going."

Angus shrugged. "This is all too strange, Man. First we've got a storm that knows where it's going and now it's picking off radio masts. Never mind the fact that I've got parents on their way here and you won't help me put together a plan of what we're going to tell them."

John considered. It was almost as if Angus thought by not telling his parents they could prevent what was happening from happening. He wondered if he'd be acting the same as Angus if he had the closeness of real blood ties. He couldn't answer. He knew he cared about Angus. He knew he had a deep affection for Manda and Paul Yeager – knew that Haziq, Sarah and Dan meant a lot. He cared about them too. But he couldn't know what it felt like to belong. He had no frame of reference to understand.

"Angus," he said. "We should tell them what we know."

"The truth – you're kidding? Ma'll go berserk."

"Angus," John stood up. "We don't know the truth – not yet." He felt the familiar speeding up of his heartbeat as he made the admission. OK so he'd identified so much of what was happening. The microscopic errors in measurement the need for the reconfiguring of optical observations, the direct correlation between the diminishing magnetic forces of the Earth, and the slow but sure shift of the Earth's axis – the equation, the Great Pyramid as a significant point of energy release. He could go on and on. He wasn't going to.

"I think we should tell them what we know." He paused. "Manda and Paul, your ma and pa, they're not fools. I…" The rolling crack of thunder and the burst of illumination in the room terminated the time for talk. Angus had frozen, statue like mid-stride in an almost catatonic postural stance. John leapt to his feet. If he was right about the waves this could be the third. He hoped that Manda and Paul Yeager were not yet airborne. If they were it was going to be a bumpy ride.

The sound of the rain as the clouds opened, filled the entire house. It was like the beat of a Shaman's drum, incessant yet strangely soporific – the chant of enchantment. John struggled against the almost hypnotic thrum of the beat and turned back to his laptop. It was running on battery. He realised the lines must be already down. He reached for the mouse. He needed to know what reports were already coming in on the Internet news channels.

# 68 EMERITUS

The ranch house was still intact. Its position, built within the curve of the hill, protecting it from the main features of the flood that had been the result of continuous battering rain and howling winds. There'd been mudslides, which had carried and upturned cars. Islands in the south pacific had disappeared. Again there'd been what could only be termed a miraculous plot to the storm that led to it evading the habited islands. Angus had stared in disbelief when John showed him its route.

"Like it knows where it's goin, Man," he said, "as if it doesn't want to hurt anyone." He shivered.

"There's buildings down," said John. "Highways submerged, but still no reports of fatalities. Either someone is keeping the truth very close to their chest…"

"Or it's warning us, Man."

"There's something I'm going to have to do." John watched Angus's eyes suddenly close as he said it.

"I don't…"Angus began.

"I'm going to speak with Franklyn," John said. "I need to key him in on everything."

"Your work?" Angus ran a hand across his head. "The weasel has already stolen everything." He resumed pacing. "The bastard is a thief, a liar. He may have even – no, Man, let's get it straight. He was behind what happened in Chile. He even tried to burn down this …"

"Angus," said John. "It matters about the house, about what happened in Chile, but the rest of it doesn't."

"Doesn't matter, you're saying it doesn't matter?"

"It doesn't matter about what he's stolen from me." He started to gather his papers.

Angus caught his arm. "You can't speak to Franklyn, John."

He felt the pressure of Angus's hold.

"The guy – the weasel will just…"

"I don't care Angus," he could hear the determination in his own voice. "He can have everything. All the calculations, the synthesis, the documentation…"

"But you can't, Man. He's…"

"He's the only one anyone is listening to. The only one with enough prestige…"

"Emeritus Professor, Man," said Angus. "Adviser to the Senate." He kicked a chair. "Yeah," he said. "Go tell the Bastard…"

"I'm going to," said John. He laughed. "But you're going to have to take me." He paused. "Once we've found out where the Bastard is."

# 69 FRANKLYN

If it hadn't been for the storm all the delegates would have long been returned to their respective governmental offices in various strategic points across the world. As it was, many of them, including Franklyn were still returning from the slopes of Kressa Peak to the hotels they'd been booked into but hadn't enjoyed the pleasure of staying in. Angus had picked up the information from a contact with one of the technicians up at the site, who'd explained of the weather and traffic warnings that had led to the majority of personnel, and those who were visiting the site, being advised to stay put. With the worst part of the weather now retreated the roads were being cleared and those with places to go were going to them.

Now John and Angus sat in the foyer of the Milton Motel, the smartest and most expensive place for travellers who required first class accommodation and food when visiting Kressa. Angus held a two-week old newspaper in front of his face. John had settled for a journal. The journal in which Franklyn had published the first adulterated extracts of the stolen thesis and called it his own.

Because of the clean up campaign; the overall confusion associated with responding to the emergency the weather had instigated, no one was paying them any attention.

"I'm starved," Angus whispered. "Surveillance sucks, Man."

John kept hold of the journal with one hand. Concealing his face, while he retrieved a wholefood mixed nut, cereal and honey snack bar from his pocket. He passed it to Angus without speaking. Keeping his eyes firmly directed over the top of the reading material he was holding and at the entrance door.

There was a slow but steady stream of arrivals. Some were booked in. Others were looking for bookings because they'd decided to cut journeys short because of damage to roads or floods en route to their intended destinations. John was finding it hard to keep his eyes open. Being still was allowing his body and mind to receive some misguided physiological signal that sleep was acceptable. It wasn't.

He was considering the necessity of moving in order to keep awake when Franklyn, and a small group of people who could only be conference delegates, entered the foyer. Franklyn went immediately to the desk. John stood up. As planned, he noted the number of the space the reception manager retrieved the key from. He sat abruptly down again.

"Good work," Angus's voice was barely more than a whisper.

John watched as Franklyn headed toward the corridor, which led to the executive suites. He stood up again. "On my own," he said. He heard the exhalation of a sigh from Angus as his own breath locked in his throat.

Making his way along the corridor he considered what he was about to do. He was going to tell Franklyn everything he'd learned and understood. It was the only way. He'd tried everything else. Franklyn was the man who people would listen to – the accepted and acknowledged authority. The person in whom, even the President and his advisers had faith. When he reached the door he bit back the urge to turn away, blanked out the intruding images of Franklyn's smirk. Closed his auditory memory to the sound of Franklyn's abusive laughter, denied the tremor in his hands and knocked.

"Yes." Franklyn emerged as the door swung open.

John felt, rather than heard, the rattle of his own breath as he prepared to speak. The words slipped away but he grasped for them before they completely disappeared.

"Dr Franklyn," he said. His voice sounded as if it was coming from a distance outside of him. Separate. It didn't matter. He had to say what he needed to say. "I need…" he began. The sudden curl of Franklyn's lip halted him, made his vision blur.

"Professor Franklyn, Begvious," Franklyn laughed out the words. "Emeritus Professor." He held up a hand. "I've no idea what you're doing here, but security will soon have you removed." He started to close the door.

John shoved his foot into the gap. Leaning the full weight of his body against the pressure being applied to close it, "I'm going nowhere, Dr Franklyn," he said as he pushed harder, "until you listen to me."

"You never were, Begvious." Franklyn was holding firm. "I made sure of that. Oh but how you tried to impress me with your genius – so very helpful of you."

John exerted all his strength. The door moved. Franklyn stepped back into the room. John moved forwards before back kicking the door shut behind him.

Franklyn made for the phone. "It's my work," Franklyn hissed as his hand hovered in the air. "Your theft of ideas, Begvious, your plagiarism, is well documented. No one is going to listen…"

"I don't care." John moved closer. "You can have everything, Franklyn I…"

"Emeritus Professor Franklyn, Begvious. Get it in your head exactly who I am."

"Dr Franklyn," John said. "Please just move away from the phone and listen to me…"

"I've had all I need and want from you, Begvious. Small-time nobody with your big ideas."

John moved toward him "There's more than you've told them," he said. "More than the information you've stolen…"

"I'd be very careful about accusations, Begvious. I think you'll find…"

"Franklyn, this is more important. The work on the capstone, the explosion of the white dwarf… Sirius is the major threat. There's something far more profound, something that goes beyond the material. I need to talk to people…"

"You're not talking to anyone, Begvious." Franklyn again reached for the phone.

"It's all here." John held out the pen drive. "You don't need to steal it. I'm giving it to you. Everything. The links with the spiritual and the mythical…they can't be ignored. The white dwarf, Sirius B is merely an energy plug, the diminishing energy of the Earth…"

Franklyn lurched forward, snatching the pen drive.

John looked at his now empty hand then back at Franklyn. Franklyn's face melded into the smirk. "There's nothing beyond the material, Begvious," he said, stepping back. "Life's all about taking what you can in the here and now." He swung an arm pressing a button on the wall behind him. "Myth and religion the soporific of fools and idiots…"

"You should have read my work," John felt the tension in his throat. "Tried to understand what it was really telling you…"

He didn't finish. The two burly security guards were already in the room. Franklyn nodded. "I found him in here."

"No!" John turned.

"He was trying to steal this." Franklyn held the pen drive in the air, as if for inspection by the security guards, as he made the accusation.

"It's not true. He's lying," John said. "It's mine. I've just given it to him." He could feel his thoughts spinning in panic. This shouldn't be happening. He was trying to make things right. He made to run. But he was too slow. The security guards were at the door before him. He felt the pressure of the grip of their hands on his arms. They dragged him outside.

# 70 VIBRATION

Manda and Paul Yeager's arrival in what was the middle of the night, felt like an early Christmas to John. He was released from his cell.

The big man, Angus's father, had crushed first Angus, then John, in a bear hug that only just missed cracking bones. Manda had waited before pressing the softness of her cheek against John's face. Folding her arms around him then reaching out to pull both Paul Yeager and Angus into the circle of her embrace.

The uniforms on duty were still waiting for autographs. John, and the charge against him, forgotten in the general amazement that a legendary Rock Star had not only paid the bail to release the skinny guy who they all thought was crazy, but was also willing to sign as many scraps of paper with his name; even agreeable to posing for a few photographs with the team.

It was beyond ridiculous, but by the time they left the station John couldn't help but feel it was like leaving a bunch of friends who'd been kind enough to let him stay over for a few nights – easy to think with the fear of arrest shrinking into memory.

"I need to get the truck," Angus said, but made no effort to move.

"No need little man," said Paul Yeager. "We're all going home together tonight." He threw an arm around Angus as he said it, and within a single beat of John's heart had an arm around him, too.

The journey back to the ranch house, with the hired car and driver Paul Yeager had arranged, was swift because of the emptiness of the roads. John wasn't sure whether it was the fact that it was the middle of the night, or whether people were beginning to become more cautious due to the sudden and unexpected weather changes. If Paul or Manda Yeager noticed that part of the highways were closed while recovery work took place on some of the damage the storms had wreaked, they didn't mention it. Neither did they comment on the huge mounds of mud, which had obviously moved with speed, taking the weight of several cars on the journey to the bend at the foot of the pass they'd travelled through. Instead they talked about how good it was to be heading home again.

By the time they all piled out of the car, almost as if they were just starting out on a holiday, John's mind backtracked with concern at the lights blazing. What if? But Juanita swung open the door, quelling the edge of anxiety that had leapt from past experience. She ran forward. Hugging them all in succession, speaking in what John assumed was quick fire Spanish. Whatever she was saying was making both Manda and Paul Yeager smile. John, irrespective of being totally unable to comprehend what she was saying, felt the shape of a smile forming on his own face too.

He glanced at Angus who, despite his dishevelled appearance after spending over thirty-six hours camped at the police station, appeared to be beaming. For a moment he felt safe – part of a family. He hadn't been asked a single question about his arrest on Franklyn's engineered charge of not only breaking and entering, but theft as well. It felt good.

It wasn't until after eating the feast conjured up by Juanita that Paul Yeager asked the question Angus had wanted to prepare for.

"What's happening?" he said, his head tilted slightly to one side. "We know…know what you talked about, the research, the evidence for cosmological threat."

John watched as Paul Yeager sought out Manda's hand to hold.

"I guess after the past few weeks," Paul Yeager continued. "We know – know that whatever it is, has begun."

"Listen, Pa." Angus gave a dismissive gesture with his hand.

Paul Yeager reached for Angus's errant fingers, clasping them with his own. He smiled, while pulling Angus toward him. "We're not scared, Angus," he said.

Manda gave a small movement of her head to demonstrate her agreement. "We'd like to help," she said. "If what you talked about…" She paused, moving the bejewelled braid of hair over her shoulder.

For some unexplainable reason John found himself thinking of Julia again. She too, sometimes had a braid. He wondered if that's how his mother had worn her hair. Wanted to ask Manda if she'd found out anything more than they already knew. Wondered if Manda had already heard about their ill-conceived visit to the Hopi Reservation. But he could see she was speaking, he just couldn't hear the words she was saying.

"Help?" he asked, retracing to the last word he'd heard.

"Yes," Manda said. "We'd like to."

"Who knows?" Paul Yeager said. "Even if it's gone beyond the possibility of changing things – gone beyond changing what's to be. There may be something we can do."

Despite being aware of Angus's agitated stance, he told them everything he knew. Everything he was trying desperately to understand. Even told them about the storm and his perception of its progress and movement across the landmass.

Paul Yeager became thoughtful. "It's not such a strange concept, John," he said after some deliberation, with no evidence of the fear or panic

Angus had wanted to prevent. "As far as I…" he glanced at his wife. "As far as we, know. Almost all ancient belief systems respect and recognise the power and purpose of natural forces. I guess we…" – he glanced at Manda again – "we always believed such things ourselves. Still do," he said, his voice warm with undisguised humour. "People of our generation…" he said, softly, his eyes locking with Manda's, "tried to do the speed course in engaging with the mysteries of the world and the Universe." He closed his eyes momentarily before opening them to focus on Manda again. "Man," he said. "Did we try?"

John caught the look, quickly averting his eyes as he recognised the intimacy of the joint memory.

"We sure tried," said Paul Yeager continuing, "tried to access the understandings and teachings of people wiser than ourselves. Those who could sense, and read, the meaning of the breeze."

"Some thinking there was a quick way," Manda offered.

"To find Nirvana," said Paul Yeager. "But drugs and mental dissipation only take you down, not up."

"But this is something else," Manda's voice quavered only slightly. "Maybe we need to enable people to make peace with each other and themselves before…"

"It happens," Paul Yeager stated. "And if it's going to," he said as he stood up and played some imaginary guitar, "I think we need to raise the vibration."

"Man," said Angus. "You talking rock concerts, Pa?"

# 71 EGYPT

They were heading down toward the small makeshift airstrip when the lights below them disappeared. The pilot circled the light aircraft.

"Control panel has blanked. I'm keeping her in the air."

The pilot's voice was calm, but John could feel the buffering of the wind against the wings. The small seating space, like the rest of the world outside, was in darkness. John thought of Berke. Experienced the innocence of his own childhood self. Remembered the blindfold; the misplaced trust; the foolish anticipation. Remembered that that was then, not now. Nothing remained static – the past could inform, it didn't need to define.

Now he was travelling out to Egypt. He was alone except for the pilot. The false papers in his pocket, Ogilvy had organised, would enable him access onto the site. Angus and Sarah were travelling overland as part of the reporting team. Sarah had managed to swing it.

"Engine's fine," the pilot's voice was strained.

He wondered if the pilot's report was as much to allay his own fears as those of his passenger. There was no visible light. John wondered if they were in the thick of some cloud. Whatever it was, they couldn't land without some sort of a signal. Maybe even a flare from below. He should have been terrified. Yet the fear of flying that had limited his existence for years belonged to someone else. This, he thought, could be his last journey. He should saviour it. Not hold his breath, till it was over.

He wondered if this is what it felt like to be in the womb, this all-engulfing darkness – this capsule with the world outside. He'd been in that space once.

There was an illusion of safety, but in truth the vulnerability was immense. He was still coming to terms with what he now knew, aware of the illusion that had driven him on.

"Your mother," Manda told him after she'd finally arranged the meeting with Joanna. "She wasn't running away. She wasn't running from anything. She was running toward something. Something she believed in. You, John, she believed in you. Your astrological chart, the symbol of your birth, the Otter child, she was running toward the hope of a future where you would find the education you needed to become the person she believed you could be."

He'd been quiet. Felt the warmth of Manda's hand placed atop his own.

"She achieved her dream, John," Manda said. "More than many people do."

That his mother's brain haemorrhage had stolen many of her faculties, leaving her without memory of his birth was clear. She'd escaped all the searches of the authorities by returning to the people she belonged to. There'd been no knowledge within the group of the pregnancy, only the shared confidences between a young girl and the woman Joanna. Joanna, from whom his mother had sought help, when the pregnancy she was hiding, approached full term.

The haemorrhage, Manda had told him, was probably the result of a clot associated with the complications of childbirth, followed by the sudden bolt to a believed freedom for the son she'd given birth to.

As was Manda's way, she had given him the space to decide. He had. Then she'd taken him. The beauty of the Hopi people had surprised. The dance had mesmerised. They'd waited till they were approached, as Manda had promised they would be. Joanna showed no indication of any previous meeting. No acknowledgment of the time when her eyes had shrunk backwards to protect the secret. She'd spoken with Manda, before leaving them once again in the hustle of the crowd.

He'd been scared she'd disappear; experienced again the overwhelming sense of loss till he saw her returning, transfixed by the slight figure by her side. The figure, who, viewed in the distance, seemed no more than a child. Manda had held his hand. It had helped to still the shaking.

It was only as they approached, that he was able to recognise the true fragility of the woman who'd given birth to him – the mother he'd searched for.

She smiled when she reached them, touched the shaking hand he held toward her, placed her tiny fingers on the curve of his cheek. "Beautiful boy," she said, and his life, his entire past, every moment of pain he'd ever experienced, rose above him and vanished into the sky before transforming into a ray of sunlight which shone directly on her face. His mother's face, now sketched into his mind forever. For a split second it was as if she knew who he was. Then she turned, and he watched her disappearing into the crowd, a child who would stay forever young, her tiny hand clutching tightly to Joanna. Joanna, the woman who had kept the secret, would continue to do so.

The 'Reach Out Starburst Concerts' had begun. The Snow Leopards had opened the first one in Central Park. Paul Yeager had captured both the live and televised audiences with his 'Reach Out' speech even before he pressed his foot on the pedal and almost blew the sky away with his signature electric guitar riff. Everyone had gone as wild as the building storms were threatening to be, the rain, the wind and, the at times unexplainable flashes of lightning, only adding to the spectacle.

The rock fraternity, and many others, were being welcomed on the bandwagon that was now touring the world for free to raise both awareness and funds. Money was now pouring in from all corners of the globe for the 'Reach Out' charity that was aiming to support all those affected by environmental volatility. And somewhere, amongst all the madness, Paul Yeager had enabled Ogilvy to realise his boyhood dream – allowing him to join the band on tour for one of the concerts.

Amazingly, many people still believed the press reports, which linked the global volatility with the so-called 'greenhouse' effects. Every day there was some expert discussing how everything could be explained in terms of known phenomena. The work being carried out behind the scenes as part of the international military and space programmes was still, as Haziq and Ogilvy had cryptically communicated, no further in providing a clear understanding of what was going on. Still, Franklyn had obviously been willing to put his name behind some, but not all, of the work John had given him on the pen drive.

The massive space defence programme had all sights pointed in the direction of the Sirius system. Ready to blow her apart if they had to – if they could.

John considered the sights he had set on his own destination. The Giza Plateau, where the desert had become almost as much of a stage peopled with performers as any of Paul Yeager's hundred plus live music concerts currently rocking across the world. Franklyn had become Donovan's second man. The research he'd stolen from John; adulterated and claimed as his own, already nominated for the Nobel Prize. He was no longer simply Dr Franklyn. His manoeuvrings, his lies, had secured him not only an Emeritus Professorship but also a ministerial position.

The massive undertaking to replace the capstone was gathering force. It was being presented to the world as something akin to a theatrical event by the American Media, and a celebratory historical event by the Middle Eastern press. Huge screens had been erected in almost every major city during the lull in the storms. The world could see history, taking place. Those making it could watch the world watching, as it happened.

Within the space of the enfolding darkness around him, it seemed impossible to believe that the world was continuing to exist beyond the confines of the configured metal boundaries of the plane within which he was travelling.

He wondered now if that was what it had been like for Thomas

Begvious. The closed order his benefactor had chosen to retreat to was little more than a walled isolated church, and yet just his being there had sparked so many things. The libraries he'd spoken of in that first letter were metaphoric libraries – the vast Akasha: the sky that held all knowledge encoded on the non-physical plane. The Akashic Records containing all history of the cosmos. John had not understood then, and was still now, on his way to the location, which was probably the first point in the end of time, barely touching on the meaning of what was called the 'Universal Supercomputer' and by others the 'Mind of God'.

Thomas Begvious had been so calm. Humble. He'd known there was very little time. He'd shown no fear. John remembered the light in his eyes, so bright. A light in the darkness of the space for prayer he'd chosen to spend his life dedicated to. It seemed impossible to imagine it dimmed.

"Purpose," Thomas had said. "Finding you was mine. I think you already know what yours is."

John, in truth, wasn't sure. But the man, Thomas Begvious, had generated such inexplicable direct energy and force in the simple but warm embrace they'd shared before parting, that he hoped, for Thomas's sake, he would.

# 72 WHOOSH

"Flares twenty degrees south," the pilot announced.

John felt the tilt in the plane as the voice intruded in his thoughts, scattering the memories of his time with Thomas Begvious to the four winds. His seatbelt was already on. He'd never taken it off. The sudden fall and jolt pinned him to the back of his seat, his breath coming out in a whoosh. He could feel the plane turning, was grateful for the blackness outside preventing visibility of the spin of the ground below.

"Taking her down."

John's stomach registered the forward lurch as the pilot coughed out the words. He closed his eyes. The picture of his mother etched itself on the forefront of his mind, the sound of her voice a tiny fist of joy and pain in his heart.

# 73 GIFT OF TIME

With his back braced against the sharp edges of the stone of the Great Pyramid John released his grip. The ropes were already searing the skin of his hands. His rapid descent was now underway – the only way possible. There had been no time for the gloves. The CNN connection in his ear informed him that the storm had already reached eighty miles an hour. At least he was on the eastward side. Here he could almost see into the distance. See the swirl of the sandstorm creating only a rising bank of what appeared like cloud moving with great power. Alternately obscuring and revealing the sun falling in the deepening night sky – a Turner landscape, wild with colour, light and force. He resisted the urge to reach out to capture it in his hands – his mind – for a painting he may never paint.

Yet still it didn't feel right. It was a sensation in his gut, a feeling across his shoulders, something nagging inside his head. How many times had he questioned his own ideas? He didn't doubt his calculations. Neither had the other scientists, they'd eventually concurred. Recognised the mathematical formulae were correct – the equation perfect. He'd identified that there was a missing link – the force; the energy.

He inched further downwards, the skin on his hands raw against the ragged surface of the stone. Strange how it seemed so smooth when viewed from below – innocuous. So many things seemed different when viewed from afar. Like Sirius – no more than light millennia away till her mask was removed. Here she now was, ready to hurtle through time and space to collide with the Earth in a catastrophic embrace, if balance could not be restored.

He needed to move faster. The helicopters were swarming the sky – covering all points of the compass. The sound, the drone of a billion winged insects, creating an ear splitting buzz of static, already muting the sound of his radio contact to no more than a penny whistle being played against the wind.

The helicopters, already several had gone down in the storm. They'd been forming an aerial highway in the sky – a massive illuminated flight path to bring in the reconstructed capstone. Franklyn had been unable to distance himself from a material answer, which enabled him, the elevated status and kudos of such a massive undertaking. John prayed the crews had survived – even if it was only for long enough for the entire world to meet their Maker together. The guys on the ground, and in the air – men and women both – giving their all, once given the go-ahead. As Angus had said before he'd left Arizona for Egypt, they all at least deserved a place at the farewell party.

Even now at this precipitous point in time the old question still gnawed at his thinking. Why hadn't they given him the space he needed?

He felt hijacked, and now the world was watching. For how long would they be able to? If his calculations were right it could already be far too late. The entire world had already experienced the first, second and third waves of destruction – the storms decimating large sections of landmass. Dr Franklyn, now Eminent Professor, quick to affiliate himself to the cause once scientists from over fifteen countries had taken the risk of being disbarred from their professional positions because the memory of Haziq's father still meant something, and Haziq had found a way to harness those memories.

Still, Franklyn had managed to secret the evidence, which had been provided to him on the spiritual links. It had all been on the pen drive. John swallowed. The man had made him waste so much precious time.

He was beyond the halfway stage. Already he could see the movement on the ground, the frantic yet co-ordinated activity of services from all corners of the Earth – moving as one massive organic operation despite the great cumulus of sand cloud veering toward them. They'd been given the signal to 'Go', from the top. The key players on the world's stage, believing everything was in place.

He considered his own pilgrimage, his experience on the summit of the Great Pyramid. The place where Sir Sieman, the British scientist, had felt the unmistakeable prickling of the shock of electric energy when he raised his index finger to test the claims of the guide who, with outstretched fingers, had heard the acute mysterious siren sound emanating from the point where the apex – the capstone, should have been.

Now the final twenty feet were behind him.

"John…"

Sarah's face swam into focus as she rushed toward him removing her eye protectors. He was flat against the rock, the climbing hoist still confining him. He let her hold him; press her forehead against his. He felt the gravel of sand and sweat stinging his blistered skin, reminding him of how glad he was to be still alive.

"They're bringing her in," she said, helping him unleash the harness. "The capstone, she's on her way," she pulled the protectors back on as she spoke.

"Good trip, Man?"

John felt the slap on his back and turned, almost laughed in disbelief. Angus, impossible to recognise in his protective gear, threw an arm around him, pulling him into a crouched position as they ran together toward the jeep.

"You don't look good, Man," Angus turned the jeep full circle, the sound of his voice poor competition for the screech of the sand filled carburettor, "but still alive. That's what counts."

John took the bottle of water Sarah handed him. Wincing as he turned the lid with his skinned fingers. He swallowed several mouthfuls, strangely conscious of the sound and movement in his throat. He wiped his mouth.

"Did any of the air personnel survive – the helicopters? I heard we'd lost some before the connection was drowned out."

"Ah, Man. It's been mayhem. No one's talking about casualties. They've got footage running of people across every continent," Angus said as he turned the jeep to join a snake of moving vehicles as they circled back toward the main pavilion where all the news channel crews were located.

John could see the makeshift stations up ahead. The screens, the hovering confluence of people, the presenters, film crews, each determined to get the best footage, even if it was the last thing they ever did.

"John…" Angus intruded on his thoughts. "Nobody is talking about what's already happened. The whole world is just looking at the sky tonight – waiting for what might appear as the biggest ever Fourth of July celebration, even if the summer is already long over…"

"Or maybe the end of time," John said.

Angus parked the jeep. Let out a long low sigh before speaking. "You don't think we can berth her. You still think…"

Angus let the question hover in the air. Sarah was silent.

John shook his head. "Something's not right." He glanced at Angus's profile before turning to Sarah, before looking straight ahead at the theatre the mission had become. "I've wanted so much to believe that I was wrong…that maybe all the other stuff…" He struggled to call up the words, which came slowly, "The myth, the spiritual, was part…"

"John," Sarah said. "It's…" She reached for his hand.

"I thought it was part of me being crazy," he said before she could finish. "But everything I've read, everything I've been drawn to, helped me recognise, as the Essenes did, the spiritual nature of the physical Universe."

"Man," said Angus.

"It's hard to…" John began. "It's hard to explain." He paused. "The summit, the top." He took a deep breath. "I felt an absence of energy when I was up there – something's off."

"Off how, Man? Off balance – the landing path – what?"

John pressed his palm against his forehead, pushing his fingers hard into his scalp. "There was no sensation," he said. "Maybe it's crazy. Maybe I'm crazy." He glanced at Sarah – the honorary sister. "I raised my arm, spread out my fingers, listened." He lifted his arm in demonstration. "There was nothing. The world is falling apart. Storms are raging. There must be thousands of radio signals blasting the night. But up there, there was nothing. Just a void – nothing."

"John, Man."

He felt the grip of Angus's hand on his shoulder.

"There's a team of scientists out there who believe it's the shield. You…your own research supported the link. Showed there was a missing factor. Maybe you're right about being wrong. Maybe the other stuff…" Angus stopped.

John tore the lid off the bottle of water a second time and emptied it down his throat before he spoke. "I never said it was the shield, Angus. I said all the co-ordinates, the mathematics – the cosmology, all fitted the equation. I've been fighting for them to listen, but all my findings just fitted too many of their own theories. He shook his head. "And Franklyn, I guess he couldn't let go of this debut, on the stage the world is watching."

"If it's not the shield, John," Sarah said. "That means…"

John closed his eyes. He could almost imagine she was still sitting opposite him in his old apartment, lecturing him about the state of the place, instead of under a storm filled desert night sky where the world was about to fracture and disintegrate.

"You were up there, Man." Angus gestured to the rising wall that blanked out the horizon. The Great Pyramid of Giza waiting to be reunited with its capstone. "If it's not the shield waiting to be charged with that 400 tons of gold being carried in and Armageddon is waiting round the next bend, what the hell is it?"

John tried to focus on a point in the far distance – the flesh of his jaw slack, his head almost shrinking into his shoulders. He opened his mouth. "It's…" He pressed a fist against his forehead. "Angus," he said. "It's not going to make any difference…The Great Pyramid…it's just…just…"

"Just a what, Man?"

"Just an empty tomb…"

"John." Sarah clutched at his hand.

He closed his fingers around hers.

"You need to be in the control station," she said.

"Me too," Angus said, retrieving his keys from the ignition. "Let's go. Join the party."

They ran together toward the tent – the main pavilion.

John caught the commentary, now free of static, as they pushed their way through the throng.

"This is CCN, live from Giza. The capstone, all four hundred tons of her, she's a big girl – is moving in. She's being guided along the flight path…"

The whole area was swarming with service men and woman – controlled madness. John focused on the silver chain around his neck, which held the silver cross, the otter charm – handmade and beautiful; the tiny stone, engraved with the Hopi symbol. His gifts – treasured links with his mother, *'I will watch over you'*, she'd written on the parchment. He wondered if some part of her, some spiritual essence that hadn't been destroyed by the haemorrhaging stroke, was in some perfect as yet unknown Universe, doing that now. He turned to Angus.

"How long have we got? I lost the signal coming down – my watch stopped."

Angus pulled his iPad from his pocket. "If what you're feeling's right, Man…" He paused, deep in concentration as he monitored the co-ordinates on the control panel.

John watched, the sound of the news channels reverberating in his head, trying desperately to believe that they could do it. Hoping they were right and he was wrong. They had to be. He had to be.

He glanced over to where Sarah now stood at the opening to the tent, her frame hidden inside the bulk of the jumpsuit, the protectors in place safely concealing her eyes. He thought of Julia again. Her soft almost always half closed eyes that gave the impression she was waking from a dream. John let the dreamlike image of her fade; wished all that was happening were a dream. It wasn't. They were wide-awake. To his left he could see the bank of monitors following the storms. They were losing trace. The satellites were being battered.

He saw Haziq, his profile sharp – focused on the monitor he was stationed against. He went toward him. The keening sound of the guy ropes straining against the building vortex of the wind. He touched Haziq's shoulder.

Haziq turned, his eyes at first distant, then warming with recognition.

"Thanks," John said. "For being with us."

Haziq smiled. "Sometimes," he said, the contours of his face almost luminescent in the reflected light from the computer screen, "I can feel my father and mother by my side. I hear the sound of their prayers. Feel the energy of their prayers. Their love and prayers lifting me from the darkness I had entered."

John felt the rush of awareness. Remembered and reached for his friend. Held him for a second. Experienced the blossoming convergence of truth. Haziq's words, the catalyst of mind-blowing synthesis. John knew. The picture was complete. Perfect. The primeval mound, the centre of the

Earth, the diminishing magnetic force that no one could explain, the key essence that held everything in harmony and balance, the reason the Universe was accelerating. It was because there was something missing. He felt the beginning of a rainbow of hope in his heart. It wasn't too late.

He turned. Saw Sarah's back curving as she held against the force of the gale, heard the panic seeping into the news reporter's accounts as he started to move.

"This is CNN, people are being…"

The static of the breaking signal and the billowing rumble of the flimsy fabric of the tents were drowning out the newsman's voice. "Take care of Sarah," he yelled to Angus as he spun toward the exit.

He heard the hail as he started to run – a rising cacophony of sound building in velocity. The fourth wave, if the prophecy was true, had begun. They had to listen to him. He had to make them.

He ran head down, across to where the main podium was sited. Ducking against the hail as it battered his face. Catching snatches of the now frenetic commentary being translated into many different languages, as he made his way to where the Hub, 'think tank' was operating.

Tank was right, a huge armoured military vehicle housing Leaders from several different countries. Those taking their risks along with the common man and woman, while the rest holed up in bunkers.

A simple side awning, a makeshift tunnel, protected by only one armed guard on the outside had been erected to enable initial access to the area that led to the podium. He scanned the tent which acted as a fall out space, still wide open to the elements, but protected from the swirling sand by the bulk of the south eastern wall. He saw Franklyn. Franklyn – Emeritus Professor and advisor to the Senate.

John closed his eyes to blank out the image. Welcomed the rage that rose up inside him, allowing it to fire every cell of his body, before holding out his badge for identification as he manoeuvred himself through the wall of military personnel and into the outer area of the Hub.

"This is CNN. The force of the storm is building. This is some scene here…"

He could hear the broken sound of the newsman speaking to the world as his earpiece picked up the signal before fading into static again; could see the bank of screens on the inner wall. The blur of the helicopters on the first screen, the 'white out' where the satellite had taken a hit on the second screen, on the third screen he saw the footage of people in the streets around the major cities of the globe. Some were already screaming and crying. He hoped that Angus was with Sarah; truly hoped that Haziq's parents, though in spirit, were with Haziq.

He waited his chance. No more than a second. The armed guard outside the Hub turned his head slightly sideways to adjust his earpiece. John moved forward slipping under the side awning. He did it. He was in. Started moving stealthily forwards. Intent. He was slipping under the second awning when he felt the weight to the side of him wrest his balance. He twisted, steadying himself, but unable to break the fall.

"You make a lot of mistakes, Begvious."

Franklyn's face loomed above him, moving in closer as John attempted to pull himself upright.

"You're too late," Franklyn shot the words out of a mouth twisted with hatred. "You just don't understand the game do you, Begvious? I've made it clear that your thesis, all you've been proposing, are elements drawn from my own work, my own theoretical stance – my research."

John abruptly averted his head to avoid contact with the spittle escaping from Franklyn's mouth. Determinedly defocusing his vision from Franklyn's wide, unblinking stare, folding his arms across his solar plexus to prevent the sudden drain of energy he was experiencing. He moved them forward, pressing against Franklyn's ribcage. He'd never realised the man was so small.

"Get out of my way, Franklyn," he heard the snarl of his own voice, deep and low, rising from someplace forgotten inside him. Franklyn didn't budge.

"You don't see do you, Begvious?" The spittle was now frothing out the side of Franklyn's twisted mouth.

John again tried to avert his head from the poison of the smell of the sharp metallic sourness of the man's breath, keeping his eyes fixed beyond Franklyn to the door that led into the Hub. He needed to get in there.

Franklyn wasn't finished. "Let's make this clear, Begvious," he said. "If anyone is going to be taking the credit for the success of all this, it's me. I'm pushing forward with the theft charge. I've already filed against you for plagiarism. It's a dirty word in academic circles. You'll never…"

"Out of my way." John pushed harder, his arms braced against Franklyn's chest. He had to move the man. He couldn't believe he'd ever feared him. He pushed again.

"It's mine," Franklyn said. "I'm the one, Begvious…"

"Franklyn," John almost laughed out the name. "Franklyn you're crazy. The world's about to explode and you're thinking about credit. People are screaming in the streets and all you can think of is your fucking parasitic self. You made me feel so fucking small while you were leeching off me, stealing my ideas, almost sent me over the edge…"

"You'll need to withdraw those comments, Begvious…" Franklyn said, his hands clutching at John's arms.

John stared, aware of the absence of light in the man's eyes, just as

Franklyn's hands made a sudden grab for his throat. Using the full force of his strength John pushed back. "Get the fuck off me before I break your pathetic scheming neck," he heard the growl his own voice had become. Saw Franklyn's hands flail as his own force of strength broke the physical contact Franklyn had made. Felt the tension snap as Franklyn staggered back. Grasping the opportunity to make for the opening door of the Hub.

"I'll see you get…"

He didn't hear the rest of Franklyn's words.

He was already through. Brandishing his ID ahead of him as President Donovan, skin on his face stretched tight across his bones, eyes wide, his body flanked by guards, came into view.

John's head reverberated, his heart raced, his limbs felt like they belonged to someone else as he called out, "Donovan – you've got to listen to me…"

The sudden jolt as he was rolled to the ground from behind, even before the air carrying his voice had exited his ribcage surprised him. He lay on the floor. His ID still clutched in his hand. A machine gun pressed against his throat.

"This is CNN," the voice in his earpiece crackled, "the force of the tempest is reducing visibility…the capstone…"

"It's not going to save us…" John heard the disappearing sound of his own voice as he was rolled over on his face. The encrusted sand of one of the guard's boots polluting his mouth before he could finish. He was dragged upright and backwards. His arms twisted and cuffed behind him. He struggled.

"Donovan," he called out, as he was rushed forward in the melee toward the Podium. The gale outside a roar, the static in his ears a knife through his brain. "Einstein was wrong," he shouted. "There's something…a greater force…faster…something that can lift us from the darkness, dark energy. You've got to tell them, Donovan…" He sagged as they faced the opening to the tunnel. It was barely possible to see. Yet the large screens were still running. "Tell them Donovan. Tell them that thought can go faster than the speed of light…" He saw Donovan turn. "The fire clay tablet – the sign; the symbol; the plus and minus; the circle, they're representing the positive and neutral forces in a magnetic field, " he shouted, desperate Donovan would hear him, "where they cross is a vortex into the next dimension. Tell them to …"

The arm around his throat, the silencing stranglehold of the guard jammed his vocal cords as they lowered the capstone against the force of the elements. Donovan's face was neutral, only his eyes betrayed him. Showed he was terrified. Just like the rest of them. This was the climax they'd been waiting for, thought John. They had twenty minutes he reasoned before the fifth wave hit.

"This is CNN," his earpiece whined. "They're lowering the…"

He looked up as the night decimated in a spewing of rock. The bodies on the podium scattered, the screams resonating with the sound of the helicopters spinning out of control. The hold of the guard was gone. He saw Donovan lying face down only feet away, blood running from a gash in his head, the footage of people from all corners of the Earth still running as a backdrop on the screens behind him.

"Donovan," John tried to roll forward using his feet as propulsion as he called out the name. "Donovan," he tried again, raising his voice above the wail of the broken night around them. "Prayer," he shouted; saw Donovan move his head toward him. "Prayer, like thought, can travel faster than light. We need the light. The capstone only ever existed on the spiritual plane. The Egyptian Key of Life, it represents the energy of life. We have the energy to restore the balance. Ta Khut – the light. It was only ever light. Tell the people to pray…"

He watched as Donovan, bewildered from shock, dragged slowly across the podium, his hand untangling the microphone still attached to his lapel. Watched as Donovan tried to lever himself up, but couldn't find purchase.

"Help me," Donovan mouthed the words.

John moved forward. Saw Donovan struggling to raise his arm – hold out his hand, realised Donovan was offering him the microphone; holding it forward so he, John, could speak. Heard the echo of sound as the sensor picked up his rapid breathing.

"Tell them," Donovan's mouth shaped the words without sound. "Tell them who you are."

John called on all his energy, drew in breath, aware of the importance of his task. His whole being encapsulated in the moment, "I am John," he said, the boom of his voice cutting through the airspace, the echo of his name filling the night. "The capstone has failed," he said. "Now all we can do is enter into prayer. Whoever your God may be, please pray."

The night stopped. Donovan slumped in exhaustion. An eerie silence surrounded them.

Donovan closed his eyes.

For a moment John did, too. Sending out his thoughts to the light.

At first it was no more than the sound of a distant forgotten generator, gathering momentum around them. John tried to free his hands, scanned his surroundings. He needed to get to Sarah, Angus, and Haziq – all his friends. He saw Donovan's eyes flicker open, saw the massive screens revealing, in flashes, the people of the world on their knees in prayer.

"The sound," Donovan managed a ragged whisper as he tried to raise his head. "What is it?"

John listened as the vibration built, all encompassing – the hidden harmonics of the highest octave. He found its name, "The Ohm," he said, hearing the hush of his words as he spoke. "The sound of balance," he took in a breath. "Balance and harmony."

"And the light?" Donovan gestured upwards.

He followed the trajectory of the President's hand. Saw the small particles of light like pinpoints coalescing into a spire above the Great Pyramid of Giza. Felt the shudder of recognition.

"The Apex of prayer," he answered, aware of the power of the truth unfurling. "Ta Khut – the light, the missing capstone," he said. "The true missing symbol and link we were searching for. The spiritual energy of the Universe." He paused, struggled against his cuffs, considered the possibility of a future. "I think it means we've been given the gift of time, Mr President. The world is back on course…for now."

# 74 EPILOGUE

Moving toward the back of the auditorium Thomas Begvious slowed his step. Aware of the distance he had travelled to arrive where he was. The world was moving forward. A torch of understanding had been ignited. Many had viewed what could only be described as a miracle.

John, the young man who had fulfilled the meaning of his name, was standing on the podium. Thomas understood that John would not be able to see him – would have been surprised to discover if anyone could see him at this time. But he was gratified to see that all eyes were focused on the stage. The hush around him palpable, the energy electrifying as John prepared to deliver his speech. Thomas had already heard it. Had helped John write it – both of them connecting in purpose in those few short days when faith and belief in destiny had made it possible to hold on.

The miracle in Egypt had been only the beginning. Sustaining the energy required to restore order in a Universe, required – no, demanded, that humankind aspire to greater levels of spirituality. Maybe The God Particle scientists were searching for existed in every living thing. It was the beginning, the essence of being – the light. Had the light been turned in upon itself as humankind had descended further and further into materialism? The cataclysmic fall from grace, the spiritual cataclysm believed to have occurred in the time of dynastic Egypt, leading to the degeneration of mankind. Had that descent created the weight of dark energy leading to an accelerating Universe and the threat of cosmological disaster?

But the world had united in prayer. The energy of sustained and focused spirituality creating a power surge; an apex of light, to stabilise the Earth, and the balance and harmony that sustained its place in the higher order of things. For a short time it would be enough. Enough to make people listen to the young man on the podium and recognise the messages myth, religion, and science offered.

How had it all come to be? Chance, thought Thomas, that bugbear of academics and statisticians. The mysterious phenomenon, which showed there was more, so much more than we really knew about. The leathered parchment with the Hopi Symbols, John's precious cloth, had been no more than a simple family heirloom. A wall hanging upon which John's mother had scrawled out her own message to the child for whom she wished far more than she could give. Yet it had sparked a journey. A search for truth, guided by providence to illuminate that indefinable unfathomable spark which could not be captured, only harnessed, that precious essence, which enlightened us all to recognise the divine in all things, including ourselves.

He listened as the sound of applause exploded and rose, creating a shimmering vibration of sound reminding him that it was time. The plus and minus – the circle, representing the positive and neutral forces in a magnetic field, where they crossed was a vortex into the next dimension – into the world of spirit. Thomas stepped once again across that threshold. Leaving only the diminishing and shimmering phosphorescence of his presence in the coolness of the night air. His work was done.

The End

*Author Request*

*I'm really happy you chose to read my novel, Ta Khut. Thank you. I hope you enjoyed the story, the characters, and John's journey. If you did, it would be most helpful, and I would be very grateful, if you would take the time to post a review on Amazon for me here at www.amazon.co.uk and type in Ta Khut - click on the title - under where it says EDITION – click on review.*

*With all good wishes*

*K.C. Hogan.*

Printed in Great Britain
by Amazon